# True Colours

Dear Anne

Hope you enjoy it as much as I did writing it

Love Susannah
x

# True Colours

*Susannah George*

iUniverse, Inc.
New York  Lincoln  Shanghai

**True Colours**

All Rights Reserved © 2003 by Susannah George

No part of this book may be reproduced or transmitted in any form or by any means, graphic, electronic, or mechanical, including photocopying, recording, taping, or by any information storage retrieval system, without the written permission of the publisher.

iUniverse, Inc.

For information address:
iUniverse, Inc.
2021 Pine Lake Road, Suite 100
Lincoln, NE 68512
www.iuniverse.com

ISBN: 0-595-28803-0

Printed in the United States of America

I dedicate this book to my wonderful Mum, Charley and Molly, my Nana and Papa, Yolande, and all my special cousins and friends.

# CHAPTER 1

❁

Abby tucked her blonde hair behind her ears and sipped from her tepid cup of coffee as she darted around the large cream and rosewood kitchen of the pretty detached Suffolk cottage. She perched on the edge of one of the breakfast chairs and searched through her leather shoulder bag. Yes, her tickets and passport were there!

"Have you got everything?" her mum asked anxiously. "You *will* phone when you arrive at the hotel, won't you?" Teresa clutched her daughter's arm with a worried hand and used the other to stroke the side of her hair in a tender and loving way. She knew her daughter had to take this opportunity, but it had been a while since Abby had flown on her own and she couldn't help feeling anxious.

"Don't worry, mum, I'll be fine. Anyway, a car will be waiting for me at the airport; then Patrick will be at the hotel later. Besides, the flight only takes an hour or so."

"I know, sweetheart. You know me, I can't help but worry." She forced back the tears that were filling her eyes.

"Oh mum, please don't get upset," Abby pleaded, seeing her mum's watery eyes.

"It's okay, honestly." She smiled. "They're happy tears. I'm so proud of you, sweetheart." Her warm and shapely body hugged her daughter with great affection. Abby kissed her mum's cheek and tried to reassure her that everything would be fine.

Teresa watched Abby head for the front door and the waiting taxi. She sank her hands into the pockets of her floral print skirt. Knowing that her sister would be arriving soon brought comfort to her worried face—a face that had well defined and attractive features in spite of the shadow of anxiety. She ran her fingers through her styled auburn hair as she watched her daughter enter the car. The taxi crunched the gravel as it swung round and filled the air with dust. With a final wave, Abby was on her way. The unpleasantly cold air was living up to expectations for January. Teresa was full of pride as she made her way back inside her picturesque cottage, though her heart was still weighted with concern for her daughter's journey. Flying was a sensitive matter as Abby's father had died suddenly in a light aircraft accident. They had both managed to face the fear of flying again since the accident nearly eight years ago and, although it was different circumstances than those that had happened to Charles, it never came easy.

Abby was an up and coming and very talented Interior Designer, though one that also had a natural flair for writing. She had written a book on the trade and, to her great surprise, it was published last year and did moderately well, largely thanks, perhaps, to the use she made of some friends and contacts. The book led to her making her mark on the industry and, with that in mind, an interior design magazine from Paris had heard of her and the book and also read some articles Abby had written for a selection of broadsheet supplement magazines. She had been asked to review a new interiors store in a very chic part of Paris. The magazine was a French based firm, though it had subdivisions in many countries. The article would be published in and around Europe in an assortment of languages. They were paying for Abby to stay four nights in a very sought-after hotel a stone's throw from the Eiffel Tower. They welcomed her fresh new style—a quality that seemed to simply radiate from the page. Abby had a distant cousin working in France and thought her visit would be a great opportunity to catch up with him, for it felt like forever since they had last seen each other.

In addition to all this a friend of Abby's mum and late father had married a Frenchman and been living in various parts of France for about twenty years now. Martha Beauville and her husband Phillip had recently bought a quite exquisite residence close to the Palais de l' Elysee on Avenue Gabriel. They were both soon to travel to St. Tropez to visit their son and daughter in law. When they knew Abby was going to be in Paris they practically insisted she stay in the their home while they were away. Not wanting to be churlish and refuse an all-expense paid for room at a stylish hotel, however, Abby decided to move on after the four nights in the hotel and extend the visit until the following Sunday. She was thus able to accept the hospitality of Martha and Phillip, and at the same time give her the opportunity to see more of Patrick. With her aunty Alice staying with her mum for a while, as her uncle Stanley was off on an indoor bowls tournament in Nottingham, her plans seemed to work for everyone.

Patrick was her late father's second cousin, except that Abby's dad was a lot older than Patrick and as it turned out Abby was in fact closer in age to him. It had been a ridiculous amount of time since they had last seen each other, although the family did vaguely keep in touch. Patrick was a brutal lawyer and relished his nascent career. His mum and dad lived in South Africa, due to the family's shipping business, which neither of Edward Daly's sons was interested in pursuing. Although they both grew up in Durban, he and his brother Jacob were half French as their father had married a French lady, Paulette. Jacob, too, was a very successful, victorious and influential lawyer, but he was based in Canada. Though he wasn't married, he was never short of female companions, so to speak. The brothers' relationship was strained, to say the least; there had always been an underlying competitiveness between them, one that as the years went by caused a fierce friction between the two.

Patrick had been living in France for about three years now, having gone there originally as a result of a job offer. With Jacob having left their home country years earlier, he went in search of the same respect and success his brother seemed to acquire with great ease, something that always grated on him, to say the least. Abby hadn't seen Patrick or Jacob since she was about twelve, and that was when Jacob was about seventeen and Patrick going on for twenty. This was while on a holiday in South Africa, long before they both moved away and long before the death of Abby's father. With each of them caught up in their own lives, the opportunity to come together before this time oddly never presented itself; but now, with Patrick and Abby both nearly fifteen years older, they were both in for quite a surprise.

Abby was due to land at 3.30 p.m. Monday, French time. She reclined in the patterned aeroplane seat, her shoulder-length blonde hair nesting on the headrest, her subtle fringe poised over her eyebrows. The seat moulded to her delightfully curvaceous figure, and as she glanced at her leather-strapped watch she was happy that there was only twenty minutes to landing. With the end of the flight in view, Abby reached into her brown leather bag that rested by her feet and sat back, having retrieved her Winnie the Pooh make-up bag—she was still a child at heart! In the midst of her touching up she noticed the seat belt sign had appeared, and calmly fastened the red belt and resumed applying her make up with her nerves still intact. She had suffered terribly from an eating disorder through her teens, and she had relapsed severely after the unexpected death of her Father. It had understandably led to a downward spiral in her confidence. Despite her progress and enjoying excellent health, she still had trouble believing she was an attractive young woman.

Her simple make-up enhanced her fresh, vibrant and slightly olive skin. Her eyes were as wide and blue as the sky, and she had an eminent smile that was never far from her cheeks, one that was a picture to look at. When Abby put her make-up back in her bag on the floor, her necklace brushed forward on her chin and it instantly brought her dad to her mind. It was a present from him for her eighteenth birthday, the last birthday present he had bought for her. She smiled and fiddled with the sterling sliver chain which hung with a bijou cross, but she didn't on this occasion feel sad—she just knew her dad would be so proud of her achievements. Abby really had made a fantastic recovery from being anorexic. Her once undernourished, emaciated, skeletal frame was now a million miles away from that traumatic past. Her long black skirt, slit at the front, revealed her jet-black warming tights and hugged her shapely legs perfectly. A white corseted shirt complemented it exactly. The whole outfit fitted her body flawlessly.

The plane landed at Charles de Gaulle airport and not a minute too soon for her. Making her way down the gangway and onto the terra firma, having indulged in the delights of business class, she headed to the baggage claim with her fellow passengers. Though the airport was relatively busy, she reached her brown checked holdall and trolley case with great ease. Both luggage carriers were packed to the brim, as Abby was never one to travel light. Making her way through the other travellers, she headed for the exit doors, hating having to walk through on her own looking to see who held her name up on a piece of card. Luckily a rather tall lean looking chap came forward in a grey suit and removed his hat and gestured to her.

"I believe you're looking for me, Mademoiselle," he said in a rich warm accent. He was the chauffer who was to take her to the hotel laid on by the magazine. He recognised her from the photograph that was given to him by World Interiors; also, her wanton expression as she arrived through the automatic doors gave her away! He reached for Abby's hand and took her bag while she held on to the trolley.

"Thank you. Sorry I took so long—my bags must have been last on." She thought that must have sounded quite lame. As she rolled her case through the end of the arrivals terminal, she needed to pinch herself that she was actually in Paris, a place she had never been to before, but a place she dreamed about visiting. The climate was typical of late January and so, as they reached the revolving doors, she quickly added her leather jacket to her already chilly body in spite of the imminent prospect of the seclusion of the waiting car that was practically outside the terminal. The stylish black door was opened by the chauffer, revealing the warm and luxurious leather seat that awaited her. She felt so important and promised herself to revel in every single minute.

"Is this your first time in France?" Eric enquired as he pulled away, leaving the airport behind and the beautiful capital beckoning.

"First time in Paris, but I did visit Normandy on a school trip." Abby fiddled with her ring, something she always did when she was anxious and when talking to someone unfamiliar.

"I believe you're doing a review here?"

"That's right, the opening is tomorrow. It's supposed to be quite something."

"Will you have time for the sights?"

"I hope so. I'm staying on after the review so I hope to see everything." Abby smiled brightly. In spite of her nervousness she was glowing with delight, thrilled with being where she was.

Once the small talk had died down she looked out of the window. The view was distorted slightly by the tinted glass, but that didn't deter her. Everything else now seemed to become extraneous. She was in awe of everything that presented itself to her sparkling eyes. It was like a child looking at a Christmas tree for the first time; her face just seemed to shine as if a bright light had been turned on inside her. She was mesmerised by this amazing and romantic city and all the sights that were capturing her glance; and even with the sound of the busy traffic and swarms of cars, it all just added to the atmosphere that radiated from this cosmopolitan city.

The beauty of Abby was that she could be bewildered by the sights of Paris and flabbergasted by it all and even see a lifestyle that was within her grasp. However, it didn't stop her from losing that innocence that she so greatly cherished. As a child and even now at twenty-five she had such a passion for everything. A new magazine that was her favourite, a TV show, looking round show houses, however big, small or inexpensive, she simply would exude with life and vitality, something that made her draw a deep breath, enjoying being alive.

She did not possess a pretentious bone in her body. She was excited about what she was seeing and had no problem whatsoever in expressing it. She was modest in every way and that was her secret charm.

Approaching the very lavish and very expensive hotel, she could see that the grand building had flags from various countries catching the cool easterly wind. Porters bustled around, businessmen and couples all entering this flamboyant residence. The time was nearly 5 p.m. and Abby had just over two hour to freshen up and get settled before Patrick would arrive to pick her up her at about 7 p.m. She had plenty of time to refresh herself and make a good impression, something she was going to do anyway. Eric escorted her in to the hotel and made sure she was happy before he left, his own kindness enabling him to go beyond the call of duty. However, Abby suddenly realised she may need to tip him. She reached into her chequered wallet and was just about to touch some foreign notes when Eric spoke.

"Oh no, Mademoiselle, there will be no need for that. I shall see you in the morning, bright and early."

Abby smiled as response to his benevolence. The wonder of this rich and luxuriant hotel filled her head as she made her way to the busy lift. Strolling with her luggage across the patterned maroon carpet with her destination in view, the change in flooring was a welcome contrast from the hard marble of the reception area.

Swiping her up-to-date key card, she unlocked the rich oak door. For a moment she stood transfixed with disbelief, for the hotel room was enormous and sumptuous. The colour scheme was nevertheless so delicate to the eye, yet also inviting to the body. It had a wonderful combination of fineness, ivory satin sheets draped over the four-poster bed accented by raspberry floral cushions and matching bedspread. The curtains picked up the colours from the floral addition with great delight. As for the cream and sumptuous carpet, the mere touch of it from Abby, as she crouched down to smooth her hand over the woven blend, encouraged her to remove the black-heeled shoes from her tired feet. With the release of her footwear it was now easier for her to merge her size six feet into the thick and obliging pile. The tasteful lighting and captivating pictures together with a fresh vase of flowers and chic accessories, gave the room the ambiance and feel of sophistication that she herself had created many times before. The aroma of the stylish room was subtle and enchanting, and emanated from the numerous amounts of flowers that were all around the room. Heading for one of the windows, she pulled back the sheer curtain and the view that crowded in to her full eyes was a view that would remain in her mind for some time. Astonishment spread over her face. Although she was only to stay in this exquisite room for a short four nights, she was going to make the most of every minute! She lifted her bags to the luggage stand, but before doing anything else she headed for the phone, perched on the edge of the bed and called reception for an international line. Dialling and fiddling with the cord, she waited for her answer.

"Mum, it's Abby."

"Oh, Abby sweetheart! How's everything? You are at the hotel, aren't you? You are okay?"

"Stop worrying, I'm fine! The flight wasn't too bad. The driver…no, sorry, the chauffer," Abby said, putting on a posh voice, "was really helpful and got me to the hotel with no problems."

"Please be careful, and don't go out on your own late at night," an anxious mum said down the long distance line.

"Don't worry, I'll be fine, I promise. I won't phone again till I'm at Martha and Phillip's place."

"No, that's fine, I'm just glad you arrived safely and that you're okay."

"You should see this room mum, you'd love it!"

The conversation continued in a light-hearted and fun way with laughs and affection and a blow-by-blow run down of Abby's first impressions of the sights and, of course, the room. It all ended with a simple, "I love you and talk to you again soon."

Wanting to explore the room fully, Abby took a few short footsteps and entered the quite exquisite and superior bathroom that was lavished in glowing cream towels, some draped over the antique chair in the corner with others resting on the edge of the deep and seductive oversized bath. The under-floor heating for the wooden floorboards made Abby's nylon-covered soles tingle with the touch. The hardness from the wood was broken up by an arrangement of soft mats, all strategically placed around the surprisingly spacious bathroom.

The Edwardian style washbasin and its chrome taps in the centre, with its miniature soaps gathered on the edge, stood close to the traditional shaped lavatory. The pearl walls were finished with some well-chosen pictures and a rusted framed mirror over the basin, all ideally placed. The circular table that was covered in an ecru cloth and topped with a lace pattern and protected with a glass circle was nearly the last thing Abby noticed. It stood tall and proud and was tucked neatly into the room, a close neighbour of the generous bath. On the surface of the table were small bottles of lovely fragrances and toiletries, ones that were dwarfed by the beautiful array of tall fresh flowers from which emanated the most delightful scent that extended the aroma from the bedroom. The very last thing to catch Abby's eye, before she made her way back to unpack and freshen up, was the two-person shower cubical in the far corner. She smiled to herself and said out loud in a cheeky manner, "Chance would be a fine thing."

# CHAPTER 2

❀

Not really knowing what to wear for her meeting with Patrick, Abby eventually managed to decide on a tweed grey knee-length skirt and a lilac roll neck sweater, finished with black stiletto long boots and her black leather jacket. She could have stayed the same but she felt better for changing her appearance from what she had travelled in. Her blonde hair shimmered as it brushed against her jacket, like silk on bare skin. With a quick spray of her Ralph Lauren perfume and an even quicker touch of lip balm to sheen her full and defined lips, she was ready. This young beauty was a picture fit for a gallery, but oblivious to what was going to happen next, let alone over the coming days. With the time approaching 7 p.m., a flutter of butterflies filled her tummy, yet she had a sinking feeling in her heart. Up till now nerves had forsaken her and the anxiety about seeing him again after all this time had evaporated; nevertheless, all the emotions were now thrust upon her, like a crashing wave breaking on the shore. Although it had been nearly fifteen years since they had last seen each other, they would still be able to recognise each other. Just then, as Abby entered the foyer and was about to sit down on one of the attractive chairs that dominated the elaborate entrance, a light accented voice stopped her in her tracks.

"Abby Raycroft!" The tone was almost one of disbelief.

"Patrick!" Abby answered in a shocked timbre, but her famous smile raced to her rescue.

"Wow you look…" He hesitated, trying to find the right word. "Amazing!" uttered the foreign-blooded dashing male, finally finding his compliment for her.

"You too—goodness, it's been so long." Her smile was so wide it could have stretched across the Sahara desert. He had stunned her and taken her unawares. She felt her face redden as his touch extended from her arm to a full blown hug. His enchanting fragrance heightened her sense of smell as her body was drawn close to his. She could feel his muscled biceps through his suit jacket, strong around her, and his stalwart hands pressed into her back. Their faces engaged as they reached for one another to further the greeting, with their lips lingering on each other's cheeks before freeing themselves from the gestured salutation. Patrick, too, was staggered; he couldn't believe what a beautiful young woman Abby had turned into and, at the same time, she was finding it difficult not to notice how mesmerising Patrick's deep brown eyes were. Coupled with his distinguished features and special sparkle, which she instantly recalled the moment she turned round, they made him a very striking man.

"So, blue eyes, what now—eat chat, chat eat? You say!" His tone was a little unsure, but it left the phrase 'blue eyes' ringing in her ears. Her dad always called her that, though somehow it didn't sound funny coming from him.

"Umm, we could eat here, or…we could have room service? My room is enormous, so we won't be cramped!" she joked

"Room service could be good, give us a chance to chat and catch up more privately." He flashed his inimitable smile like a deadly weapon.

They made their way to Abby's room, their arms intertwined around their backs with Patrick bringing his hand to Abby's shoulder in a very natural way as he escorted her into the lift. He looked at her as she lent over to press the floor number. He was so taken aback, not just by her appearance but also something that shone from her, that it almost made him lose for a moment his slightly cocky and arrogant manor. She was breathtaking and had an air of serenity about her, an inner calmness, something that was disarmingly attractive. Patrick's arrogance was not completely intrusive but it depended on how it was directed. With Abby standing before him, however, he really was aware of something he had never felt before and it almost seemed to unnerve him. Although having had many past relationships he had always cunningly managed to elude this feeling; but there was something about Abby that touched him, something that wasn't meant to, and not because they were distantly related.

The lift travelled quickly to the tenth floor and as they left the square enclosure, walking through the brass doors and onto the landing, their eyes met. Abby took the lead with Patrick walking behind her, his hands resting on her shoulders. Despite the instant mutual attraction, they both seemed to have a certain comfortableness with each other. They were so natural with one another, and so quickly, too. It all managed to happen very spontaneously, with no planning or awkwardness, and certainly no discomfiture about any of their actions.

"Here we are," she said, opening the door. "I couldn't believe this place—they must think I'm something special, that's for sure. To give me a room like this for a review and for only four nights!" Her facial expression carried her disbelief.

"Of course you're special, did you only just realise that?" Patrick spoke with cheekiness in his voice, and once again flashed that sexy grin.

"You check the menu, I just need to use the bathroom." It was more of a need to calm herself and to divest herself of some of the redness that still dressed her face, rather than a need for urgent necessity. She removed her jacket and draped it on the bed as she aimed for the bathroom, and added, "Order what ever you want—it's on me; oh, and make yourself comfy." The last of her words faded as she reached the bathroom and closed the door.

Patrick took off his designer pinstripe single-breasted jacket, loosened his charcoal tie and undid the two top buttons of his white shirt. He ran his hands through his thick and luscious styled hair before sitting on the edge of the patterned sofa with his elbows resting on his knees. Remembering the menu, he leaned over to the clear glass table and started to read. After a few minutes, when he heard the toilet flush, he moved round and saw the door open, making him stand up, drop the menu and bring his lightly bronzed hands to his hips to rest them on his gold buckled leather belt. What a picture!

"So what are we having then?" Abby said, making her way to the sofa, having calmed herself down a tad as she paused at the mini bar along her way. "Would you like a beer?"

"Love one. Listen, how's your mum doing?"

"She's great. She's retired now but still dabbles in the odd dressmaking for friends—that sort of thing." She passed him a cold beer

"Good, I'm glad. If you phone her perhaps I could say hello?"

"Sure, she'd like that," Abby answered as they both sat down at opposite ends of the sofa, slightly turning their bodies towards each other as they did so. Patrick rested his arm on the back cushion while Abby slipped off her boots, then curled one of her legs underneath her bottom, making her body a little more comfy for the evening's chatting.

"Unfortunately I can only have the odd day here and there, but I want to see you as much as I can. No rest for the wicked, as they say." He was feeling annoyed he didn't have more time with her. "But when I'm not working, I'm all yours."

Abby smiled to herself glancing at his soft and inviting lips and thought, "If only." But she answered with a little more subtlety. "No, that's fine, whenever you can will be great," she said, sipping her beer and giving a million dollar smile that was mirrored by Patrick's. Their eyes held for longer than the smile lasted and, not knowing where to look and suddenly forgetting how to speak, Abby ran her fingers through her loose hair—another nervous habit—and fiddled with her single ring that adorned her right hand. It sat on her third finger and was her mum's eternity ring, which was an anniversary present from her dad. Patrick, sipping his beer, glanced down at her hand, noticing her fiddling.

"That's a beautiful ring, where's it from?" The words led him to lift Abby's fingers with the palm of his large hand to see it closer. It was a happy excuse to touch her angel-like skin.

"My dad bought it for my mum for their twentieth wedding anniversary."

The ring was antique silver and had a single amethyst stone in the centre surrounded by fresh water pearls and inscribed with an elaborate and complicated pattern, typically of late sixteenth century art.

"My mum and dad loved the work of Beethoven, so my dad engraved the same words he had written to his own love."

Before Abby continued she withdrew her almost trembling hand from his palm and wriggled off the ring from her finger to recite the words that were encircled around the inside of the beautiful ring. "Ever Mine, Ever Thine, Ever for Each Other." She could feel some tears welling up in her slightly saddened eyes, all at the remembrance of how special her parents' love and relationship had been. She wondered if she would ever be lucky enough to experience such pure unadulterated love and devotion.

"Sorry, I didn't want to upset you," he said, concerned.

"No, no, it's fine, I'm glad you asked." Abby replaced the ring on her clammy finger.

"So tell me more of your news," Patrick said, wanting to change the mood. "Especially about this book you've written—and where is my signed copy?" All said in a very winning way, opening his mouth wide enough to show just enough teeth and at the same time brightening Abby's teary eyes.

They talked about everything and nothing, pausing every now and then to remember to eat the dinner they had ordered. The time was nearing eleven and as Patrick looked at his Armani wristwatch he voiced his dilemma.

"Well, as much as I'm enjoying your company, I should be getting home. I've got a couple of things to finish off before the morning." By now, standing and towering over Abby with his just under six foot height, he stretched his arms out and turned his palms up, inviting her to hold them so she could stand up with ease, which she did gladly.

"I guess I should get my beauty sleep for tomorrow."

"Well, you do need it," he said seriously

"Cheek!" Abby responded with a playful tap on his arm.

He turned and reached his jacket and slipped it over his opened shirt and tapped his pocket to check he had his keys.

They both headed for the door, but there was one thing they hadn't talked about, the one thing Abby was curious about, and that was that of a partner. However, she was worried that if she were to phrase it she would sound either noisy or obvious. But she went for the kill.

"I'm not keeping you from someone at home, am I?" she said in a breezy, uncaring way, but waited with baited breath for his answer.

He smiled with a faint laugh

"Dust sheets and cans of paint—I decided to have a bit of a revamp."

She smiled, trying not to look too relieved. She tried to remember, though, that although distant, they were still related—but there just seemed this rightness between them, a feeling she had only thought happened in films or in fairytales. She wanted him to ask her if she was with anyone, but of course he didn't; whether he had come to his conclusions or not, he didn't share them. It felt very much that he was the one at the helm, so to speak—but Abby was happy to go with the tide.

"So I shall come by tomorrow evening?"

"Yeah, great."

"It will be earlier than today, about…6 p.m. I hope?"

"Sounds good."

"I'll take you to this fantastic Bistro I know. The food is out of this world. You do like French, don't you?"

Abby thought with her cheeky sense of humour, which she defiantly inherited from her dad, "more than you know"—but she replied with a simple, "love it!" They stood by the door facing each other and making very deep eye contact, both in their own way feeling a little uneasy as to how they were feeling and how well they just clicked.

"So," Abby said in a bright and free way.

"So," Patrick said, paralleling her, but with a mischievous expression. They both hesitated before embracing one another with a hug. As Abby's chin rested on his shoulder, her cheek having grazed his tasteful stubble along the way, she inhaled his alluring aftershave, sending a rush all through her body. As they both released themselves from the embrace Patrick caught the feminine coconut smell of Abby's hair. Before leaving the room they shared kisses on each other's cheeks in a very European way.

Patrick soon passed through the foyer and the brass revolving doors and so out onto the Parisian street where he waited to hail a taxi. He turned his head to glance up behind him at the formidable building and smiled, as though in recognition of the great evening he had had and what an amazing and beautiful woman Abby was. She had, somehow, by just being her, made him drop the big bravado he carried round with him, drawing out his softer and gentler side, a side not many people saw but a side he didn't show to many people.

While he was heading for his apartment on Avenue Montaigne, Abby removed her appropriate outfit. In keeping with her efficiency and tidy nature, she hung up her clothes in the deep white built-in wardrobe. However long she stayed anywhere, one night or ten, she had to unpack everything and feel settled. While Abby was at the wardrobe she brought out a finely tailored suit in deep purple and scanned through the tops she had brought and matched the single-breasted jacket and long pencil skirt with a coordinating striped shell top. Closing the doors of the wardrobe, she made a point of looking at her toe-capped black court shoes, which she thought would be perfect to complete the look. She posed awhile in the full length antique effect mirror, modelling only her under-wired plunge black bra and matching deep full briefs. She then walked over to the bed, reached for her red tartan pyjamas from under the pillow where she had placed them earlier, the place where she had kept them since she was a little girl, released her final garments and welcomed the warmth and softness of the nightwear on her velvet soft skin.

She snuggled into the sumptuous softness of the duvet and lent over to reach the TV controls, smiling at the framed photo of her mum and dad and herself in the middle of them. She had brought it with her for added comfort; it had been taken on her eighteenth birthday in their summer garden. The death of her father had undoubtedly brought Abby and her mum even closer together, and she treasured their special bond and relationship and never once took anything they did together for granted. Nestling back into the bed and downy pillows, she closed her eyes and said her prayers silently, finishing by saying, "I love you mum, and I love you dad." With those words she felt a little lonely. She hadn't ever really been away from home, and it all felt a little alien. She distracted herself by flicking through the mass of stations, privilege of the Satellite TV, although Patrick had not disappeared from her mind. She muted the sound and gazed over to the sofa, the place where they had sat and talked for nearly four hours. It helped her not to feel so isolated in a strange city and not being in her own bedroom. Remembering how comfortable and confident she felt warmed her face, and with that in mind she elicited a drowsy memory.

She remembered how she had looked so deeply into Patrick's eyes and thought back to when they had hugged and how well their bodies seemed to fit into each other. She recalled how soft his lips felt on her skin, how fantastic he smelt and how it had been a long time since anyone had had such an effect on her, and so quickly. Even though she was twenty-five, she was still pure to the touch of a man—well, nearly. With many troubled years the love of a man had taken a back seat, but the way she was feeling now she was open to falling in love.

Lying comfortably smack bang in the middle of the double bed, she thought back to when she had a very passionate crush on her English lecturer—a memory awakened by her languid mood. Her impish and rosy cheeks flushed as Joshua Green's face drifted back into her mind. He'd had an athletic body, a very cute and young looking face, big blue eyes and, despite being only just in to his thirties, receding short blond hair. His soft and slightly accented voice, as he originated from New Zealand, echoed in her head. But what she remembered most was that no matter what he wore, his lightly blond tanned hairy chest always seemed to put in an appearance. When reviewing her final course work alone together one afternoon in the empty study room, it became blatantly obvious that the attraction was mutual. Despite the fact that she was close to graduating, she was still his student; he was still her lecturer. He had already made plans to go back to New Zealand at the end of term and then backpack through Australia. Nevertheless they did share a very tender and almost fairytale-like kiss before he left. She recalled how it took her months to get over him and she was afraid of going through that same pain again with Patrick. However, *was* it too late, even if her new-found feelings were unrequited?

# CHAPTER 3

❀

The February sunrise shone through the Georgian style window of the sophisticated hotel room. Abby always left the curtains open when she needed to get up in the morning; she always thought, what better alarm call than Mother Nature herself! The cool morning sun poured across Abby's sleepy face on a day that was to be a strange phenomenon. Despite her growing nerves, she was so looking forward to reviewing the store. Voicing her opinion was something she loved to do and now she was being paid for the pleasure. She thought the day was going to be pretty much taken up with the review, not really knowing how long she needed to be at the store; plus, she had to have the final copy of her review to the magazine by the following morning.

Abby's reverie made her lose sight of what the date was. Looking in the bathroom mirror and brushing her teeth simultaneously, she remembered, coming back to reality. It was the first of the month and, after rinsing her mouth, she shouted, "Oh Rabbits!" She also remembered she needed to take her contraceptive pill for the pure purpose of regulating her very erratic periods, something that was a result of her past extreme loss of weight. The time by now was nearing 8.30 a.m.; the car was due at 9.30 a.m. and just then the phone rang. She quickly rinsed the rest of the toothpaste away, which, despite one rinse, still clouded her mouth. She dabbed her face on the luxury hand towel and reached for the phone by the bathroom door. Clasping the slimline receiver in her hand, she spoke.

"Hello," she said in a hesitant pitch, unsure who would be calling.

"Bonjour, Mademoiselle," the sexy voice enunciated.

Abby knew straightaway it was Patrick! Her face flushed and at the same time she felt a wave of relief, relief that he couldn't see how flamed he had made her face with just two words.

"Hey you, Bonjour ca va?" Her voice tried to disguise her excitement and her awful accent. Luckily her review was in English, as her writing of the language was about as good as her speaking.

"Ooh, tres bien! Hey, good accent!" he said, laughing. "I just wanted to wish you luck for today."

"Thanks, that's really thoughtful of you." Her tone expressed some surprise by the gesture. But it was a welcome thought of kindness and she really appreciated it. Catching her reflection in the full-length mirror attached to the back of the bathroom door, she relaxed a little, her face now a cooler shade of peach. Her coy bare body was wrapped in just a towelled gown, which was still partially damp from the hot power shower that had woken her up for the day ahead. At the same time the shower had also washed her lengthy hair, which was now wrapped up in a towel and balanced on the top of her head with a final tuck to secure it in place. She was going to be late if she wasn't careful, but she couldn't bring herself to tell him that.

"I'm just at my office checking emails and faxes," he said. "Then I am heading off to court; but tonight I have to take someone out for dinner. Her name seems to have escaped me—you might be able to help me."

"Well, at least your trying to be funny," she laughed. "I'll give you a point for effect."

"You'll love it really."

He was right, she did, and she couldn't wait to see him later that day.

"Good luck, gorgeous, and see you tonight."

"Thanks again for phoning." She quickly added the words before the receiver on the other end was replaced.

"No problem. Au revoir."

Dressed in her classy suit, ready and raring to go, Abby grabbed her key card, zipped it into a compartment in her black shoulder bag, and checked she had her notepad and pen. The photographer was meeting her down there, so that was everything. With the door closing behind her she chased the lift, just catching it in time. Entering the lift she passed a middle-aged woman just getting off on her floor, and as she settled into the travelling cube two men entered. The first was a fifty-ish businessman with balding hair and a dull grey suit and the second a rather intriguing looking man, maybe thirty-five or so. Although he was quite striking it was as if he had an aura about him, something that almost compelled one to look at him. Abby was not long in the lift when the older man got off at the seventh floor where the conference suites were.

With the doors still waiting to close, Abby was left in the mirrored and spacious lift with this eye-catching guy. He wore black mid-thigh sport shorts and a logo t-shirt. He was very suntanned with mottled brown hair, styled to a suitable length and at the same time complementing his slender, defined and familiar face. He had some tasteful facial hair, which was making a beeline for his upper lip and chin and which highlighted his mossy green eyes. He towered over Abby with his predominant height, and as she felt his shadow lean over her as the doors finally started to close, she seemed to recall him from somewhere but couldn't recollect from where. Glancing at his sports bag that nudged his new looking snickers, she saw a tennis racket poking out of the side—and it was then she knew who he was. The realisation must have spread on her face as quickly as butter on hot toast. She looked over at him, and by now, smiling with admiration, his eyes were clearly drinking in the beauty of this young woman who apparently knew who he was. He was surprised, considering he had not played professional tennis for a few years now and was doing time backstage, so to speak, as a coach. Abby took a deep breath and acted quite out of character.

"I know you must get tired off this…," she began, trying to avoid a cliché and ending up with a classic. "You're not by any chance Pascale Cluzet, the international tennis star and all round champion winner, are you?" She completed the question with a gush of enthusiasm and excitement.

"I'm flattered," the stylish Frenchman answered simply with a debonair air, radiating charisma and a magnetic allure.

"You couldn't sign this, could you?" Abby held out her notepad and pen that she instantly produced from her bag. She eyed him hopefully, wondering what his response would be.

"Of course," he smiled. "I never could say no to a beautiful woman."

Abby blushed. She sensed his compliment was said merely out of kindness and politeness, but it was nevertheless a nice thing to say, she felt. The lift reached the foyer as he handed back the notepad.

"Thanks ever so much, really—thank you," she said warmly.

"My pleasure," he said. "You know, it's only fair as you know my name." He added with a cheeky grin: "I don't know yours."

"Abby, Abby Raycroft," she answered, smiling.

"Nice meeting you, Abby." His French accent radiated friendliness and sincerity, making her blush again.

"You too."

He headed for the sports complex and Abby met the car and, as they say; that was that.

Sitting in the car as it passed through the morning traffic, she felt exhilarated and apprehensive at the same time. She needed to pinch herself as to where she was and where she was going. She took a deep breath as she steadied her nerves, consciously relaxing in the plush leather seat. Her excitement was added to her other feelings like a shopping list, but she tried to contain herself. She didn't want to give the impression of being an amateur, or look unprofessional, knowing that there would be rival journalists all over the new store and much more hard hitting than herself. Her mum had always told her that "no one intimidates you without your say-so," but as the car reached the exclusive store, garlanded with people, photographers, TV cameras and even some celebrities famous for the trade, her mum's advice wasn't cutting much ice. Eric turned to her as the car ground to a halt just a few metres from the door of the store.

"Well Mademoiselle Raycroft, here we are."

"Thanks—well, I guess it's now or never."

As a result of many episodes in Abby's short life she did actually have a slight problem being among big crowds of people. Determined not to let her anxiety prevent her from making the best of this opportunity, she took a deep breath and braced herself. The realisation of how many people were going to be inside hit her like a bolt of lightening. With her face starting to flame and her chest heaving uncontrollably and with a sinking feeling in her heart and stomach, she was unable to disguise her panic attack from the Eric. She took some more deep breaths and concern creased the driver's face.

"Mademoiselle, are you all right? Is there anything I can do?"

"No, no, I'll be fine—nerves are getting the better of me—I'll be okay in a minute."

"Take your time," he added in an understanding and patient way.

"Thanks—listen, can this be just between us, it's just…"

Before she could finish he interrupted and reassured her, allaying her anxiety. She alighted from the car a minute or so later and was greeted by the cold daylight air. She paused at the driver's window and thanked him again, at the same time ensuring that he knew what time to collect her.

The sleek and stylish design of this new venture could not be faulted, and the layout was exactly right. Classic fabrics were married to modern ones, up-to-date looks merged with classics, and just the right tone for the environment—unpretentious and comfy, and all in a setting that was truly memorable. The collection and displays illustrated great thought and style. The team behind it all were welcoming and friendly and the mood of the whole area was that of calmness. The style they had opted for was quite unique in the sense that one could buy brand new fabrics, furniture and collectables, along with antique pieces and dated pastime additions. One could even bid at an auction, which happened in a magnificent glasshouse adjacent to the perfect covered courtyard with open seating for the warmer days. An array of drinks and nibbles were on display and, to add to the efficient running of the business, there were in-house professional designers, soft furnishing experts and a made-to-measure service for all their designs—nothing had been forgotten. Abby later came across an entire section dedicated to world interiors, fabrics and styles from all over the world and a layout similar to the Epcot Centre. You could travel round a globe style room and stop at different country displays and view all their treasures and styles and, of course, buy them too.

Luxury seating for use while ordering and stacks of books on the subject in question finished the approach that was really quite delightful and all under the same roof. There was an air of curiosity, emanating from different sources. Passers by that wanted to air their views, the wealthy, which were invited, and not forgetting the critical designers and journalists that wanted to nit-pick—they all filled the air with their opinions. However, this did not change the ambience that ignited the flaming store. It was all so bewildering, one didn't know where to look first, or second, come to think of it. Abby loved it. Although she was easily impressed, there was no escaping the fascinating idea, which had a lot of hard work behind it. The creation, in Abby's mind, would be a defiant success.

The day seemed to go so quickly, talking to other designers, interviewing the majestic staff, joining in with the finery at the auction and taking home an Art Deco vase which she knew her mum would love but wondered how on earth she would pack it. Circulating and sipping strong and flavourful coffee and using all her senses to make the best review within her capabilities, Abby continued to jot down her thoughts. The aroma of the fresh flowers that adorned every spare space possibly camouflaged the entire area with a faint yet worthy bouquet. The exquisite feel of textures from the kaleidoscope of coloured fabrics, the sound of the cultured water feature coming from the

China display, the sighting of the grandeur that oozed out of everything possible, and the brilliance and opulence spilling out of every corner, it was all noted by Abby. The taste of sophistication fed the air as if it had been ordered from a menu and no one seemed to be rejecting the delicacy. Abby enjoyed every minute and her nerves faded as quickly as the money in her purse did. With a complementary review finished and resting in her bag and her arms laden with high quality shopping bags, she was ready for home. Making her way through the glass doors the cold air was so intense that it seemed to slap her in the face, bringing an instant pinkness to her checks. Her body, icy in just a suit, moved swiftly to the waiting car.

# CHAPTER 4

❀

The Jaguar made its way through the noisy rush-hour traffic, the pavements full of bustle. People descended on to the city like falling snowflakes and, before you knew it, a few snowflakes had collected together and become masses of white predominance. She went past street cafes, which were full to the brim, and newsstands with the sellers cold and shivering in the chilly air. There were swarms of cars everywhere, the sounds echoing throughout the popular and lively city. Abby looked at the variety of individuals as they all went their separate ways, moving through all the bedlam. Some of them were in suits carrying briefcases and coming up from the stations, some dressed down, some lost and wandering, and tourists that you could spot a mile off with their cameras round their necks and the fetching bum bags. The bright lights reflected on the glass of the car and cocooned in the warmth of the vehicle Abby felt lucky to be out of the frosty sharpness, which had peaked in the polar atmosphere. The temperature, though, was far from being anything like the way Abby was feeling inside, a warmth was touching her everywhere. As the car pulled up in front of the palatial hotel, a smile spread across her contented face—and all because of her rendezvous with Patrick.

It was nearing 5.45 p.m. by the time she reached the hotel. She hadn't allowed for the traffic that had been atrocious. Charging through her hotel door and dumping her bags on the chair, she removed her suit with speed, catching the time as it edged close to 6 p.m. She really wanted to be ready for when he arrived, not wanting to keep him waiting. She ran her hands over her bare legs, sporting just her black briefs and matching lace bra. She wished she had shaved her legs that morning. She had planned to put on a new dress that her mum had made for her, but the sprouting hairs on her toned legs deterred her from doing so. Instead she threw on a black satin Jacquard trouser suit, removing the straps from her multi-functional bra, and slipped on a black faintly patterned halter neck top along with an Art Nouveau necklace to complete the effect.

Having added some dramatic make-up to her eyes to enhance the look, which she did with perfection, she was ready. Noticing that the time was 6.05 p.m., she swiftly brushed her hair and swept her fringe, which she wanted to grow back over her face. She had completed the look in less than fifteen minutes, and could have given any model a run for her money. Abby examined her reflection in the full-length mirror that was on the inside of one of the wardrobe doors and was pleased with her substitute and quick thinking.

Meanwhile, downtown, a confused Patrick was still in his office.

"Hey Patrick, I thought you would have left by now," said a friendly colleague. "I thought that case had been dropped."

"It was," he replied in an frustrated tone. "I just wanted to finish a few things off, that's all."

"Are you okay? You seem a bit distracted?"

"I'm fine, really."

"It wasn't that phone call you had earlier, was it? You seemed a bit fraught after that."

"Listen, Paul," he said with a hint of sharpness, "I appreciate your concern, but I'm fine." He added in a modulated tone: "I'm sorry, I have a few things on my mind, that's all."

Paul, a British lawyer, accepted his half-hearted apology and returned to his office.

The truth was Patrick was fraught and frustrated and bedevilled by a lot of other emotions too. The morning's phone call was on his mind, but it had nothing to do with work—well, not entirely. Patrick had strong desires and knew what he wanted and went after them at any cost. Selfish? Quite possibly, but strong desires sounded better and less self-centred. He had a number of things on his mind, and perhaps a pang of guilt was the result of a little of his conscience coming in to play. If it was, it didn't stay long. A passionate person tends to feel every emotion in a very intense way. Abby and Patrick were both similar in that sense, although Abby expressed herself differently to Patrick. This intense combination of their highly-strung feelings was to later add fuel to an already flickering fire.

Abby looked at her watch. The time was already 8.45 p.m. Though she conjured up a list of reasons as to why he was late and hadn't phoned, they were far from comforting. Just then the phone rang. Abby's heart sank as to who it was and why Patrick was not there with her.

"Hello?" she said as she picked up the phone, her voice strong but inquisitive at the same time.

The reply was immediate if not abrupt. "I'm really so sorry, work went crazy this afternoon!" Trying to redeem his rudeness, he continued, "I should have called before, I really am sorry." There was sincerity in the apology and regret in his tone, but the reason was not altogether the truth, though the apology was sincere. Whatever the real reason he was regretful and if it hadn't been for the fact that Abby detected his regret, she would have felt a lot more hurt.

"It's okay, these things happen." She tried not to betray how upset or bothered she was.

"I'll make it up to you, I promise, but now I have to go. Talk to you soon."

Before Abby could say anything else he had gone. Disbelief spread across her confused face. What had changed since yesterday? Then she worried—did she come on too strong? Was her attraction too obvious? Already on the edge of the bed, her body fell back so that her eyes peered up at the pristine white smooth ceiling. She was angry with herself for being so open. As she pulled herself off the bed she thought the only thing to relax her tense body was to have a hot bath and to get her surplus clothes off. Making her way to the bathroom, she started to run the hot water, adding her favourite scent to infuse some bubbles at the same time. After loosening her clothes and a twisting of her hair to dress it into a pleat, she reached for her towelling gown and was ready when the bath was.

Immersing herself into the deep bath she reminded herself that the review had to be with the magazine by 10 a.m. Planning to have done it in the morning she figured that with the evening free she would alter her plans. Lying in the hot steaming water she thought back to the simple yet significant things that made her feel there was an instant rightness and mutual attraction between the two of them. How could she have got it so wrong, she thought? She was convinced he felt the same; in fact, she was so sure it was like it was written on his forehead, and now it felt like he was blowing her out. Remembering how amazing he made her feel in such a short space of time, and just thinking of him, sent a shiver down her spine and a quiver across her shoulders. The subtle odour of his skin, the contact of his face on hers, the way his body pressed against her body and the tenderness of his caress. Her whole being ached for his touch again, but she had a feeling it was wishful thinking. Nevertheless her body did start to feel relaxed and at the same moment very tired. She rested her head on the back of the bath and closed her eyes. A second or two later there was an abrupt knock at the door. Startled by the dull sound, she sat up and paused to see if the knocking would persist, which it did. She climbed out of the bath with annoyance yet with a little secret wish that it might be…

She made her way out of the bathroom, tying her robe before opening the door.

"Sorry to disturb you, Madame, but there was a fax for you with instructions to give it to you immediately." The young and nervous bellboy handed the piece of paper to her. He saw the look of displeasure on her face. Having to leave her bath only to find it wasn't the man she yearned for was irritating, though she hardly blamed the bellboy.

"Thanks—um, I mean, merci." Stretching over to the dressing table she grabbed some money and tipped the young hopeful.

She closed the door and glanced at the fax. It was a few details for the article and also clarified that Mike Brampton from London would be at the hotel earlier than first arranged, now 9 a.m., to collect the review. With not much to do to the article, having fiddled with it while she was waiting for Patrick, Abby was not worried; she dropped the fax on the table, lost her robe to the bathroom floor and resumed her position in the cooler bath.

Her cushioned bottom rested on the enamel of the bath again. The ends of her hair around her neck became covered in bubbles as she sunk further into the water. Noticing her razor on the edge of the bath and her shower cream, she remembered her need to shave. Lifting her legs up one by one she freed then from the growth of hair contently, running her hands over her muscled thighs and calves to check for lingering hairs. Finishing with her under arms, the bath had fulfilled its purpose and she pulled out the plug. After some loud gurgling noises, the bath was empty.

Abby stood on the 100% Egyptian cotton bath mat and dressed again in her robe, damp from her earlier premature departure. Walking away from the hardness of the bathroom floor to the soft depth of the bedroom carpet, she paused at the vase of flowers on the bedside table. She was loving and enjoying the perfume and the combinations of buds, all beautiful and bright in spanking raspberry, with a perfect accent of green leaf. Dropping the gown on the floor her naked body quivered from the change in temperature. With a slap of expensive moisturiser all over her goose-pimpled body, she grabbed her pyjamas to warm herself. She released her hair, reached her notebook and headed for the sofa, all in an adroit movement.

It was 11.30 and the review was complete and ready for the morning. She lifted her agile feet up to relax her tired body on the sofa. She was still confused as to when she would hear from Patrick. She still felt bad about the whole thing for some reason and was wondering when she would see him again when another knock rang on the door.

"Oh, what now?" she said, recalling her earlier disappointment. But when she opened the door—there he was, all 170lbs of him in an exquisite suit, standing in the frame! To say she was confused was an understatement. One minute he was on the phone saying good luck gorgeous, the next he was on the phone again cancelling with no real explanation—and then he materialises like magic!

"Well, look what the cat dragged in!" she said, still annoyed and wondering why he had come round at 11.30 p.m. and not five hours before. But she ended her statement with a smile, nevertheless. It was as if to say I could be persuaded to forgive you if you try!

"Can I come in?" With no verbal answer and just a smile from Abby he walked in. "Listen," he said, flashing his disarming smile, "I wanted to explain my rather erratic behaviour. However I say this it will sound like an excuse, but I've just had a few problems at the moment, work things." He wanted to make it all better, realising he must have confused her with his mixed signals. But he still couldn't, or more accurately wouldn't, be forthcoming with the complete truth. "I promise it has nothing to do with you. It's just matters that have been going on before you arrived, but I have them under control now." Which was not really true, but he continued: "So, can we start again and just enjoy the days we have together?" With his French accent mixed with his barely detectable underlying South African accent he was sincere, even though not completely honest. Abby couldn't help but forgive him. With them both standing by the sofa at the far end of the room, Patrick reached to hug her when she said, "You're forgiven."

He felt her naked breasts through her nightwear pressing against his well-dressed chest, and a surging rush of desire ran all through his body. His attraction for her had grown even since the day before, and by now he was finding it difficult to ignore. Although she was now without any make-up with her hair undone, she was naturally radiant, which had an added effect on Patrick. Sitting on the sofa mirroring their earlier positions, they chatted about the day's review and the conversation led to his enquiring what her plans were for the coming days.

"I've taken some time off. A case was dropped, so I don't have to go back for a few days. I could pick you up in the morning and we can start doing the sights?"

"That's great, are you sure you can spare the time?" A little sarcasm crept in, though not enough to offend since her smile softened the edges.

"No problem—and besides, you're worth it," he said, adding a smile. "I'll come by about ten in the morning. That way you should be finished with that guy from the magazine."

"Okay, brilliant." She felt much happier and excited, once again feeling drawn to him like a bee to a honey pot. She really was feeling very somnolent after all the activity of the day but didn't want to say anything in case he left. Just then Patrick asked:

"Can I use the bathroom, I had a really rich lunch and…"

"No more information needed, go ahead." Both of them smiled.

With Patrick in the bathroom, Abby dropped her head down involuntarily and, feeling drained, cuddled up on the thick chenille fabric of the sofa. Her head sank into the soft luxurious pillow kept in the corner of the expensive furnishing, and she began to drift into sleep. Not even the flush of the toilet or the opening of the bathroom door a few minutes later could wake her. Making his way silently over to Abby, Patrick was warmed by the sight of her sleeping figure. He perched on the edge of the sofa and just gazed at her for a while. Then he moved her falling hair back off her face and drew his finger across her soft cheek. Realising the time and that she must have been very tired, he scooped her up in his more than capable arms and carried her, still asleep, to the bed. He lowered her down and simultaneously pulling back the bedclothes, Abby still oblivious to his affection and sleeping like a baby. Her semi-conscious body nestled in to the warmth of the sheets and, as Patrick finished covering her, he reached to kiss her rosy cheek. Her other cheek was submerged already in the feather-rich pillow. Scribbling on the pad by the bed, he wrote a reminder note for the next day's plans:

∞

*I'll be here at 10 a.m. I'll wait in the lobby for you. Be ready and wear something warm and we'll have a time you'll never forget. Patrick x*

# CHAPTER 5

It was what only could be described as the most appropriate yet incredibly sophisticated outfit Abby had ever modelled that she chose to wear for her day of sightseeing with Patrick. Warm and comfy and at the same time in its simplistic way, purely stunning. Her silver checked trousers rested on her comfortable black loafers, the whole outfit dominated by her impressive and close fitting knee-length black leather coat, which aptly moulded to her nubile young body. Abby's black cashmere roll-top sweater, which completed the look and caressed her long and elegant neck with charm and precision, added just the right touch. Clutching her compact shoulder bag, filled with womanly essentials and her automatic camera, she wriggled her fingers into some suede and leather black gloves. Her shoulder-length and freshly laundered hair was dressed in a simple single loose plait and flowed down her back. Her cultivated fringe sat elegantly on her shapely eyebrows. She felt so calm and not poised, not a worry in sight, just a clear open road for her travelling along—and she was doing it in style.

She left her room just as Patrick arrived in the lobby. Despite his casual appearance, he had acted quite out of character and had been undecided since he got up as to what to wear. His final choice was very precise, however—tanned twill designer jeans, a v-neck knitted sweater with an easy white t-shirt popping into view around the base of his substantial neck, all finished with the cherry on top of the cake: a deep brown leather sheepskin jacket. Stepping onto the lobby carpet with his weighty Bellow lace-ups shoes, his lingering aftershave wafted through the immediate vicinity. His longing brown eyes wandered over to the approaching lift and in a matter of seconds the doors opened to reveal Abby. With no hesitation from either, they embraced with a kiss on each cheek. In their glances they mutually acknowledged the impact of each other's eye-catching appearance.

"Good Morning," she beamed, her cheeky tone and pretended coyness expressing confidence.

"All ready then?" When he received a nod from Abby he posed his next question: "Was the review okay? No problems, were there?"

"No, no problems," she smiled.

"Great—well, let's go!"

The sights of Paris were calling out to them like a loud foghorn. Heading for the outside the comfort they felt with each other reached its peak. With their arms looped, their body language spoke before they did, and as they joined the pavement and all its bustle, the day's adventures were about to begin.

The capital and opulent city might be said to have enjoyed Abby and Patrick as much as they were enjoying it. Abby's eyes were new to the wonder that filled them. With that drop of sugar that sweetened the whole day, Patrick, she was on cloud nine. They shared moments she knew she would always remember, moments, however, that she was afraid would always mean more to her than to him. She felt so close to him—something she never knew before. All the sights, the Arc de Triomphe, the unforgettable Eiffel Tower and the beautiful River Seine, along with all the other earmarked sights, were all going to be complete because of the increasing desire she had for the man sharing every minute with her. She had a desire for him that was growing and spreading as quickly as ivy; but at the same time it was as unsure and as frightening as a roller coaster.

The views were memorable, the company dreamful, and the day was disappearing so quickly; but the day was not short of fun, laughs and some tender moments. Stopping for a late coffee at a delightful café, Patrick indulged in a French pastry and cappuccino, while Abby favoured a black and bitter coffee that came to her by courtesy of a miniature white cup and saucer. Momentarily tempted to skip the calories, Abby's mischievous mind succumbed to an impulse, and without further thought, as Patrick brought the large pastry to his month, she lent forward, lifting slightly from the old slatted chair, and took a bite from one end of the large pastry just as Patrick brought it to his mouth. She resumed her seat, still managing to smile gleefully as she chomped away at her portion of his sweet pastry. Patrick appreciated her humour, and when he finished his own mouthful looked quizzically at the end she had just bitten from. In jovial mood he added his own contribution to the banter.

"Well, I'm not eating that bit *now*," he said with a playful look of disgust while Abby, in response, aimed a red paper napkin at his chest.

With too much to see in one day, they concluded Tuesday with a boat trip on the Seine, combined with a passing glance at the Notre Dame Cathedral, an attraction they reserved for another day. Sitting on the hard inside seats of the French riverboat, a silence fell between them for the first time in practically the whole day. With only smiles from each of them while they relaxed on the floating marvel, Patrick lent forward and reached for Abby's hand—not a romantic gesture as such, but more a way of getting her attention and diverting her from the scenery for a moment.

"I…um…," he began with hesitation and uncertainty, "I have to tell you something." The hope and anticipation in her eyes made it difficult for him to release the words from his mouth.

"What is it?" Abby's face was still bright and colourful.

He still held her fragile hand and gazed into the blueness of her eyes, which were like drops of the ocean. A squeeze from her hand reassured him that he could tell her, whatever it was. But he still didn't want to tell her and spoil what they were enjoying and how he was feeling. Instead of relieving the confusion and seeking the firm ground of truth he swum deeper into the sea of deceit. Without her consent or knowledge, she was left swimming with him.

"I guess I wanted to say, I've had a great day and I…I really enjoy your company." It was true he did enjoy her company, but it was a large generalisation of what he should have said, far from his real intention.

"Thank you, you had me thinking it was going to be some deep dark secret for a minute then." Releasing her hand from his, she lent forward and kissed his cheek. "You're great to be with too," she added. Leaning back in her seat and peering out of the opened window, she took in all the beauty with the passing current of air.

Patrick, having failed to say the right words, gazed at her beauty, his selfishness having got the better of his conscience again.

The evening was descending upon them and, having touched on the elegant districts of the Champs-Elysees and sampled the delights of the many shops, dinner was next on the agenda. With a mass of selection to choose from, they opted for a chic bistro just a short walk from Abby's hotel. The low lighting, the tea-light candles on the tables, and elegant décor, gave the bistro a special charm. The setting imparted a romantic and intimate feeling to the proceedings. The candles were burning calmly and as they took their seats in their designated places, the antiquity of the finely crafted table creaked comfortably.

The padded chairs grumbled a little as they grated against the stone flooring, but were silent once in position. The blue checked tablecloth spilled over and rested on Abby and Patrick's laps, and with the enchanting smells from the food and wine and the faint sound of music, the atmosphere was typically French and exquisitely superb.

Sitting opposite one another, still dressed in their day wear but free from their coats, which were now draped over the back of the matching chairs, they studied the menus. Patrick made some welcome suggestions to a bewildered Abby, and when the time came he ordered with great ease and exactness. He even went to the trouble of explaining the way the food was cooked and served, endeavouring to impress someone who was impressed by him anyway. With the order taken and the mature red wine being poured by the over zealous waiter, the bistro was full of life and character, with a sense of culture from a variety of backgrounds. The sense of magic and contentment that seemed to sit in the two empty chairs at the table with Abby and Patrick was created by the obvious attraction and connection they had between them. Their voices didn't need to speak since their eyes did it for them. Waiting for the starters and sipping at the wine poured in advance from the half bottle, the conversation was easy and flowing.

Abby listened intently to his revelations of being a lawyer. At the same time she looked at him, trying to see deeper than all that he showed. She wanted to believe he was experiencing the same conflicting emotions and confusion that she was. However, although she recognised a feeling that was the same as hers cascading out of him, she felt she sensed something else—but was none the wiser as to what, even though she probed with subtle questions. She had tuned in to him more than she thought possible and as she listened, something popped into her head. She recalled a time when she went to see an opera with her mum and dad. She was worried she wouldn't understand it all because of the language, but her dad had reassured her that even if the words were confusing and didn't always make sense, the way the people spoke, expressed themselves, and by the way they looked with their eyes when they spoke, could say far more and be more readily understood than the words themselves. With this in mind she felt as if some of Patrick's innermost feelings were singing out to her like music from an opera, and she found herself understanding him more than she thought.

The conversation continued around the wild mushroom tartlets, herb salad, and warm dressing. With the starter plates clear and already heading for the kitchen, Abby brought her elbows up and rested her chin on her overlapping hands, clicking her knuckles along with the process. Patrick lent further forward and, with the candlelight on his face, their eyes locked. But a puzzled and inquisitive look appeared on his striking face. He lent back into the wooden cushioned chair and voiced his confusion.

"You know, I have to be honest. I thought you might be with someone. I mean, a partner, maybe even a fiancé. I was expecting you to talk about someone."

"Why did you think that?" she answered confidently, yet pleased.

"Well, the fact that half the men in here, including the waiter, for that matter, can't help but notice you. You're an intelligent and very beautiful woman. I guess I thought you would be taken."

Seeing her opening and seizing the moment, she asked her own question instead of responding to his. "So are you one of the half of those men?" Her tone was breezy, as if she were asking the time. With raised eyebrows, she tilted her head slightly to assert the question and ensure an answer.

"Maybe," he beamed.

"Just maybe?"

"Well, I best not show all my cards." He was diverting but still flirting.

"This is nuts!" Abby gave a wide smile and fiddled with her plait, breaking eye contact. Was she playing with fire?

"What makes you say that?" he asked with a nervous, faint laugh.

"Well, for one thing, we are related, however distantly; and secondly, I don't know…There's more to you, more than you reveal…Something runs deeper. It's like you're…" She lent on one elbow, her hand cupping her chin slightly, and smiled.

"Go on," he said, "I'm curious as to what you think—please."

"Okay." Her tone implied, well you asked! "I don't know, it just seems like you're lost or something. I mean, I know you have a great career but it seems like you are still looking for something—but you don't know what, or maybe you do, I don't know. It's just the way you look when you talk about Jacob, or your work and what you want for the future. It's like you're trying to prove something and prove yourself and in the process maybe you're forgetting what it is that you want, instead of what *you* think you should want." Emphasizing the "you" in the assessment.

"You got all that from my eyes?" he said with a dismissal smile and tone and a little chortle.

With a little headshake she replied simply: "I guess I just got it from you."

Staring into his eyes and not breaking contact, making him do it first, she knew she had struck a chord. With no more than just a smile from Patrick, which said enough, he dropped his head down and rubbed his hand over the base of is neck. He knew she was right but it wasn't her being right that scared him, it was that no one had ever been able to read him like that before. He wanted to say something, but at the same time wanted to keep his conflict private as he was unable and unwilling to confront it.

"Maybe you're right, but it's not always that simple."

"Why not? Surly it's as simple as you make it."

He looked distant and almost worried that his battle had come to light.

"Look, it doesn't matter," she said with a shrug of her shoulders. "But you can talk to me if you want to."

Abby's words made him wrestle with his conscience once again. But he was someone who went after whatever he wanted and that was the ultimate downside to his character. He went after what he wanted regardless of whom he hurt and the consequences. His desire to be a mighty success and achieve more than his estranged brother and to beat him to the top had taken him over. He had set himself goals and sights so high that even on a clear day they were hard to see. He didn't care how he got to the top of the ladder and who he had to leave behind along the way. However, he hadn't bargained on a complication—Abby. She had got under his skin and he was battling to stop her getting into his heart. And with moments of enlightenment such as he had just experienced from her, the battle was hardening. Never one to show his true emotions, he tried to dismiss it all, and with the welcome arrival of the main course he reached out his hand to hers.

"Best not try and understand me," he said lightly. "Just love me." And so he passed off the whole thing as if it were nothing, and tried to dismiss the nagging fact that she was right. At the same time he tried to reassert his more arrogant side, the side that didn't feel or hurt as much, the side which was unaffected by things, especially matters of the heart. His variance with Jacob was not really that deep or complicated; there were no hidden skeletons in the closet—it was all just a result of a very big rivalry that they shared between them. But the fact remained that Jacob, who was a few years younger and had a very successful career and prosperous future ahead of him, was an immense threat to Patrick, as his career was far from as successful. He had changed law firms three times since arriving in France and couldn't bear being told what to do. Over the years they were always trying to out-do one another and it always seemed to result in hurting or involving some innocent party. However, with

Patrick having plans of his own and Jacob still revelling in his success, it was like the calm before the storm.

Strolling back to the grand hotel in the prestigious district, the hot-blooded pair became chilled by the minus-degree air. They passed café bars filled with an array of people all sipping at their coffees and chatting together. Watching them as they passed, everything seemed to look so simple; maybe that's what it looked like with Patrick and Abby to passer-by's, just two people who were enjoying each other's company and strolling along freely. Patrick and Abby had undoubtedly become incredibly drawn to one another and just had a knack of bouncing off each other. It all had a look of simplicity but that was merely the surface, for if one were to delve deeper there might be complications and hidden secrets. Behind every face and every lover there is a world yet to be discovered and explored; however, should one find that world, it might not be what one expects—and by then it might be too late.

With some friendly teasing and banter exchanged between them, along with some playful pushing and a final locking of entwined arms, they enjoyed the late evening sky as they neared the hotel. The night heavens looked like an embroidered quilt. The stars shone with a sharp accuracy, as if they had just been hand stitched to deep black fabric. Abby and Patrick both paused and stopped at the side of the pavement, taking a minute to fix their eyes on the sparkling magic crammed into the darkness.

"It seems so peaceful up there," Abby sighed, her head tilting back as her eyes filled with the starlight. She turned her head to glance at Patrick and her heart quickened as he moved forward to stand closer to her. With both their faces staring straight at one another, with inquisitiveness as to what was to follow from Abby, she smiled lightly to ease her tenseness. With as much emotion and honesty as he was capable of giving, puzzled too by what was going on and what he was feeling, he reached towards her and simply took her into his arms, receiving an instant response. He forgot everything, just enjoying her closeness, knowing how much he was drawn to her. Abby's head rested neatly on his shoulder, while her arms scooped beneath his underarms and held him as closely as he held her. The warm soft collar of his jacket cushioned her cold pink chin as she nestled a little closer. Her refined and alluring perfume rubbed off from her neck, lingering on him longer than she did. The hug had such power, as if they couldn't get close enough to each other, and for a time they remained motionless in the embrace. Patrick was the first to break the silence.

"You're great," he said. The short and simple declaration may not have been something out of *Romeo and Juliet* but it had a power of truth. In its own uncomplicated way the words were special and seemed to be more poignant, thanks to his mixture of accents. Abby's response was to merely echo what he had just said, and with the same sincerity: "You're great too."

The moment was concentrated with feeling. Breaking the hug after a few minutes, Patrick held Abby's arms firmly, feeling the expensive leather in his grip. Abby waited for what was going to follow. He covered her dainty ears with his large and strong hands, cool from the cold air, and with anticipation in her eyes as to what he was going to do next, he planted a kiss on her forehead. Thanks to the light breeze her fringe had blown to the side joining the rest of her locks and leaving it clear for Patrick. His lips left a lasting impression on her exposed skin and, with no further words, they hooked arms again and a few minutes later arrived at the stylish hotel.

Outside the grand hotel the cold hard grey pavement was covered partially by a majestic red berry carpet, sheltered by the white and green-striped appropriate canopy that hung over the entrance. In addition to the sound of cars arriving and going from and to the hotel, the area around the building exuded with life and, despite the cold night, voices of people still out and about could still be heard, occasionally interrupted by the odd horn from passing vehicles. With no further advancement on the emotions and expressions already shown by Patrick, Abby thanked him for a fantastic day. With the same response from a mystified Patrick, they arranged to meet at the earlier time of 9 a.m. the following day. They went their separated ways, though not before a final hug and, instead of perfunctory kisses on each cheek, one lingering kiss took place on just the single side of each of their faces. That loving exchange gave the finale to a revealing day.

# CHAPTER 6

❀

The weather for Thursday was a complete contrast from the previous days. The early year temperature may have risen slightly but with it, seemly from nowhere and out of the blue, it had brought torrential rain and gusty winds. The drumming of the heavy falling rain against the windowpane harmonised with the whistling of the blustery gales. The hotel room was filled with the sound of the harsh weather. Abby lay snuggled up in the warmth of the hotel bed, still unaware of the turmoil outside. The time approached 7 a.m. and, with a sudden burst of harder rain on the windowpane, she awoke to a dark and gloomy room. Her mood was quite unlike that of the room, however, and as she swung out of bed and burrowed her bare feet into the depth of the carpet, she felt fresh and happy. When she walked over to the window it felt like she was walking on air. Her face was so bright it could have melted stone. The day's weather didn't dampen her mood and, with quick steps and joyful movements, she raced to the bathroom for her morning ablutions.

At the same time Patrick stood at the window of his lavish apartment, located in the discerning district of Paris. Wearing nothing more than his grey Calvin Kline briefs that hugged his firm body, he was thinking of one person only and, for once, not himself. His thick dark hair remained uncombed with his face partially covered with appealing stubble. He was also gauging their plans for the day, now taking into consideration the severity of the weather. His subtle yet adequately hairy chest covered his modest peaks and torso with pride. After a moment of reflection and sipping a much needed cup of coffee, he decided to call Abby.

Meanwhile Abby, thinking along the same lines about the day's activities, was just about to reach for the phone when the ringing stopped her in her tracks.

"Hello?"

"Hey you!"

"Hey, I was just going to call you! Do you think we should alter our plans?"

"Well, I could still come to you and just see how the day goes. We still have plenty of time. Oh, and I might have a little surprise for Friday."

"Ooh, sounds intriguing. Any clues?"

"Just that we will be together and having a good time," Patrick said in an almost touching way.

"Okay then, so when will you be here?"

"Say about 9 a.m., as we agreed. We might as well still make the most of the day."

"See you soon then."

"Okay blue eyes." Brief but to the point and with both of them needing to get ready and less than two hours to spare, they got moving.

Patrick rolled down his only garment and headed for the shower. With the steam and heat bellowing from the large showerhead, he basked in the force that powered onto his athletic body. Running his hands several times through his hair to rinse out the shampoo, he couldn't shake Abby from his head. With a final lather of shower gel over his rippling muscles, he turned the tap off and pulled back the screen to just cover himself from the waist down with a navy blue towel that was waiting for the pleasure. Abby, still relaxing in the tingling warmth of her shower and enjoying the comfort of the large cubicle, she too couldn't get Patrick out of her head. He made her feel so at ease and had a way of making her feel so alive and vibrant. She stepped out of the spacious shower having refreshed her day-dreaming self. She slid back the glass doors and wrapped her dripping body in a white cotton towel, overlapping it around her chest and making a knot to secure it in place. It was a change from her usual gown. Moving back to the bedroom to sit on the edge of the bed, still yet to be made, she hand dried the ends of her washed hair while half listening to the TV news station that she had found.

Abby searched through the drawer where she had housed her underwear and bras and selected a simple stretch t-shirt bra and a coordinating pair of bikini briefs, both in fresh white. As she slipped them onto her slim body and added underarm deodorant, she gazed into the mirror above the dressing table. Abandoning the hair towel from around her neck and, still bare of any other clothes, she set about brushing and drying her hair, and then applied some simple foundation. Nothing else was needed for her naturally radiant face and skin, something she inherited from her mum. Padded by the kindness of the dressing table stool, Abby continued to dry her growing hair with the provided hairdryer. With a final brush and her makeup all finished, she set about getting dressed.

Sitting on the floral slipper chair adjacent to the four-poster bed, the time neared 9 a.m. Drinking some morning tea and reading a requested English newspaper, she reviewed her chosen outfit. Looking down to her grey loose flannel trousers, accented by the simple pink wrap-over shirt, she was pleased by the superb way the two garments complemented each other. She was happy and comfy with her decision. Adding an extra two and a half inches to her five foot six height, were her black ankle boots; and, with a few final touches of jewellery and a second addition of her designer perfume behind her ears and a rub on the underside of her wrists, she was ready and waiting.

Standing outside Abby's hotel door, Patrick acknowledged a passing twinge of nervousness about seeing her again. He admitted he was plunging himself deeper and deeper into something beyond his ability to escape. As he stood moments away from Abby his whole body tensed and, as he was about to knock, he stopped himself and moved away from the door. He leant on the wall next to Abby's room. With his head tilted back and resting on the faint patterned textured gold wallpaper, he paused and, with both his hands sunk into the pockets of his dark textured jeans that were secured by a thick brown smooth leather belt, he stopped to ponder.

His chunky turtleneck jumper, delicate to the touch thanks to the added lambs wool and subtle light, sat with ease on the denim material and fitted his upper body with exultation and meticulousness. Despite his body being camouflaged to some extent by his waterproof jacket, which still had traces of the rain on it, one could still see how good he looked. There was only the distant sound of the arriving lifts and some faint footsteps from the other guests that filled the near empty hallway. However, lost in a moment's thinking, he was in a state of oblivion and unaware that two people had walked by and wondered what he was doing. However, whatever he was reflecting on must have reassured him somewhat, because all of a sudden, with one swift movement, he pulled his body up from the hardness of the wall, pivoted his stylish and robust shoes on the bordered patterned green carpet and knocked with a self-assured bang, right on time—9 a.m.

The greeting between the two of them was simple and polite, with a quick kiss on the cheek. Having shared more intimate moments than that yesterday, reverting to a peck on each cheek would have seemed awkward and false. With the breakfast trolley finished, which they had just shared and enjoyed—a simple continental breakfast—the mood was light; yet at the same time the atmosphere was intense with the chemistry that was brewing between them. The weather outside was still unchanged, and although not a disaster to the day, it threatened to make it less enjoyable. So with a day or two to spare, just relaxing in Abby's comfortable and all expenses paid for room, which she only had for one more night, was still a great choice. Besides, Abby didn't care where she was as long Patrick was there too. In the far corner of the room, away from the other furniture and the slipper chair that Abby had enjoyed earlier, there stood two upright armchairs fixed in a woven striped multi-shaded fabric. Separating them was a wrought iron glass side table, and a convenient freestanding lamp stood behind. It was there that the two of them sat finishing their beverages.

"I have some photos with me I thought you might like to see, just some old family ones." Abby leant forward, perching on the edge of the comfortable chair, anticipating his response.

"Okay," he said a little hesitantly. He wasn't one for nostalgia, but was nevertheless intrigued.

Abby had removed her boots for more comfort and moved with agility across the floor, creating foot patterns in the extra thick luxurious carpet. Delving into the compartment of her case the thought struck her that she would need to pack up soon as the rest of her stay would be at the Beauvilles. She pulled out an envelope of photos, none in an album, just some she had grabbed at the last minute from her drawer at home.

"Here we are," she said, making her way back to Patrick. "There should be some when we visited you in Durban." Instead of resuming her previous place she knelt down beside Patrick. Sitting back on her legs, her bottom resting on the soles of her feet, she handed some of the various pictures to Patrick, adding that they had no order whatsoever. The selection of pictures varied from the Abby growing up to her graduation, some old family ones, which included a picture of Patrick and Abby from way back when they had first met all those years before. They glanced through the distant memories rekindled by the photos, Patrick enjoying the experience more than he thought he would. In one photo Abby was eleven, on a primary school trip. Seeing her sitting on some open greenery eating a packet of crisps, her hair even longer than it was now and her cute appealing childlike face beaming with life, he couldn't help but say: "You were such a pretty girl!"

"What do mean, *were*!"

"You know what I mean." And just then his view of her as a pretty healthy girl changed to someone unrecognisable.

"Who's this?" He was referring to the picture that was partly sticking to the back of the one he was holding.

"It's me," she said, shocked at the discovery that that one was in the envelope.

"You! Were you ill or something?"

"Something like that," she answered in a light way to dismiss any further questioning.

His shock was caused by seeing the figure of a tiny, unrecognisable girl standing in the foreground of the picture, which he still clutched in his fingers. Waif-like in appearance, timid in stature and painstakingly thin, it was Abby. She stood dressed in white shorts and a loose pale blue denim shirt. Her gaunt and wasting body was nevertheless more than detectable. Unbelievably, she was in fact three years older than in the previous picture, a far cry from how she looked there. Her features were distorted by the hollow and sunken look that haunted her face. In spite of the distanced view it was possible to make out the faint sallow shade that seemed to appear on her once contented face. Her deep-set eyes were shadowed by an unhealthy pallor that circled them. Struggling to weigh six stone, her tired and cold spirit looked lifeless and feeble.

"What was wrong with you?" Patrick asked with concern and regret as to why he had never known about it. Although not on her top ten list of things to talk about, she felt that she wanted him to know. So she answered with confidence, not wishing to sound ashamed of what she had gone through.

"I was anorexic till about sixteen and then I was better, for a while, that is; and then, when my dad died, I fell apart all over again and it all relapsed."

"You were anorexic but you were always so happy, I mean, when you came to South Africa."

"Sadly things changed. When it all reoccurred when my dad died—that was probably my lowest ever point." She sounded awkward talking about it, not because it was to Patrick, but because she never really spoke about it to anyone other than those involved. But she also wanted him to know that she had persevered, that she had wrestled with her condition with dignity and grace.

"The first time started a year into secondary school. Long blonde hair, blue eyes, all mixed with a naïveté, made for an interesting combination. It was an all girl school and the friends I thought were friends turned out not to be on my side. I may have been a tad on the chubby side, you know, with puberty and all that, but compared to everyone else I was construed as fat, fat and ugly. I ended up by listening to it all, feeling ashamed and taking on board what they said. I became so ill, and I started to really struggle with my studies. Having a group of girls constantly bothering me, it all became too much. The stupid thing was even when I was ill and losing weight, they still didn't want to recognise me as being any different. When I told my mum and dad eventually, they told me it stemmed from jealousy—but I didn't believe them, I wasn't open to believing anything. I didn't have enough belief in myself. Even when the school was informed nothing changed and because of my deteriorating health, mum and dad took me out of school and I had a private tutor until I went to university.

My dad paid a fortune for that and for private treatment but my parents just wanted me to get better and to be their healthy little girl again, instead of this fear driven creature they no longer knew. Even though I wasn't at school and I was being taught at home it was too late by then—the seed had taken root. The treatment was such that it controlled the anorexia and, though it somehow enabled me to put weight on, I barely ever got over eight stone. With my broad frame that was still very thin. But I was never what you'd call 100%. I guess I only just had it under control. University was much better, though—nothing like school; maybe just being that much older, different people, I don't know."

"What happened the second time? You said you were worse?"

"It was different than what happened the first time. When it first happened to me, looking back, the symptoms were more of classic anorexia, if you like. I had cut down to an extreme the amount I ate, but I still had a fascination with food. I would want to be around it, cooking it for other people, seeing them eat; and I even used to read recipe books while I nibbled feebly at my dry crackers. It gave me a buzz that I was in control, when, in fact, I wasn't. But when it reared its ugly head again it went from an obsession to a very powerful fear, one that just drove me to distraction. I would exercise to an incredible amount. So much so that I even developed shin splits. It was a really, really bad time as I couldn't even put any weight on my legs in order to walk. I remember the only exercise I could still find to do was cycling; I mean, I couldn't even swim, that's how painful they were. However, somehow I still managed to cycle. I was underweight and couldn't even walk up the stairs. I had crutches to help me walk. My legs were strapped up, yet I still had to exercise. It was like I had been taken over. I also had this thing about being lazy; I had set amounts of time that I could sit in a day and sleep. I remember being out one day in the car and we got stuck in this traffic jam; because I'd sat for so long I had to stand up for most of the evening. I just lost all rationality, and the more the fears took me over the harder everything was. The fears created a suit of armour over me. Not only could I not get out of it, I couldn't let anyone in.

The problem this time was not only whether I limited the food I ate or whether I was choosing to eat enough to just survive; the problem was I couldn't look at food, I couldn't smell it and I couldn't be near it! Food became my ultimate enemy. It's funny, you forget things and I never kept a diary, but I remember how my mum even had to cover over fruit bowls, and eventually limit what food we had in the house. I just thought *everything* was going to make me put weight on. I thought food was conspiring against me or something. I couldn't walk past people eating, dustbins, litter on the path, anything that had a link with food, even in the vaguest or obscure way. I was just so scared of food; it was like I had been taken over by this stranger. I'd became this person not only I didn't know but I didn't like, and when you have that many fears and such paranoia that you can't even sit down for more than ten minutes at a time, life just seems so pointless and endless. I couldn't bare the thought of living the rest of my life the way I was.

When my dad died the shock was just unbelievable. One minute I was on the phone talking to him in Scotland, where he was on business, with him saying he had a surprise for me and that he would be landing at 6 o'clock, and the next thing…well, you know. It was like something just snapped inside me, something that was fragile and vulnerable to start with. By the time we got to the funeral I was so dosed up with sleeping pills I didn't know what was happening. I was in a complete daze and, to be honest, I can't even remember the day very well. From then on it was just a downward spiral."

"I'm sorry I wasn't at the funeral," Patrick said with a sudden pang of regret.

"It's okay, best you weren't—it wasn't a pretty sight. I feel really stupid now telling you all this. You must think I'm a bit strange." She had no tears, not even a saddened face, just a sudden realization that she had possibly said too much, and she wondered what he might now think of her.

"There's nothing to feel stupid about," he smiled sympathetically. "What's stupid about being honest? All that is part of who you are, and being able to talk about it is a great gift. It shows how far you've come. And I don't think you're strange. I think you're an amazing person, to have lived through all this and survived to tell the tale. It just makes you even more special."

With that reassurance from Patrick and a prompt from him to continue, Abby carried on with her story. She wanted to explain more to him as best she could and opted for the best metaphor she could think of.

"It was like I was this tired weary old boat that had been damaged by a passing storm. It had been fixed, sort of, but had only ever sailed again on calm water. It hadn't been tested again in a storm. So when the next storm came out of the blue, totally and utterly unexpected on a normal day, the boat couldn't cope and started to sink—deeper and deeper." As the painful words came out of her trembling mouth she changed her position and sat crossed legged. Having moved her body round somewhat and now looking up to Patrick as she spoke, she also looked past him, seeing with her mind's eye all those past events that had caused so much anguish. Tears welled up in her eyes, but she controlled them, preventing them from trickling down her face, so open and sincere.

"What happened to the boat?" He smiled and leant forward.

Straight faced, bringing her knees up to her chest and wrapping her arms around her calves, she dropped her hands down to her ankles and continued. In a sense her rearranged position was comforting.

"Somehow the boat was rescued and brought back to shore. It was badly wrecked and needed a lot of repairs, but with time and patience it sailed again. This time it was stronger and tougher than ever before."

"What changed, though? I mean, how did you get completely better after being so ill?" He really wanted to know and had such concern in his voice.

Abby took a deep breath and prepared herself for her very personal revelation, but wanted to add something first.

Patrick slid down from his chair with his back resting against it, his legs stretched right out in front of him. There was something more intimate about their positions and, despite the wide selection of seating, the soft floor seemed most fitting.

"The thing is," Abby began, "With it all I've learnt this: I may never be 100% again—in a way I can't be. There will always be that two or three percent of me with those fears; the difference is they are now outweighed and no longer dominate my thinking. However, it never goes, not really—you learn to live with it and you find your way of keeping it at bay. That's something that I've now managed to do. But I'll have days when things are on my mind, a sudden pang of guilt about what I have eaten, or a worry if I haven't exercised as much as I would have liked; but those days are fewer and far between now. The fear of food itself eased as I started to grieve properly for my dad. It was as if I used the fears to hide behind, avoiding my true pain. But as for my first steps to recovery, it was strange how it came about." Abby paused a second and then resumed her tale.

"I was sitting in the garden one afternoon, tired, with my whole body aching, and I was wearing one of my dad's old jumpers. I was on this spot near where my mum and dad had once made me a teddy bear's picnic—it was for my fourth birthday. I remember it all so clearly, as if it were yesterday, I think because it was so special and important to me. Anyway, my dad did this treasure hunt for me around the garden. I had to find all these little teddy bears and at the end of the trail, hidden in the garden somewhere, there was an enormous one and each teddy bear was leading me to him. I'd found quite a few and was close to the end, when it just started pouring and pouring with rain. This dark gloomy cloud covered the garden so abruptly—it was like someone had just thrown a thick old blanket over the once blue sky. Mum was rushing to gather everything up, taking the basket and rug along with all the food inside, and dad was telling me to wait in the house until the rain stopped. But I wasn't having any of it and kept saying, 'I must stop the rain, I must stop the rain!' So I ran to the cupboard in the hall and got out my wellies and my green waterproof coat, which had this yellow umbrella on the back, and I said to my mum and dad, 'I'm going out to stop the rain, I won't be long,' so matter a fact! Seeing how determined I was they didn't even try to stop me. Mum pulled my hood over my two plaits—they were supposed to be like Goldie Locks—and off I went." Abby spoke with glee and warmth. She wasn't recalling the story with sadness but with a big beaming smile right across her face. Patrick mirrored her smile at appropriate moments.

"So there I was back out in the garden with my hood up and plaits poking out a bit and my yellow wellies protecting my feet, and I said, 'Please God, can you stop the rain so I can find my teddy and finish my picnic?' I only asked once and I stood and I waited and I closed my eyes. Then, a moment later, as if by magic, the rain stopped! It was like the clouds had been personally lifted from the sky and squeezed out just at my request. The sun reappeared and the sunlight poured over my face. I pulled back my hood and there, filling my eyes, was the most beautiful, beautiful rainbow I had ever seen! I remember it so well, even to this day. At the end of that rainbow—well, to me, anyway—was our garden shed, and for some reason I just instinctively ran over to it and opened the door. Inside, sitting perched on our lawnmower prouder than any king on any throne, was my big teddy! He was light brown and had a yellow bowtie and I called him Sunny. The thing is, I believed in what I was asking. I believed that someone would hear me and, having that belief at four years old, is what proved to be my turning point fifteen years later. From that day on mum and dad always called me their little rainbow."

The revelation, for Abby, had been so meaningful and profound, that she felt she had given him an insight into her very soul. Both still sitting in the same position, he pressed Abby to finish.

"Well, like I said, I was sitting right near this spot and I longed so much to go back and be that little girl all over again; but a voice inside me said, 'Don't go back, go forward. Be that girl as she would have been *now*.' I wanted that so much, as much as that day I wanted it to stop raining, and I just said to that voice, 'I don't know how to be that girl'. I mean, I didn't just get up and go and start eating and stopped being frightened, but from that day on I wasn't dealing with it on my own; I'd given it to someone else, I'd shared it. I know that might be hard for someone else to understand, but from that day on I never felt I was on my own, and the hardest thing when you're in a place like I was, is to let go and say, take it all from me and help me. You have to give it up and let it go, otherwise you can't be helped. It's like that thing you do when you fall back into someone's arms; it's having complete trust and letting go and letting somebody else catch you. Not only did it help me but it helped my mum too. Dealing with my dad dying in the way he did and seeing me destroying myself all over again and coping with her own grief, it was a tough time for both of us. We got through it together though."

Abby's eye-opening revelation finished on a happy note. Patrick was touched by her trust in him, telling him something so personal. However, at the same time it made him feel even guiltier about his lack of honesty; but right now he wanted to forget that.

Patrick stood up from the carpet, pulled Abby up to a standing position by holding her hands, and said decisively: "I think we need livening up."

"What did you have in mind?" she smiled.

"Can you dance? Of course you can!" Answering his own question, he headed for the compact stereo.

"Have you got any tapes?"

"I've got CDs." She reached for her hand luggage where she had a travel CD case brought for her CD Walkman for the flight and for when she stayed at Martha's.

"Okay, let's see what you've got, Mademoiselle."

"Are you serious?"

"Of course. Okay, let's try this one."

With some quick pressing of buttons and adjustment to the sound, he forwarded the track to number nine and the music began. Bellowing out of the micro system came Abby's favourite track. She loved this song and strangely Patrick had instinctively gone straight to it. Despite her youth she loved sixties music and, as Neil Sedaka's *Oh! Carol* played, her face lit up with a large smile. Patrick took her hand, just clasping her fingers, and pulled her with one positive motion to start the dancing. With instinct leading before talent or experience, they both just enjoyed the close contact and danced to their hearts' content. With twists, turns and some shaky moves, their laughter filled the room with enchantment. With their hands married, their breathless bodies close and their eyes locked at every opportunity, an indescribable feeling gripped them, something that was difficult to put into words. It was as though they saw a part of each other in each other, a part that was so mysterious and profound, a feeling so rare between two people. It almost made them hurt and ache; even when they were together the need for each other was ever-increasing. For Abby, though, there was an addition to her feelings. She felt that although she was standing or dancing so close to him and within arm's reach of him, it felt like she would have to cross a chasm to really get to him.

# CHAPTER 7

Patrick pulled out the casual chair for Abby as they sat down for lunch in one of the many restaurants in the hotel. The morning had been full of heart-wrenching revelations, but with their peppy dancing and a quick freshen up, a late lunch was next on the list. They had chosen the informal seafood eatery, which had an impressive range of extremely tasty sounding dishes. The whole mood was lighter and as they enjoyed the flavourful dish they had both decided upon, and with only a few other people seated in the compact yet charming eating place, Patrick remembered his surprise.

"I didn't tell you my surprise. I have two tickets for the Gala Ball on Saturday night which is being held here in the Monet ballroom. I know you are leaving here tomorrow, but I know how impressed you were when you saw the ballroom yesterday."

"You've got tickets! They must have cost a fortune! How did you get them?"

"I have this client who owed me a favour. When he couldn't go he gave them to me, so are you pleased?"

"Pleased? I've always wanted to go to a ball, for as long as I can remember, but…what will I wear? I haven't got a dress."

"Well, Cinderella, we will have to buy you a dress."

"I suppose the review paid well and I haven't bought myself anything here yet."

"Don't be silly. I'm buying you a dress—my way of saying thank you for the great time I'm having."

"I can't let you do that! It will cost the earth for a ball gown—and how will I get it home!"

"Okay, we'll compromise. We'll hire the dress and that way you won't struggle to get it home, and you won't feel so bad about me paying. Done!"

"Okay then." Abby still felt awkward about Patrick spending his money on her; however, he seemed so adamant she agreed.

"So how do you want to spend the rest of the day? We could look at some boutiques, see what dress you like."

"Sounds good."

Their late lunch was complete and, as they headed for the main foyer, Patrick's mobile starting to ring, leading Abby to take her cue to visit the rest room. Patrick stood to one side of the foyer talking to the caller, not far from where Abby was still powdering her nose. As the restroom door swung back, Abby only heard the final words from his call, "See you Monday night then." With a choice of shops in the hotel complex, it was there that they started to look. With drenched people still flocking into the hotel shaking their umbrellas, they had made the right choice in opting for the dry and warmth. It had been a strange last few days and with Abby knowing she was leaving Sunday she didn't want to think about what was going to happen when she had to leave him. They had not just got on well with each other; the way they were together and the chemistry they shared was what one dreamt of finding in an ideal partner.

It was bizarre; this was the man she had played with when she was eleven. She remembered how he taught her to dive while in Durban, and considered how much older he was than her, how much time he took to look out for her the whole month they were there. Now she had this burning passion for him—a desire so strong it could have turned the current of the sea alone.

With window displays laden with designer names but not a hire shop in sight, buying was the only option; however, not opting for something so flamboyant would make it easier for Abby to get it home. With Patrick still insisting on paying as they prepared to enter the first shop, Abby reached to his smooth cheek and kissed him with tenderness and thanked him with great sincerity. After admiring the window view they went into what looked like the most lavish of dress boutiques. As they wandered round the sparse area Patrick's sense of humour surfaced again and, holding up dresses to his own masculine body and hooking them over his head, he pretended to file his far from ladylike nails. His antics elicited suppressed giggles from Abby, even more so when the shop assistant gave him a stern look.

They shared laughter and playful teasing and some extremely intimate moments, one in particular. It was when Abby approached a very tasteful purple patterned taffeta skirt adjacent to a coordinating sequin silver shaded bodice. They were beautiful and just seemed to call out to Abby. The iridescent fabrics shimmered and changed in colour as Abby lifted them off the peg and raised them both to the light; for a split second, as the light caught the garments, she saw her rainbow in her mind's eye, brighter than ever. With the interior light beaming from the ceiling it mirrored the sun that had once poured onto her face, and with her memories close to mind because of the morning and the garments seeming perfect, it was a good enough reason to overlook the cost. She beckoned Patrick to come over so she could show him her choice.

"What do you think?"

"They're gorgeous."

Abby wandered across the wooden floor to the freestanding mirror, her boots making a confident sound on the hard floorboards, with Patrick following behind, having taken the top for her. She rested the taffeta skirt against her tailored trousers and, as Patrick lent in closer behind her, the fragrance of his aftershave preceded him and sent a shiver down her spine. As he spoke, his lips directed to the back of her neck, the hairs on her body stood to attention.

"Let me hold the top so you can get an idea." His offer had a hidden agenda, any excuse to be close to her irresistible self. With his chest pressing to her back, he held the top against her blouse, leaning over her shoulders. As Abby gazed into the mirror she found herself looking at how well they looked and had to remember to look at the outfit.

"I best try it on to be sure and to check the fit." She made her way over the stylish changing area, removed her own clothes and dressed her confused body in the designer skirt and top. The fullness and long skirt covered her inappropriate footwear and, as she arranged herself in the mirror, she un-tucked her hair from behind her ears and pulled back the curtain to reveal a pacing Patrick. As she stood just outside the changing area, the shop near empty, she said, "What do you think then?" She remained in her position, waiting for a response—but her nerves made her tuck her hair again.

"You're stunning!" His eyes were mesmerised by her dazzling appearance.

"It's very expensive," she smiled, still happy from his compliment.

"As long as you like it—that's all that matters."

With Abby changed and back in her clothes and carrying a very classy bag out of the shop, she thanked him again—and this time the kiss on the cheek was mutual. The afternoon was fading fast and, undecided on what their next move should be, they thought it best to take the outfit back to Abby's room first. Abby suggested an Art museum, but with the best part of the day over that was something they'd best leave for another day. With Abby wanting to pack up her things for her change of venue, the direction they were travelling in seemed the right one—and something else was on the horizon.

The brass doors of the lift closed and they stood close by each other, Patrick just a little behind her. With the bag in Abby's hand and the lift still moving, the silence was unusual for the two of them and with a now or never impulse, Abby turned and smiled at him and they shared a look that said it all—and the moment finally came. Passion and desire came into play and with an overwhelming thirst for each other's lips they met at last. Abby, still holding her bag, swung it over Patrick's shoulder, her free hand caressing the back of his thick hair. His hands were on either side of her mouth, but as the kiss became deeper they slid down her body.

The kiss was strong and powerful and acted as a match igniting the fire, with the heat intensifying and the flame strengthening as the lift stopped at the landing. The arriving noise of the lift and waiting guests interrupted the kiss but, only momentarily, for as soon as the bedroom door closed, the bag and key card were lost on the floor and the passion restarted—only this time with even more craving and urgent need for each other. The dull and darkened room needed some light and with a quick flick of the switch the illumination filled the room discreetly.

Their hungry bodies stopped by the bed, their legs just detecting the smoothness of the sheets. Their lips still touching and their bodies breathing at an increased pace, they both knew where they were heading. Their arms were so entwined in the embrace it was difficult to tell whose were whose, both very much anticipating what was about to happen. With no words spoken they just lost themselves in the moment, resting from the kissing for a second to lock eyes, their pulse racing with anticipation. Patrick drew Abby closer, his searching lips avoiding her lips as they explored her soft angelic, fragrant neck, covering it with delicate and patient kisses. They responded to each other, sensing their mutual and intensifying desire. His heightened feelings for her aided him in giving her the pleasure he wanted her to feel. She dropped her head back as a sign of acceptance of the bliss he was succeeding in giving her, letting him know how effective his touch was; nevertheless, she knew she had something she needed to tell him.

"Patrick, I have to tell you something." She tried to sound serious in the midst of the pleasure.

"It's okay," he murmured. "I think I know what you're going to say." He paused and gave her a reassuring look that told her he knew this was the first time she had been touched in this way. The way her body responded to his contact made him aware that her body was pure to the touch of a man. After that she said nothing else, just happy to respond to the new life he was bringing to her, like a wilted flower receiving water. Patrick's soft kisses travelled lower, to Abby's chest, and with his hands assisting him, he lifted her wrap-over blouse over her head. His eyes took in the simple yet enticing lingerie that covered her modest breasts, leaving her trousers still to conquer. However, with Abby's bare midriff and Patrick still clothed, she followed his example. She lifted up his over-thick jumper in unison with the white t-shirt he had on underneath to reveal his inviting chest. She wanted to feel his body on her lips and as she laid the first kiss around his right nipple, Patrick felt so alive, as if with that one kiss she unlocked a part of him that had lain dormant for a long time, as if forgotten. She covered his chest with tender kisses and, in spite of the circumstances being alien to her, she was guided by the instinct awakened by the love she had for him—a love that had developed so quickly, yet a love that stepped in and aided her along the path to fulfilling Patrick. She wanted to make him feel how incredible he had started to make her feel; but this was a big thing for Abby and she didn't want it rushed, and so she pulled back from the intensity, curtailing the touching and leaving him to contain his desires a little longer. Through her naiveté she didn't know it would drive him crazy with suspended passion.

Telling him she would be back in a minute, she headed for the bathroom, clutching a garment she had quickly grabbed from the drawer, the only thing she could think of that she had with her. She wanted it to be special and, unwittingly, she was setting the pace. After a moment she reopened the bathroom door, seeing Patrick sitting on the edge of the bed and the covers pulled back. He was free from everything other than his briefs. She walked over to him and stood between his lightly tanned and hairy legs, with her body now dressed in a simple ivory satin chemise. She bowed down her head and met Patrick's lips again, her hands on the smoothness of his clean shaven skin. Time had stretched and it felt longer than just five minutes since she had last tasted him. He wrapped his arms around her waist, hesitating and breaking the mouth contact to make sure this was what she wanted. Then he slowly moved his hands under the weightless fabric, which in a moment had slid midway down her shapely thighs after her confirming eyes told him what he wanted to know.

Their lips met again as Patrick moulded her velvet like buttocks with his imperious hands—but he wanted more of her. The passion was brewing and as their bodies fell back onto the crisp clean sheets, her head sank into the luxury pillow, with Patrick covering her lightly with his rampant body. His gentle hands touched all of her chaste skin with tenderness and consideration. She received his touch and caresses willingly. The chemise lay abandoned on the carpet along with Patrick's last garment, their naked bodies writhing with zeal. Abby felt a burning need to touch more of Patrick and manoeuvred herself with grace and, protecting his body with her own, she lowered herself to his waist, kissing every available part of his supple skin along the way.

Whatever experience Abby lacked she had a great ardour for Patrick, and that outweighed any inexperience. She had an instinctive ability to drive him crazy. From his waist she avoided the next milestone and instead kissed deeply down his inner thigh, leaving her succulent taste behind as she did so. Patrick quivered in the intense and titillating delight that brought his eager body close to boiling point. He wanted to take Abby further along the path of euphoria and explore her being more, so he took her back to where she lay before. Sacrificing the pleasure she was delivering, Patrick returned to her chest, taking both her supple breasts in his hands. They were unspeakably soft. He simultaneously kissed and embraced them in an intensifying way, then lightly dragged his lips down her tingling body, his flickering tongue never far from her skin as he descended.

Long past her waist, his hot lips and magical tongue began to melt Abby's already thawing femininity, making her lift her rounded hips from the mattress as the provocative excitement electrified her. His sensitive exploration sent surging currents through her already charged and aroused body. They had taken each other to the place they could share together and with gentleness and patience they moved slowly and naturally together. They had no inhibitions and their youthful bodies responded readily and with ease to each other. Her hands fervently gripped Patrick's lightly perspiring back while her responsive legs locked around his waist. Then, with mutual eye contact, the moment of pulsating sweetness swept both of them to a new and sudden height of ecstasy. Their chests remained heaving and their hearts beating as one, Patrick's body collapsing to the side of Abby. As he kissed her stomach he travelled further up to her neck, and then their mouths met for a warm lingering kiss. Lying close together, arms and legs entwined, Abby felt she was in a dream, one she never wanted to wake from. Patrick stared up at the smooth white ceiling, his thoughts taking a different direction. He knew he had just been very selfish, but nevertheless wanted her so much; and this growing feeling he had for her had just spiralled completely out of control. It had left logic, thought and consideration a long distance behind.

CHAPTER 8

❈

Patrick and Abby stepped out of the chauffer driven car; courtesy of the Beauville's luxury and fabulous lifestyle and were amazed at what they saw. Disbelief spread across their faces, as the Beauville's Townhouse was absolutely outstanding. The four-story white building stood proud as punch on Avenue Gabriel, with the trusted and long standing housekeeper Maria and Butler Franc waiting at the darkened double doors. Abby and Patrick had to pass through a small front courtyard before reaching them. The area was simply decorated with some exquisite potted plants and secluded by the four-foot high hedge, which was entwined in a black spiked metal fence. They both made their way though the grandeur, Patrick's hands now free from Abby's luggage, as the conscientious and particular Butler had taken it from him. He was at the same time very welcoming, as was Maria. The entrance hall was merely the tip of the iceberg and, as they entered further, they saw a striking staircase which curved round impressively to reach the first floor, dominating the extensive reception area. The convoluted black metal design of the staircase was finished with a shiny brass rail and superbly complemented by the opulent décor. The style the Beauville's had chosen and captured so well followed through the entrance area to the first of the grand and spacious salons.

The area was adorned in rich antique wood and scattered with oiled canvases, the most predominant being the Jean Baptiste Camille Corot of Ville d'Avray. With historic furniture from around the world, privilege of their wide travels and large bank balances, everything was very elaborate and very intricate. As Abby and Patrick took it all in, it didn't feel like a home as such but more like a museum: one half expected to see a sign saying no food or drink to be consumed on these premises. However, she was grateful they had trusted her and didn't want to seem unappreciative. The atmosphere was very sombre but with the two of them standing among the old and treasured pieces, they brought new life to the porcelain-like room.

With some Louis XV furniture incorporated with eighteenth and nineteenth century masterpieces, the quality and elegance oozed out of every square inch of the whole townhouse. They wandered around jokingly trying to outdo each other as to what they came across. They thought they had found the ultimate discovery when they were shown the guest suite by Maria. The sweet unassuming housekeeper stood tall despite being less than five foot; her very petite body showed experience and politeness, which came from her mature years. As Maria headed for the kitchen dressed in housekeeping attire and her long greying hair twisted into plaits and then a bun, Abby headed for the second door within the bedroom suite and the ultimate find stood before them.

The Salle de Bains was just beyond their imagination—affluent swags and tails titivating the period restored window, a bold pale green wallpaper with a gold pattern motif hung proud and tall, thanks to the incredible high and decorative ceiling. The beautifully moulded cornice that ran round the top of the slightly domed room did so with exactitude and married very well with the mural painted ceiling. The reproduced detail of one of Michelangelo's paintings added the most unique quality to the outstanding bathroom. The room had a bit of everything, French, Italian and even some English touches brought from Martha's original background. The sumptuous velvet cream carpet, partially covered by the Louis XVI pure wool rug, which added light tones and an additional floral touch, could have been overlooked by the other superior views. Abby passed the fine Victorian roll-top bath that stood superior on its decorative claws as she wandered over to the crescent table that was propped against the wall and finished with an oval charmed mirror above. Laid across the George III mahogany demi-lune table were guest toiletries and decorative glass bottles and, glancing along the way, one spied a salient regency chair that had the most exquisite throw draped over it, typical of the inspiring rococo period. Patrick wandered across to Abby who was feeling the texture of the seat cushion of the stately chair and scooped his arms around her waist.

Abby clasped his casual yet designer navy shirt, which tucked into his dark denim wear flawlessly. Cradled in each other's arms and admiring the view out of the window, their bodies simultaneously swayed in motion; and as Patrick dropped tender small kisses down Abby's neck, she giggled and wriggled, since he was making her tickle and he knew it. Not wanting to reject the affection, though, she guided him to place the delicate kisses upon her cheek instead. He adorned her silky-smooth skin with the same delicate kisses, the ones that had previously tickled her; however, her neck wasn't good enough—he wanted her lips. He turned her face with a gentle touch of his hand and, as they propelled themselves to each other's lips, it became very tempting and most leading. Having been left to their own devices and the staff far away in their own quarters, the kiss steered them to the bedroom and suddenly had more urgency about it.

Their embrace began to stir both their dormant passions and, having directed their eager bodies to the grand bed, they allowed their bodies to land on the perfectly made posted-bespoke double grandness. Lying casually across the bed, Patrick ran his powerful hands over Abby's clothed body; the touch was made even more compelling by the yearning and unbridled enthusiasm from Patrick. There was no ennui about his touch, just pure and utter passion. Abby's various shaded pink multi-striped sweater didn't stay long on her aroused body and, garment-by-garment, she was divested of the most important items. Their mutual carnal desire was brewing up nicely and taking over, and, notwithstanding their plans for the morning, they lost themselves in the overwhelming moment. As Patrick made love to Abby the rightness between them shone ever brighter and must have been visible from a distance of ten thousand miles!

The rest of the day consisted of some final sightseeing and, with plenty of photos later, they strolled the cosmopolitan streets. The late afternoon sun was far from view, the darkened 6 p.m. sky introducing a suspicion that rain was once again on its way. Maria had insisted she cook for them that evening, so they planned to be back at the Beauvilles in time for the kind gesture. As they walked side-by-side they just seemed to be enjoying being with one another, almost mesmerised by each other; they could have been the only ones in the capital. Having exhausted all they wanted to see they headed back for dinner.

The superb and magnificent dining room accommodated a delightful three-pedestal table with seating enough for ten. The floor was a magnificent marble but became softer by the period rug that overlapped from housing the table, as well cushioning the legs of the chairs in the process. Various fineries decorated the perimeter of the room, and as they sat at the mighty table they were severed like Royalty. The diffused lighting and the romantic candlelight brought intimacy and closeness to the large and oversized stateliness. They sat at right angles to each other, Patrick taking the head, and as they wined and dined they enjoyed the experience in spite of feeling a little underdressed for such a grand room.

"I had no idea they would have a place like this, it's just another world!" Abby said, sipping from the crystal brandy glass at the end of the meal.

"It really is some place," Patrick said. "I hope I have a place like this one day."

"What—exactly like this? I mean, it's stunning and all that, but it lacks a bit of personality and character. They've decorated to impress, to keep up with their high circle of friends. I mean, they're lovely people, don't get me wrong—but they are a little ostentatious, don't you think? Money, that's all that interests them. Okay, having money is nice, but don't let it take you over so that's all you think and talk about; they used to drive my dad nuts!" Abby's reply was made in her down to earth, girl next-door way, then smiled self-consciously, having stepped down from her soap box. Patrick returned her smile, not really listening to the words but just captivated by her appealing simplistic views that made her special; and when she finished talking he just lent over to her and kissed her lips.

"What was that for?" Abby enquired, smiling.

"You're just so sweet," he said, almost sentimentally.

The evening was passing and as they relaxed in front of the fire in the smaller of the two salons, digesting their exceedingly tasty dinner, they naturally snuggled up to each other. Comfortable on the luxury rug close to the burning fire and flickering flames, the scene was faultless. Patrick's back rested on the giltwood canapé seating, which stood facing the fire all at a suitable distance away. The elaborate carved detail had been pressing hard into his shoulders, but he relieved the pressure by reaching for a cushion from the far corner of the antique structure. Abby sat in seventh heaven, nestled between Patrick's legs, sipping at their after-dinner coffees carefully from the chinaware.

The blazing fire lit the imposing room with no additional lighting needed, and with just each other's company they relished the limited time they had together. Abby's head rested on Patrick's chest and, as she dropped her head back to gaze up at him, he kissed her tilted forehead and buried his chin in to her parted loose flowing hair. The time together was evaporating speedily and with her return to England nearing, she wanted to know what was going to happen after her departure. The few days had been the most exhilarating time for her and she couldn't bear the thought of it ending. They had shared so much, their thoughts and minds, their bodies and their souls. The question was on the tip of her tongue but, as Patrick kissed the back of her head in a very seductive and sensual way, the words just seemed to vanish.

It was almost as though Patrick sensed the moment's silence would lead to the unspoken question, which for different reasons he wanted to avoid for as long as possible. Abby turned her ardent body round and met his passionate lips head on, her agile legs becoming draped over one of Patrick's thighs with the dominance of her body framed in Patrick's capable arms and the base of her spine supported by his other searing leg. As he lowered her body further to the rug, lost in the delightful kiss, the scene was romantic and oozed sensuality. Their bodies were now lying parallel to the demanding flames and were padded by the sumptuous carpet, which covered part of the majestic wooden floor. Patrick's rampant body covered Abby's half dressed self lightly but dominantly. She could feel his hard enthrallment pressed against her equally aroused body. She raised herself up slightly with the kiss to help him free himself from his shirt, longing to feel the intensity of his overwrought chest pressing up against her nipples that were taught with desire.

He planted seeds of kisses over her terrain of soil, touching every inch of her quivering nakedness. Her body responded to every touch as the seeds took root. He then approached her longing female essence, amplifying the pleasure he was giving her, of which he was reassured by her tight grip around his wrists. Wanting to reciprocate the warmth and glory, she turned his body over and sat positioning herself lightly over his hips. With her upper body tall and her lithe legs either side of his thighs, she loosened his belt and freed him of his trousers and undergarment. She fell onto his awaiting chest, caressing his responsive body and delivering some much anticipated mouth contact to his heated skin. She took her time before she slowly moved her lips further down to his enduring readiness and, with great appreciation from Patrick, she embraced the area with tenderness and charm before allowing his urgent need to slip into her receiving warmth. His need for Abby was urgent but she stayed just where she was and used her newfound confidence to lead the event. They manoeuvred their passions to the point of no return and fell deeply into the advancing moment, and it was only then that they lapsed into a state of pure, unshaken fulfilment.

Their contented bodies lay huddled close together, Patrick wrapping a blanket over their touching nudity. His arms swept the chenille fabric right around them both, Abby sitting so comfortably in the atom of Patrick's raised legs, with his knees locking her in to his irresistible allure. Her relaxed back pressed against his torso and the strong hold he had over her physically extended emotionally and she knew she had fallen deeply in love. The evening had long since passed but before heading to their bedroom they just sat close in body and close in soul, just gazing at the waning fire and taking pleasure in the romantic atmosphere.

Friday morning dawned and it was the day of the Ball. With the sights long since covered the day was free to enjoy with each other. However, as Abby rolled over on the expensive white sheets, the only trace of Patrick was the faint lingering smell of his aftershave on the oxford pillowcase. With blurred vision as a result of not yet having put in her contact lenses, she could just about make out a scribbled note that stood on the nightstand propped against the clock. She read the time—a fuzzy 11 a.m.—with disbelief, and read the note:

> *I didn't want to wake you as you looked so peaceful and we had a long night! I left early as I was worried about something at work, plus I need to check the decorators are finishing off ok . I'll be at the office but I'll call your mobile at about 12 am, that's if you are up by then! Don't worry, I haven't forgotten tonight. Talk to you soon, blue eyes.*
>
> *Love,*
>
> *Patrick xx*

As Patrick lay and held Abby in his arms earlier that morning he had gazed down at her face, his whole body aching with torment and confusion. He was holding in his arms the most amazing woman and someone he felt so deeply for, but knew it was someone he was going to have to let go, and not because of her pending departure. It was, in fact, because of a lack of honesty on his part. The pain of telling her the truth and the pain of losing the loving feeling that was saturating his body was driving him to distraction. With the excuse of work he found a temporary reprieve from all his anguish.

Abby lay back in the warmth of the bed, having read the note and given way to many smiles that spread over her waking face. After she had filled her mind with his words, she pulled herself up from the mattress and headed for the special bathroom. With pangs of hunger, she dressed modestly in her chambray robe and, with her hair twisted into a quick loop, she headed for the open staircase. Wandering down the cool marble stairs, happiness lightened every footstep as she recalled the memorable night that made her eyes sparkle. Maria greeted her cheerily as she entered the maple kitchen, having prepared a late breakfast for Abby who ate with leisurely indulgence, sitting less formally at the kitchen breakfast table. Moments later, with a final mouthful of brioche, Maria reappeared with the portable phone, as Abby had asked if she could phone her mum. She kept her mobile free for Patrick and dialled for England.

"Hello!" Teresa had such a bright telephone voice.

"Mum, it's Abby."

"Abby, how *are* you!"

"Very well," she replied with cheekiness, longing to divulge her news.

"I know that tone—so what's brought a sparkle to my little girl?"

"Let's just say things with Patrick took an unexpected turn."

"You don't mean you and him are…?"

"I do," she responded a little hesitantly, unsure of her mum's reaction.

"Well, that's great!" she enthused, expressing surprise.

"Do you mean it?"

"If you're happy, which sounds like you are, then I'm happy. So come on, tell me everything!"

"Gosh, I don't know where to start, everything's happened so quickly." Abby's smile couldn't have been wider. She updated her news from beginning to end, and as they shared in Abby's newfound happiness, she felt even happier. Now that her mum knew, it was as if her relationship with Patrick was a *fait accompli*. They had a lovely chat, and went on to speak with her aunt. As the time approached 12 a.m. she said goodbye to her mum, just in time to respond to the ringing of her mobile.

"Hello?"

"Well, hello!"

"Hey you, what are you doing?"

"I'm just sorting out a few things at my office." As the lie came out of his mouth he quickly changed the topic. "Listen, I'll be back with you at about 2 p.m. I just have to pick up my suit for tonight. Is it okay if I change at your place—it just saves me going back to mine again later?"

"Sure, no problem; are you okay? You sound a bit distant?"

"No, I'm fine—it's just not easy to talk here; there are people milling about. Anyway I'll be back soon and then we'll have all afternoon together." He tried to convince himself that he was okay as well as trying to convince Abby.

"Okay, I'll see you soon," Abby replied, sounding concerned as to his uneasy tone. As she fiddled with the mobile in her right hand, running it through her fingers against the maple wood table, her elation dropped a little. She pondered a while as to what could be causing his subdued tone, not really believing his reason. She thought maybe it was because of the fast approaching return to England. She didn't want to delve any deeper than that, so she dismissed her worries and headed for the bedroom to dress.

When she walked through the door of the grand bedroom her feelings for Patrick and the built up emotion of the last few days just seemed to catch up with her. Sitting in her coloured robe on the side of the bed where Patrick had slept with her all night, she reached for the pillow that had supported his head and caressed it in her arms. Burying the side of her face into the fibres and inhaling the aroma of the man, she realised she was uncontrollably in love with him. Her face flushed as she gave way to panic, thinking she might never see him again and that the part of him she felt she couldn't reach was the reason he was avoiding the question of what they'd do when she left. With all the overwhelming love and concern in her bewildered body, emotion took over and tears flowed freely from her anxious eyes, all the way down her flushed reddened face. The pillow caught each tear that fell, acting as a support to her lonely body. The plan had been not to think of leaving him in Paris until she had to, but that plan held no water anymore. Abby wanted to know whether she was going to lose the one man she could see herself spending the rest of her life with. Would it be the end of their intense love affair after the weekend, or was this just the beginning?

The beautiful two-piece outfit that Abby was wearing for the dance hung on the outside of the decorative wardrobe. However, having bucked herself up a little from her earlier tears, she needed only her comfy clothes for the day. She fastened the belt of her washout jeans, straightened her close fitting diamond patterned sweater and composed herself for answering the door, which had just that second rang. Wandering down the numerous steps, the sound of the knock still echoing slightly, she took a deep breath and tried not to falter from her decision to later ask him point blank where they were going. Tucking her undressed hair behind her ears, she opened the door to the dry but chilly conditions and to Patrick.

He stood dressed casually in dark denim jeans and a white shirt, which had a small emblem on the left top pocket, and with a few buttons left undone, his rugged hairy chest tantalised her eyes. With his suit hanging over his arm he leant in straight away and kissed Abby, using his free hand to press the back of Abby's head, intensifying the contact that he wanted. She had all afternoon to pose the question, yet she had fears and apprehensions because as long as she didn't know the answer she had hope, and at the end of the day, when it came to the crunch, he would have to say something before she left. So as she wavered again, she bit her tongue and lost herself in the presence of the man who was having the most irrepressible affect on her.

They relaxed in the salon with the only requirement being to enjoy each other's company. They relished in the fun they were having playing cards—a simple game but they were making it entertaining, making one another laugh to the point that their stomachs and jaws ached from the hilarity they were sharing. The game they played could have been anything; however, it was the togetherness they were enjoying that mattered. While Abby assessed her next move for the card game, Patrick just fixed his eyes on her. He took in the happiness that could be his if he wanted it, yet despite his overpowering love and passion for Abby, which in a way was selfish love, in his mind there was another passion that was stronger and one that was going to completely vanquish his love for this amazing girl. The aspiration and necessity to be bigger and better than his younger brother was to cost him his one true chance of happiness and long-term contentment.

Later in the afternoon, having enjoyed the simple pastime, they relaxed on the aging golden chaise longue. Patrick sat upright with his unperturbed body leaning in the curve of the furniture, while Abby laid lengthways, her head resting in his lap. Her face was staring over to the far wall while Patrick spoke of his ambitions with work. He may have been trying to lay the foundations for his pending revelation. However, Abby was just lost in his accent and the warmth and intimacy she was feeling, unaware of his possible intentions. His hands wandered over her contented being as he continued talking about the success his brother was taking pleasure in and how he had his own frustrations about that. Abby responded, turning her head, her face staring straight up at Patrick's tormented expression.

"You're happy though, aren't you?" she queried.

"To a point. But there is so much more I want. If you had the chance to have the one thing you had always wanted but you had to sacrifice something to get it, would you still take it?"

"I guess it would depend on what I had to sacrifice and whether I thought the reward was worth the loss."

"But you would consider it?"

"Maybe, I don't know." With a confused smile she added, "Where's this come from?"

"Just me thinking out loud." Dismissing the opportunity he could have so easily have taken, he lifted Abby's mixed fibre v-neck sweater in his winning way, dropping a loud and tickly raspberry onto her bare skin, covering her belly button with the teasing gesture. Her knees curled up with laughter and in a light-hearted way they just messed about and enjoyed the fun—for the time being, anyway. The playfulness carried through as they headed upstairs, as it was time to get ready for the evening. It was as if Patrick was in quicksand and was sinking deeper and deeper. He had ignored his chance at the beginning of being honest, and all the way through the last few days. He was playing with Abby's heart and now the game was spiralling out of control.

# CHAPTER 9

❁

The hazy morning sun struggled to shine through the collective clouds, but the light through the open drapes was enough to wake Abby who was far from sleeping anyway. She crept out of bed, not that early, though early enough for Patrick to still be asleep. Sitting at the breakfast table having made her way downstairs just dressed in the warmth of her robe, her hair in a ponytail and her fringe flicked and messy, she sipped at the Darjeeling tea that she had prepared for herself. The evening of the Ball had been very memorable: Patrick had told her how she looked even more stunning than when he saw her in the outfit in the dress shop. The way he looked last night in his black dinner jacket and white dress shirt, along with a sharp bow tie, was a vision she would never lose. When he stood before her dressed to kill, it was just one of those moments when one knows things will never be the same again.

Deep in thought and finishing the last dreg of tea, Abby turned sensing the feeling of someone close by. She was right. Patrick had started to approach the kitchen. Dressed in just a pair of checked woven burgundy boxer shorts and a cotton navy t-shirt, he paused, scratching his head through his thick dark hair, then made sleepily towards her.

"What are you doing down here on your own?" he smiled, raising his hands to her shoulders and gently massaging them through her towelling gown.

"I woke up so I just made a drink."

He sat down beside her as she replied, tilting her mug to see if any of the drink was left, hoping for a taste.

"Why don't we go out for the whole day?" he said. "We could go to the museums or do the Eiffel tower again, whatever you want."

"Yeah, sounds good." She just looked at him and then words just came out of her mouth involuntarily. "Why won't you talk about me leaving? We know it's going to happen. Why can't we talk about what we're going to do?"

"Abby…" His tone was still reluctant. "It's not that simple."

"What's not that simple? Why do you keep saying that?" Her voice became frustrated and a little annoyed, but that came from her unexplained love for him.

"Don't do this."

"Don't do what? What am I doing? You tell me."

He paused and tried to gather himself, rubbing his forehead and exhaling some breath. "I wanted to tell you but…I just couldn't, and the longer it went on the closer we got, and the harder it was."

"Tell me what?" She stood up and walked over to the sink, leaving her mug there before going back to the table to stand opposite a seated Patrick. She leant on the back of one of the chairs opposite and waited, repeating the sentence. "Tell me what? For goodness sake, Patrick, just say it!" The suspense was aggravating her normally patient self.

Patrick buried his exploding head in his hands and ran his fingers through his hair, all before lifting his eyes to Abby's intensive stare. His eyes wandered over the smooth white ceiling before he dropped the bombshell.

"I'm engaged." He waited for her response.

With a release of breath and a faint laugh of incredulity, Abby responded: "What do you mean, you're engaged?" Her face expressed confusion.

His continued silence made her snap and with the passion that was Abby's driving force, her composed voice lost its control. "Answer Me!" she said forcefully.

"Just let me try and explain," he said, tying to ease the anger that was filling the concentrated air.

"Explain! What is there to explain? What was this, then, just a last fling to get it out of your system?"

"It wasn't like that. Look, I want you to understand and for that to happen you have to let me explain."

"Why should I listen? It seems pretty clear cut to me!"

"Because it's not, and I want you to know why I am doing this. Please, sit down." There was pleading in his tone as he gestured to the chair.

Sitting opposite Patrick's taut body, Abby's body language expressed reluctance.

"I met Laura a year ago. She was involved in a case I was dealing with. We got talking and one thing led to another. Dinner led to another dinner and then we were dating. I knew she was falling for me and I guess I took advantage of it."

Abby's face showed that she was far from impressed. "Is there a point to this, or is this as good as it gets?"

"Abby, please, I am trying to make you understand," he continued, despite her comment. "It's not that I wasn't attracted to her; but I was more attracted to her name." He paused, not so much out of shame but on account of Abby's unconvinced face. "She's the daughter of Samuel Cooper-Davis." He knew Abby might have heard of the name through her dad, so for the moment he didn't elaborate further.

Cooper-Davis was probably the largest legal firm in Canada, with headquarters in Quebec and mass divisions far and wide. It was an incredibly lucrative firm, one that had had many high profile cases and one that Abby had heard of, thanks to her late father's many connections and dealings as a corporate banker. The picture for Abby was forming; however, Patrick continued before she could say anything.

"I couldn't believe my luck. I'd met this woman who stands to inherit a fortune and is part of one of the biggest law firms there is, and not only that—she was besotted with me. She became my one chance to have a bigger and better success than my brother could ever have."

Before he could carry on Abby responded: "So you'll marry this woman just so you can have more than your self-centred brother? You're no better than he is!"

"You don't get it," he shook his head. "This isn't just about who has the biggest toy, or who had the most girlfriends; this is about winning—winning a game he started, a game that I'm going to finish!" His voice changed when he spoke about his brother; it went from calm to pure frustration—but it went back to pleading as he continued to make Abby understand. But she abruptly interrupted him.

"Listen to yourself!" she said with contempt. "This isn't about winning! This is about marrying someone you don't love, walking away from what we've just shared and never probably being happy as a result of it; and it's for the sake of looking the big man! Are you seriously trying to tell me that's what's going on here? It would have been easier if you had said it was some cheap affair and you really did love this Laura! Where is she, then? At the apartment with the imaginary decorators?"

"She's in Canada sorting out the final wedding plans and the apartment is being decorated, that was true. We're getting ready to lease it when we move to Quebec."

Abby's face became ever more distraught. When he added the part at the end about moving, it all became too real and the certainty of losing him was sinking in. As she pushed the chair back with all her anger and stood on the cool solid marble floor, she felt a lump welling up in her throat as she tried to speak. Her heart was racing at the speed of light, with her stomach feeling vacant yet sick. She didn't want to cry and with all the strength she could find she fought back her tears. Still standing with her arms loose by her side and her body away from the table a little, she fired her next shot.

"Do you have no integrity at all? You've involved this innocent woman just because she has money to settle some petty competition. Don't you think she deserves better?"

"It's not like I'm not fond of her," he said lamely, trying to redeem whatever he could. He rose to his feet in a bid to try and make the sentence more convincing.

"Fond! You actually think that makes it okay?" Abby was forgetting her own pain and actually feeling sorry for the woman he was lying too.

"You don't know Laura like I do, she's cold and hard, tough even; she's got her motives too, she not some naïve…"

"Oh! Not some naïve virgin like me! Is that what you were going to say?"

"I didn't mean it like that." He walked over to Abby to clutch both her arms, but she responded by breaking the hold and walked back to the sink, leaving Patrick the other end of the kitchen, his body leaning on the integrated fridge.

"I just meant she's not like you. Her way is just so different. You're looking at it how *you* would feel, but you can't do that because your way of thinking is completely different to hers. Her love is a cold love, formal. She doesn't feel things deeply, not like you do. That's why, when I saw you last week, you were like a breath of fresh air in a stuffy old room. Abby, I have never in my life felt like this about anyone! You are the most amazing person I will probably ever meet; but I have to do this." With that mixture of feelings in the words he spoke, he had managed to approach a calmer Abby. He carried on talking gingerly, not sure as to how long she would let him stand so close to her.

"I didn't set out for this to happen and I never wanted to hurt you. I just wanted you so much. I wanted to forget what I was doing with Laura and just be with you. I wasn't meaning to fall for you, but I did and I'm glad I did." He moved himself to lean against the sink adjacent to Abby and as they both stared down at the floor, Abby rubbed her blurry eyes and responded.

"You let me open myself up to you knowing you had absolutely nothing to offer. Do you know how utterly humiliated and stupid I feel? Why couldn't you have let me decide what should happen instead of you making the decision for the both of us?"

"Because I knew if I told you I was engaged we would never have had the week we just shared." He turned his body and held Abby's slumped shoulders.

"So what are you saying? It's better to have loved and lost and all that?"

"Maybe I don't know; at least, we will always have this week—doesn't that help?"

Abby looked at him with shock and amazement that he could have said something so insensitive. She freed her shoulders from his touch and, using her arms to gesture and express herself, she reacted to what he had just said.

"No, it doesn't help!" Her tone was firm. "I love you and I think you might love me. We've shared the most amazing week together. We've laughed, talked nearly all night just so we can hear each other's voices, made endless love and fallen deep in love with each other—and you're saying you can give all that up! You can marry someone you don't even love just for the sake of some stupid obsession you have with beating your brother. Doesn't what we've just shared mean anything to you?" Abby had disbelief in her voice that his answer could actually be yes. But through her release of words, she emphasized certain parts with force and might. Patrick stood still, as calm as a cucumber, while Abby's passion and fury, brought about by her disappointment and pain, broke loose, bringing a redness to her cheeks and making her whole body tense and uneasy. She could feel her entire body panicking and her heart racing; and what was the most infuriating thing for her, and what was adding insult to injury, was the coolness displayed by Patrick.

"I'm not saying it doesn't mean anything, I'm saying…it doesn't mean enough."

Abby just stared at him and, although hurt and even angrier from what he had just said, she spoke articulately, verbalizing her incomprehension of what she was hearing.

"I don't even know what to say to that! I never imagined *you* could be this supercilious." Despite the language barrier he still understood the meaning of the last poetic word.

With all that spoken, Abby knew nothing she would say would make a blind bit of difference. With her heart broken so suddenly and her mind confused and disorientated as to what she was trying to swallow and digest, she moved her aching body past Patrick. Not allowing her eyes to lift to his, she headed for the stairs. Patrick just stood in the kitchen and rubbed his hands over his face, knowing he had stooped incredibly low to achieve all that he wanted; but that feeling wasn't going to stop him doing what he had planned.

Abby climbed the stairs at a sudden, increased pace and stormed through the bedroom door; she became like a thing processed, wanting to rid the room of every trace of his existence. However, as she scoured the room to find all his clothes, she stopped and froze in the midst of her search and just stood and stared at the slept-in double bed—the bed that only last night he had carried her up the stairs to and where he had systematically removed all her garments and made love to her for hours. That night seemed a million years ago and the pain of how he had completely misled her hurt so much she didn't know what to do with herself. She felt so injured and ashamed that her body seemed to go from weak to tense with annoyance—annoyance for having been so blind and trusting; but more importantly, annoyed with Patrick. She bent down and gathered in her arms his articles of clothing that were left around the bedroom. While she was thus engaged Patrick appeared at the door and walked in, watching a frantic Abby move around the bedroom.

"What are you doing?" he said in a matter-of-fact tone.

"What does it look like! I'm helping you to leave." Abby meant no rudeness in her reply; her tone attempted an unfelt politeness, but the pretence was obvious.

"But we still have until tomorrow lunch time," he said.

Abby stopped and laughter broke her anguish. "You really are something else, do you know that! You're either incredibly naïve, or just a complete and utter egotistical, self-centred bastard!" Laughter still creased her face but it sprang from disbelief about what he had just said.

"What?" he said, innocent to it all.

"Did you really think I would want to spend another minute with you after what you've done? Because, if you did, then there's absolutely nothing I can say to you. Words fail me, they really do. I've never met someone so insensitive!" Abby pushed his things at his chest but realised there was something missing.

"I don't want it to end like this," he said.

"Tough!" Abby knelt down by the side of the bed closest to Patrick and recovered both pairs of his shoes. She stood up flicking her hair back and with force pressed one pair into his chest and threw the other at his feet. "You made the decision the last time; well, now it's my turn."

"Abby, can't we be adult about this?"

"Adult! That's rich, coming from you!" She stood in front of him with her hands on her hips while he started to dress. "I just want you to leave! Can you at least do that?"

"I'm not going like this."

"It's a bit late for trying to do the right thing, don't you think? For goodness sake, Patrick, I'm human. If you cut me, I bleed! What more do you want from me?" With her arms all over the place and now standing a modest distance from him, she waited for his next move.

"I'm sorry—I'll go; but Abby, I really am sorry and I wish you could believe that." His tone suggested that Abby was the one in the wrong.

She didn't make eye contact as she knew if she looked at him, the tears that were well on their way, would just burst from their hiding place. She tried to act aloof and distant, anything to ease the pain from the disappointment that had washed over her drenched body. But as Patrick eventually left the room, she dropped her act.

Patrick walked down the Avenue with his few clothes over his arms and searched for a taxi. He re-acquainted himself with his brasher side so he could ease his own hurt as to how things had turned out. He was so blinkered by wanting his victory over his brother that he was oblivious to anything or anyone else that could have made him happy. His obsession with money and power had made him so narrow-minded that he couldn't see anything beyond that. He couldn't even open his mind to the fact that there could be something or someone else far more fulfilling that would make him happy, and in a way that was the hardest thing for Abby to understand.

The moment Patrick entered his apartment he didn't look back. Instead, he focused on the victory he yearned for. Abby was far from being in the same place of togetherness, but she had packed her things up and dressed her discontented body, for she couldn't stand being there a minute more knowing he was only a car journey away. She heard the door slam for a second time, but this time it was Maria returning from the shops. Abby headed downstairs and, keeping the truth private, she explained her new plans to the friendly housekeeper. With her bags packed and an earlier flight booked but no phone call to England, as she didn't want to share things over the phone and cause unneeded worry, all Abby wanted was to be at home and be hugged by her mum.

The short flight home seemed like an eternity. Looking back over the last ten days, the upset and soreness from the deceit and dishonesty made her belittle everything she and Patrick had ever shared. She didn't want to believe that he never meant to hurt her and she didn't want to believe it was just that his desire for her outweighed his integrity. She felt so infuriated with herself that she had fallen in love with a man that was so proud and mendacious. He was marrying someone else purely for superficial gain and it managed to slip his mind to tell her! She had given him herself but he had taken just that little bit more, and with her innocence lost and her dreams destroyed, the dividing line between love and hate was evermore apparent. To love Patrick was to worship him, but to hate him was to abhor him. Her feelings for him were extreme, but that came from her highly-strung personality and because she felt everything to a great depth. To Abby it almost felt like a big game he'd played, but a game where only he knew the rules. The moment she looked in his eyes it was like rolling the dice. Abby had played blindfold, but now, in all her heartache, she knew she had lost; but if she had the chance to gamble and play again, would she succumb to his charms? Time will tell.

# CHAPTER 10

Eight months had passed since Paris and Abby had not entered into any correspondence with Patrick. She was rebuilding her life, although at times it felt like she was taking two steps forward and three steps back—but she was getting there. Career-wise, though, the last few months had progressed significantly. As a result of the contacts she made doing the review in Paris Abby had become assistant editor to a home furnishings magazine, which was based in London. Her character was very much like a butterfly and the freedom and independence the position gave her was ideal. Her dreams were still alive, only deeper, under the surface for the moment, so the new opportunity was perfect for what she wanted for now. She still had hopes of writing another book and maybe even dabbling in fiction; however, the security and stability of this job was just what she needed. So for now she just went with what presented itself.

The October evening's weather was cruel and harsh. However, with Abby and her mum dressed in their nightwear and relaxing happily in their living room, it didn't concern them. Sipping at their hot chocolates and snuggled up in the depth of their velvet-covered sofa, they read contentedly from a selection of magazines, welcoming the fact that they were cuddled up in the warmth.

"*Are you suffering from anxiety?*" Teresa read out loud from one the magazine. "*Do these symptoms ring true?*" the writer of the article wrote. "*Apprehension, worries about misfortune, restlessness, inability to relax, tension leading to headaches....*" Teresa carried on down the list, making it more fun than serious.

"Sounds just like a normal day!" Abby replied in a light-hearted vein. She had a sense of humour that really did see her through times that could have been a lot worse. She never belittled anything or anyone's feelings, but just used her mischievousness to lift the mood whenever possible. Teresa naturally was concerned about her daughter when she came back home from Paris, shattered and broken hearted. She didn't want her remarkable recovery to be tested and for her to lapse back again in a state of disaster. She worried that she wouldn't be strong enough to take it all again—her mind was too fragile and could easily be broken; however, the way she handled the whole thing gave Teresa confidence that she really was stronger than she had given her credit for.

For Abby there was some much-needed new light on the horizon steadily making its way towards her. The next morning she heard the post drop through the letterbox and, curtailing her morning ritual of tea making, she headed for the hall. Crouching down, her red dressing gown brushed on the patterned stone flooring as she gathered up the mail. Searching through for anything of interest, she came across an airmail envelope with an American postmark. She headed back to the kitchen, staring at the envelope inquisitively, where her mum was just coming out from the walk-in pantry carrying some preserves. Abby sat at the kitchen table and started to open the distant mail.

"Who's that from?" Teresa inquired.

Abby's face smiled as she discovered the name. "It's James," she said with complete surprise, for she hadn't heard from him in ages.

"What does he say?"

Abby read out the welcome letter:

*Dear Abby,*

*This must have come as quite a surprise as you know I never write! Kentucky is still as fantastic as ever but I guess there's nowhere quite like home. I'm sorry that I have not written very much. Writing letters isn't one of my strong points, as you well know, but I never stop thinking about you. I have been getting your letters though but you never said how the review in Paris went. Are you famous yet? Anyway, you can fill me in when you see me. I am back on the 28$^{th}$ of this month, so we have a lot to catch up on. I wanted my return to be a surprise and to come from me; that's why I gave mum and dad strict instructions not to let on. I'm staying with them until I decide my next move, so I will call you as soon as I am back. I can't wait to see you. it will have been two years nearly since you came out here. It's been too long but we never were any good at this long distance thing, were we?*

*Well, bye for now, Abby, and see you soon. Big hug and a kiss.*

*Love,*

*James.*

James was James Foster, Abby's life long friend; they had been friends since they were five. They became friends as James's mum, Rosemary, was at school with Abby's mum. With the two school friends staying in touch, the families became good friends again when the Fosters returned from the States where they had been living for the early years of James's life. James had horses in his blood and followed in Michael's footsteps, his dad, who ran a very successful family Stud a stone's throw from Abby and Teresa's cottage. James had the chance four years ago to go back to the States and work with horses in Kentucky. The visit kept being extended, but now he wanted to come home. Abby and James's friendship was such that even if they hadn't spoken in months, years even, they would instantly be able to pick up where they'd left off.

Prior to leaving, James had been pursued by a very wealthy young lady who actually ended up proposing to him. Apart from the fact that at the time he was too young to think of settling down, he didn't love her, and no fortune or horse connections could change his heart. His departure came at the right time but that wasn't the reason why he left; however, the reason to everyone else was just that he had a bug to travel back to the States and distance himself from this obsessed woman and no one questioned that, and so the real reason was still private. The irony of the circumstances about the wealthy woman was actually quite unbelievable, but the truth was James was just so different to Patrick and not just in appearance. He just had this quality about him, a special essence that was rare to find in many people. It was hard to define, but he just had this way of making anything seem possible. Whenever he entered a room he had a strong presence and a way of bringing life to anything he was near to. At times through Abby's troubled life that was a welcome relief, one that she so needed. To Abby he was like the sun to her clouds, the perfect friend and someone she trusted and adored and someone she had greatly missed.

On the 28th October, as promised, Abby received a phone call and as soon as the two of them spoke it was just like old times.

"Hello?" Abby said as she picked up the portable phone from the handset in the hall.

"Um…hello, could I speak to a Miss Raycroft, please," a male voice uttered

"I'm afraid she's out at present. Can I take a message for her?" Abby knew who it was but responded to the joking instantly and enjoyed the messing about. As she spoke she wandered to the stairs and sat on the second step.

"Ooh, just tell her that her incredibly handsome friend called. She'll know who it is."

"Will she now? I think I can manage that." They broke into a warm and light laughter, with Abby's face beaming with happiness that her childhood friend was back. "It's good to hear your voice, James. So then, how are you?"

"Great, actually," he said with a little surprise, as he had some trepidation about coming home and adjusting. "I thought it was going to be strange, but in fact it feels like I've never been away. So that's good, I guess. So what about you?"

"Good, I'm good."

"You don't sound too sure." In spite of the time spent in the States his gentle well-spoken English accent was still very apparent.

"Let's just say we have a lot to catch up on. So when are you coming over?"

"Well, I could come by later, or you could just open the front door right now."

"What?" And with that "what" Abby walked to their country cottage front door and opened it. To her a surprise there stood James! With the phone still in her hand and James moving his mobile from his ear, they hugged one another instinctively and without hesitation.

The hug felt like it lasted for a while but it was a pure and wholesome friendship hug. They had really missed each other and in two years a lot had happened. Having added a big kiss to each other's cheeks to complete the greeting, they looked over one another, taking in any changes. James had had his once flowing hair cut to a completely contrasting shaven look, which drew attention to the beginnings of a receding hairline; however, the severity of the cut didn't detract from his gentle and soft loving face, which radiated the joy of seeing his friend again. Abby escorted him through to the kitchen where he sat at their breakfast table and watched while she put the kettle on the Aga. She was dressed casually in jeans and a knitted jumper, courtesy of her mum's handiwork. She felt a little scruffy but, working at home, she hadn't thought she needed to dress up. She was nevertheless glad she had been at home. She wandered over to the table, having placed the coffee mugs on the work-surface ready for when the kettle boiled and pulled a chair and just enjoyed the fact that her best friend, who knew her inside out and back to front, was sitting next to her.

While they chatted about casual things and James's stay in the US, she knew she would eventually tell him about Patrick. However, she was not sure she could just yet, plus she didn't want to spoil the lighter chat they were having. The right time would no doubt present itself. James's soft and oval face just lit up the room; his tall and well-built body, which had restricted him becoming a jockey, perched politely on the cushioned kitchen chair. His soft and delicate features along with his piercing blue eyes and fair colouring made him the spitting image of his mum. Dressed in simple yet stylish attire, he listened to Abby talk about everything she could think of, though she still tried to avoid the subject of Paris. The apprehension was that by talking about Paris and the review would inevitably lead to Patrick.

Swallowing the last sips of their coffees, Abby took the empty mugs to the sink. James followed her and leant on the neighbouring dresser as she rinsed them. Teresa was still at the hairdresser but she too would be pleased to see James. Still close to Abby by the sink he quizzed her a little but in a friendly and concerned way.

"So, what happened in Paris?" He knew her too well and always had done. She knew that she couldn't hide anything from him.

"Am I that transparent?" She stopped rinsing the mugs and turned and smiled.

"Only to me. You don't have to tell me anything, just as long as you are okay. I know I'm hopeless at staying in touch and I think I phoned about five times in the last two years, but I do worry about you." He had seen Abby at some of her lowest points and when one has seen a friend that low, there isn't anything one can't tell them or talk about. However, also from James's point of view, he never wanted Abby to go through again what she had done.

"I know you do. It's a long story—perhaps we can talk later."

"Okay." He was contented for now.

"Where's your car? I didn't even hear it come up the drive."

"I left it just outside the turn. I had to make an entrance and surprise you a bit."

"Mum will be pleased to see you. She'll be back any minute." They made their way back to the table and sat again, Abby just drying her hands on the chequered tea towel, which she left half falling off the rail.

"Tonight mum and dad are inviting some friends over for a welcome home dinner and they wanted to invite you and Teresa."

"Yeah, that will be great. You know, I can't believe they kept it a secret; we only saw your mum last week."

"You're right, it is amazing actually." He joked with fondness.

"It really is good to have you back." Abby felt so relaxed, realising just how much she had missed their friendship. "You don't realise how much you've miss someone till they're back again." And as Abby made James feel he had done the right thing coming back, Teresa come in the front door calling out before she entered the kitchen.

"Some twit has only gone and left their car right outside our drive. Do you know who it is, Abby?"

"Sorry, Resa, that was me." And as Teresa came through the door taking off her dark navy coat, James stood with his words.

"Oh James! It's good to see you!" She grabbed and hugged him in mid-flow of her sentence. "I'm sorry, if I'd known it was you…"

"Don't be silly, its okay, it was a daft place. I was just trying to surprise Abby and it worked, I think."

"So are you back for good?" enquired Teresa, draping her coat over the back of the chair as they all sat down again. Teresa patted her Godson's knee affectionately, but also to make sure he was really there.

"I think so. I have to convince dad I can help him run the Stud again."

They all sat together for a while chatting and reminiscing. However, with plans for dinner later on that evening and the dark and bleak afternoon advancing, James made a reluctant move. With some more hugs at the temporary goodbyes, he headed off, leaving Abby and her mum to get ready for later. With some e-mails and faxes to send, Abby concluded her day's work, thankful that she hadn't gone to the office; otherwise she would have missed her much-needed boost.

Abby soaked her body in her en suite bathtub and evoked memories of her and James as children. She remembered the games they played, how he helped her when she learnt to ride a bike and how, although the same age, just by being his wonderful self, he felt like her hero. Sitting now at her dressing table, her gown no longer quite as damp on her body, the ends of the tie that wrapped around her waist were still sodden as they had accidentally dangled in the draining water. She applied some unpretentious make up and set about fixing up her hair in a pleat before heading to her wardrobe to find her outfit. Selecting an uncomplicated mesh print shirt and stretchy dark bootleg trousers, she decided the outfit was apt but not over the top. She reached for her black astrakhan coat, for warmth from the cool night air, and then called to her mum to see that she was nearly ready.

Elsewhere, at the Foster's superb period country residence, set in over ten acres, Rosemary was making some finishing touches to the grand table that was set for twelve people. The lavish dining room, which Abby in fact designed, was perfect in style and comfort. The heavy beamed banquet area had a natural and homely feel, yet was redolent of class and sophistication at the same time. The uneven stone walls were covered in a ripe and ready plum, the windows dressed and finished in a multi-patterned woven jacquard fabric, the droplet brass and crystal chandler, along with the burr oak table and chairs, which sat comfortably on the hand-woven rug, all wedded together so well in a perfect marriage of interior design. The presence of the aging grandfather clock in the corner, along with several other pieces of collectable antiques and large overstated pictures, gave the room a deliberately cluttered feel—a satisfied and tangled look which was just what Rosemary had fancied having and what Abby had managed to achieve. Michael was busy making some final decisions about the wine down in the cellar, thereby also escaping any of the final duties to be done that he'd rather avoid. Rosemary could have been mistaken for looking quite quiet and placid; however, underneath that unassuming exterior, she was someone quite strong in personality and knew what she wanted from life.

Michael may have had success with the stud and come from a well-educated background and have many moneyed friends, but he was the most down to earth, warm and inviting man you could meet, and he never forgot his ordinary background. His towering height, maturing blond hair, along with striking features and an appealing smile, all combined with his sturdy build and modern dress to make him a very handsome and charismatic man. He was a bit like fine wine—he kept improving with age, and for his mid forties he had a lasting urbanity. Rosemary was more fragile and petite in appearance and had delicate characteristics, but was still an attractive and vibrant woman. They seemed the perfect couple. However, appearances can be deceptive. What can look like perfection can be familiarity, and making the best of what they have can be mistaken for contentment. However, to everyone else, Teresa, Abby and even James included, they seemed happy and satisfied.

The evening was a great success and with the formalities over and the majority of the guests on their way home, Michael, Rosemary and Teresa along with Larry Golding, a wealthy trainer and one of the guests yet to leave, retired to the conservatory. While the mature group enjoyed their chatting, James and Abby proceeded to the study, carrying with them the remains of their cognacs.

The two chestnut leather armchairs in the corner of the lavish wooden study was where James and Abby sat down and with the moment seemingly so fitting, having had some chit-chat along the way to their seats, Abby thought about approaching the subject of Patrick. James slivered down in the sumptuous chair, the leather creaking as he comforted his slender body, his cerulean checked shirt enhancing his intense blue eyes. With the crystal brandy glass resting just above his belt, he turned his head as Abby spoke.

"I met up with Patrick when I was in Paris."

"Patrick?"—said with a little confusion as to who she meant. "What, not Patrick that lives in South Africa, your dad's cousin or second cousin?"

"Yeah, that's the one. He moved to Paris with work four years ago and he's the reason I avoided the question of Paris." As Abby relayed the tale of the brief French dalliance it wrenched a little at her heart but she wanted James to know. However hard it all still was to talk about, she didn't leave anything out.

"So there you go, all sad and all true." Abby swirled the last few sips of the cognac and then, in one gulp, the warmth of the liquor ran down her throat, warming her chest and inner body, leaving some of the intenseness on her lips and visible traces of her crimson lipstick on the rim of the tumbler.

"Abby, I'm sorry. I didn't mean to push you into telling me." James leant forward and placed a consoling hand on Abby's arm. The contact with her skin was prevented by the fabric of her shirt. Just moving his thumb back and forth in a sign of care and solace, he tried to bring some comfort to her, just letting her know he was there for her. She lifted her flushed face and smiled.

"Don't be silly, course you didn't. I wanted you to know."

"Have you heard from him since?" he asked, reassured, and with sensitivity.

"No, nothing, but I guess I didn't expect to. Anyway, I don't care anymore."

"I wish I believed that."

Abby gave a half-hearted smile, knowing she wasn't fooling anyone with her last remark. However, she felt thankful that the revelation was over and that James knew everything now.

The soft lighting of the spacious yet well organized study camouflaged Abby's dewy eyes. It wasn't until James rose from his chair and crouched in front of her, with just the tips of his lace-up shoes in contact with the pure woollen deep brick rug, that he saw the pain in her eyes. The experience was still very much in evidence. Abby's hands, free of the glass, were clasped together on her lap. James shuffled forward, still on the tips of his toes and his knees mirroring a frog position, used he hands to cradle Abby's.

"It still hurts, doesn't it?"

"Yeah, it does. It's not just remembering what we had; what hurts even more is what we could have had, but because of this, ugh…oh, never mind, no point going over it again." She finished with a faint smile and a little glint in her eye that said, I'll be fine. And on that final note James concluded:

"I think I'm going to have to stand up. I'm getting too old for this position." As he lifted his aching knees he pulled Abby with him, and with a great big hug that was as warm as the desert and as comforting as a great big blanket, she just let the unexpected tears flow from her hurting eyes. They streamed done her reddened face, surging onto James's shoulder, camouflaged by the darkness of his shirt. Although still full of anger about what Patrick had done, Abby still missed him. Her emotions went through stages—love, hate, hate, love; however, she missed the way he made her feel and, despite what he had done, she longed to feel his touch again. She believed that one day he would realise that money and winning wasn't everything and he'd come back to her. She had to believe it at times to ease the pain of losing him. She turned her head and let it rest on James's shoulder and just let the disappointment and upset flow away with each teardrop. She was happy to be in James's comforting and inviting arms, a place which was uncomplicated and very safe.

# CHAPTER 11

The kitchen table at Teresa and Abby's country cottage was covered with empty mixing bowls, several packets of ingredients, traces of flour, crumbs of pastry and messy teaspoons covered in fragments of mincemeat filler. Abby, Teresa and Aunty Alice had, with their baking expertise, filled the whole house with the delightful aroma of homemade baking. Uncle Stanley, however, was keeping himself occupied by reading his paper in the study and enjoying a tot of whisky, leaving the ladies to their own devices. With the mince pies, ready for the festive season, which was now upon them, along with butterfly buns and sponge cakes for the church's Christmas fair, plus some to keep for home, the house smelt good enough to eat. With the Christmas cake having long since been made, they were very well organized, with only the decorations left on the agenda.

Stanley really could have given Santa a run for his money, with his portly frame and whitening facial hair, sunny smile and ruddy complexion; he really was a dead ringer for the cheerful chap. He sat relaxed and subdued in the study, or what Abby called the morning room, due to the position of the house that allowed the sun to fill the area with light and warmth at the break of day. Alice was five years older than her sister, but it didn't alter the fact that Teresa was an uncanny double of her elder sister, just a slight difference in hair colour separating them. Having nearly reached the end of their kitchen activities, Alice wandered into the study carrying a plate of samples for her husband to taste. Lowering his broadsheet newspaper past his dark brown cardigan and resting it on his sage cord trousers, his small-framed glasses looked tipsy, balancing on the tip of his wide noise. He quickly greeted his adored wife. The cottage was to be the venue for quite a few people over the celebratory season.

James, Michael and Rosemary had already booked their seats for Christmas day, as had Alice and Stanley. However, that was just the way both Abby and Teresa loved it, the house full of special people that they loved, along with the laughter, happiness and joy that they brought with them.

With one of the three Christmas trees designated for the hall, Teresa and her sister along with a reluctant Stanley, set to that task of decorating it, and with the arrival of James and his parents, Abby talked them into helping too. So they set about the one in the living room, leaving the dining room tree a conjoined task. The rich and lavish smell of pine filled all the rooms, and with the lingering aroma of baking still wafting through from the kitchen, the house had a unique scent, one that couldn't be sprayed from an aerosol.

Abby pulled out more boxes of decorations from the stair cupboard and delegated further duties. The house was by no means finished after the trees and there was plenty more to be done. With everyone occupied with new responsibilities, Abby stood back a little, as if looking in, just watching everyone with a smile of happiness lighting her face. Aunty Alice and Uncle Stanley were getting in a muddle with the remaining tree lights, her mum sat on her knees sifting through the tinsel and garlands, Michael and James were undertaking the job of the lights for the front of the house, and Rosemary was hanging mistletoe at every doorway. Christmas was a time of new beginnings and, with Patrick far from her thoughts; Abby drifted over to her mum to help her with the glittery adornments. Nevertheless, in spite of her happiness, she was desperately trying not to be saddened by her happiness—a sadness that her dad was not there to share it all with them. She consoled herself with the thought that she knew he was with them in spirit and enjoying the fun and laughter, though just from a distance.

"I think a grand ceremony of turning on the lights is needed, don't you?" Stanley suggested.

"I agree, why not the guest of honour," Alice proposed in a light-hearted way.

"Come on, James, this is your moment!" Abby jested.

So as everybody gathered outside in the dusk of the day, all huddled up for warmth from the sharp winter air, they waited with baited breath. As James flipped the switch, and as if by magic, the family home lit up in all its brilliance. James stood back with everyone else and brought his strong and warm-hearted arm around Abby's shoulder, which made her feel sufficiently at ease to instantly extend her arm around his lean waist. Everyone's eyes sparkled as they fixed them on the single row of tasteful lights that decorated the front of the house. The moment felt magical and wonderful, and Abby couldn't wait for Christmas Day and all the merriment and togetherness it would bring. With the moment enjoyed, the group of family and friends made their way back in the warmth and with no one having any pressing plans they decided on their next move. They all sat around the dining room table, in the heart of Abby's rich claret décor, and participated in a game of scrabble. The words spelt out happiness and friendship, along with laughter and enjoyment; but there were no words in the dictionary to spell out how much all this special time and fun meant to Abby.

Later on that same evening Alice and Stanley were heading back to their home, which was not far and just about in the same county. Rosemary and Michael were doing the same, leaving James and Abby talking in the living room and Teresa soaking in a hot bath. The living room was at the back of the house and was bursting with memories and mementoes of Abby's family past, from pictures of Abby growing up, to her mum and dad's wedding day. The adequate walls were covered in a weak shade of patterned gold wallpaper, with cosy and country style fabrics on the two windows and the double doors, which happened to lead out to the garden and the immediate ha-ha. With the open fire blazing with strength and bringing an orangey glow to the cosy room and with the seclusion of the drawn drapes resting on the reconditioned wooden floorboards, along with the comfort of the chenille sofa, James and Abby just enjoyed the chat and memories that they were provoking. With Abby one end of the sofa, which was flush up against the side-wall, and James the other side, they sipped at a mature of red wine as they talked about the old days. Laughter erupted as James recalled a funny childhood memory, which he knew would bring a laugh to Abby's face; she tried to speak through her amusement to add her own contribution to the fun.

"I've got one. Do you remember when we wanted a day off school and we made each other eat some leftover food from one our dustbins so we would be sick, and when our mum and dad's took us each to the doctors he said we both had food poisoning? We were off school for week!"

"I do remember—that was so awful! We felt so guilty and we didn't tell anyone what we had done. Our mums threw everything out of the kitchen and scrubbed it for hours thinking it must have been their fault. We were like the terrible twosome."

"But they were good times," Abby's voice said with mawkishness.

"I was telling Catherine about some of our antics. I think she thought we were a bit crazy."

Catherine was Catherine Harper, someone James got to know when he was at the Stud in Kentucky. She was an instructor at the neighbouring riding school. When James wanted to return to England she was reluctant to leave with him, despite their relatively serious relationship. However, she was soon due to visit England for a holiday after the New Year and James wanted to see if he could persuade her to stay.

"You'll never guess who I saw the other day when I was coming out of work." Abby sipped at the last of her wine and reached for the bottle for a refill.

"Who?"

"Only Claire."

"You're joking! Did you speak to her?" His tone expressed shock and surprise.

"Briefly. She asked how you were and what you were doing, but she hadn't changed; she looked at me and said, 'Still trying to model that style you so favour?' followed with, 'Are you still playing with your fabrics?' in the way she always did; so I just bit my tongue and said, 'Good to see you then'—in a slightly false way, I guess."

"Goodness. I wonder how many exes you bump into in a lifetime. Oh Abby, I didn't think—I'm sorry." His apology was elicited by seeing the sudden frown that had appeared on her face, creating creases on her refined forehead and between her eyebrows.

"Its okay, don't worry. I don't want you to feel you're walking on eggshells around me. I know it's been nearly a year, but at times it can feel like only yesterday. Anyway, I'm fine, more than fine, in fact. I honestly feel much better about the whole thing. It may have taken me a while but at least I've got there. Slowly but surely."

"Come here and give me a hug!" he said with a great admiration for Abby's new found strength, even though he knew if Patrick were to walk through the door right then she would run into his arms without a second thought. As Abby shuffled over to her wonderful friend and soul mate, she rested her head on the softness of his cashmere roll neck sweater, his arms locked around her coy body. She felt at ease and relaxed in the arms of her James, her hero and with the warmth and love from the embrace, she felt special and needed. Ever since they were little they just had this special connection, one they both treasured and one that couldn't be explained—or could it?

Christmas and the New Year came and went with the much imagined jubilation and delectation. With the decorations back in their boxes and the trees planted in the garden and the pantry back to stocking a more modest amount of food, Christmas was becoming a distant memory. Catherine was due for her visit at the beginning of February and with the day fast approaching James was very much occupied with preparing for her stay. Abby on the other hand had been asked to attend an interview for the position of deputy editor, a few steps up from her currant placing. Over the moon with excitement, Abby was offered the job with immediate starting due to the currant holder deciding not to return after maternity leave. This was totally unexpected but it gave Abby something more to get her teeth into, although the workload would increase and she would have to travel more frequently to London; however she accepted the new position and with it the conditions as they were for the time being.

Catherine eventually arrived on British soil and James was keen for Abby to meet her. The plan was for Abby and Teresa to join them at the Stud for dinner along with Michael and Rosemary. Meeting Catherine for the first time was to prove to be a real eye opener for Abby and everyone. To say that appearances can be deceptive was an understatement. Despite her sharp features, which were slightly softened by her somewhat curled golden-brown hair, she looked as though butter wouldn't melt in her mouth. However, as the evening commenced, that tongue of hers would have burnt and scorched the butter, let alone prevent it from melting. It was not that she was rude in a direct way as such, but more in an obscure way; and considering this was her first visit to the Fosters, she came across as almost sarcastic and rude, though Abby thought that might just have been her way. Perhaps that was her way of dealing with her nerves, and maybe she felt awkward because of her friendship with James. However, when some of the comments became directed to Rosemary and Michael, it became clear it was just her personality. Rosemary nevertheless gave as good as she got, though she remained polite when keeping up her defence. Michael, however, with his reserved manor, seemed bewildered by her, and by the time Abby and Rosemary were making the coffee at the end of the meal, they were wondering what on earth James saw in her.

"She's not very easy to talk to, is she?" Abby said politely.

"You're not wrong there, she only ate the vegetables; did you hear what she said when I asked if she was a vegetarian?"

"No."

"She said, 'I'm not a fan of charred meat, I prefer to tell what I'm eating.'"

"You're joking!"

"No, she's very out there, isn't she?" Diplomacy oozed from the sentence.

"James seems quite taken; she's not someone I would have put him with though."

"Me neither, unless she's some wild thing between the sheets."

"Rosemary!"

"Well, there must be *something* that we can't see!"

"Need a hand?" James entered curtailing their shared laughter, having left Michael and Teresa trying to chat to Catherine about her work in the States.

"No, we're fine, sweetheart. I'll just take this through." Rosemary passed him with the tray of cups and saucers, along with the freshly ground, smooth tasting aromatic coffee that was odorising the whole of the kitchen.

"So what do you think, do you like her?" he asked Abby.

"I think she's great," Abby responded lamely, seeing in his eyes the longing look for her approval. "She's a live one, that's for sure."

"Yeah, she's very direct, but she's a big softie underneath." Abby's face looked a little amazed that a seemingly tough cookie had a part that might crumble. She never liked to judge people, though her first impressions of people were never usually wrong; but if James liked her, then she would too—for his sake. If he thought a solid rock had a heart as yielding and soft as a marshmallow, then who was she to argue? As they resumed their places around the grand dinner table, Abby, for the sake of her friend, tried to befriend his new love interest.

"Catherine, have you visited England before?" Abby uttered, staring longingly at her for a reply and trying to ascertain if her frosty exterior was merely a cover, or was she really the ice woman she appeared to be? If so, James must have found the defrost button, she thought.

"Yes, first time." Her strong accent answered but with no elaboration to keep the conversation going.

"I'm showing Catherine some of the countryside tomorrow and taking her to some of the villages, Abby," James put in. "Did you want to come along with us? Give you the chance to get to know Catherine better." He had such simplicity in his tone.

"That would great, thanks."

"Looks like I'm going to be seeing you again sooner that I thought," Catherine replied with dripping sarcasm, adding a false smile that stretched her long pale face. The sarcasm remained undetected by James. Abby could read her friend like an open book; it was as if he was going over the top with Catherine to convince himself that her qualities, so to speak, didn't matter, when she knew they would to him. After all, that was why things didn't work out with Claire. His soft and gentle manner seemed to attract the opposite qualities—not just the opposite but the extreme opposite! It was bizarre. However, there was a reason for the bizarreness.

"Come by for breakfast, Abby," Rosemary said, then addressed Teresa, remembering her with concern. "Teresa, we have to finish those curtains for the Hearts and Larry's dinner jacket."

"I'll come by with you, Abby," Teresa said. "There's not much to do, but we best get them finished as I leave for Vienna next week."

"Oh, that's right, I bet you're excited. I did drop hints myself to a certain deaf ear, but nothing."

"What!" Michael defended himself. "We haven't long been back from Venice."

"That was October last year, Michael."

"Well, it's not that long ago, plus we've been busy."

"I'd rephrase that if I was you. *You've* been busy." Rosemary was intensifying the atmosphere a little and so Teresa broke the chain of retaliation.

"Maybe he'll surprise you for Valentine's Day," she suggested wryly.

"I doubt it. The last time Michael surprised me, James was just going on to solids." Rosemary laughed with her own words but she was the only one, but it was in a way to lighten the dig she was having at her husband, not because it was especially funny.

Teresa, Alice and Stanley were off to Vienna for ten days on an opera trail, plus a glance at the sights. Teresa loved the opera and used to go a lot with Charles. This was a combined Christmas and birthday present from her sister and she was determined to enjoy the affluent trip. With the coffees finished and the chat drying up, the goodbyes came next. Abby and Teresa thanked Rosemary and Michael for a great dinner and confirmed they would see them in the morning. Bravely Abby then gave Catherine a dodgy hug but as she tried to kiss her check Abby's lips ended up half way down her ear, due to the sudden turn she gave in response. None the less, she added, "It was great meeting you"—to which Catherine replied with a simple, "Likewise." With James, on the other hand, when Abby gestured to him their arms comfortably met each other's, finishing with a big soft kiss on one another's checks. However, the relaxed ease they felt with each other proved to be threatening for Catherine, who's sharp brown eyes almost cut straight through the hug and kiss like a knife, leading Abby to curtail the touch more speedily than intended. She didn't understand that Catherine could feel so threatened about their contact, for they had known each other over twenty years; it was a hug and kiss of pure friendship and what they always did when they said goodbye.

Morning came round soon enough. The day was bright and sunny, but there was a definite bite in the air, along with a lazy wind that, instead of going round you, went straight through you. Abby and Teresa headed to Stud for breakfast, with Abby knowing the day of chilly sightseeing in the countryside and brisk walks around villages with the happy couple would soon be upon her. Abby and Teresa met at their friend's house with morning greetings from just Rosemary, as Michael, who was strongly dedicated to the stud despite the many staff he employed, was out in the stables and James and Catherine still upstairs. So it was just the three ladies that headed to the stupendous kitchen and eatery.

The kitchen was not really what you might have expected from the country house. Rosemary had wanted something a little flamboyant and so she had opted for a Roman theme, and, with that in mind, Abby had created an exceptional masterpiece. The walls were covered with dramatic murals with a terracotta backdrop. The carefully chosen ivory cupboards with ornate handles were imported from Europe and the solid marble flooring had been shipped in from a distant land. The thick speckled granite marble surface added an even more luxurious touch, and with the feature cornice circling the hexagonal room and plenty of accessories, the theme was like a theatrical stage—but surprisingly tasteful with it. The central breakfast table was filled with morning fineries. James and Catherine soon emerged from the hallway and joined them for breakfast. With coffee and the third degree, Catherine seemed to have swallowed a different juice, as it was just one question after another.

"So how come you still live at home?" Catherine said casually as she poured some orange juice. James was over at the percolator with Rosemary.

"I'm sorry?" Abby was stunned by the unexpected question.

"You still live with your mum?"

"I actually don't look at it like that. My mum and I live with each other—it's different." She tried not to feel intimidated by the line of questioning.

"Yeah, but you're what, twenty-six? I would have thought you should have a place of your own by now."

Abby could feel herself about to blurt out something rude but she stayed calm and answered with surety. "Actually, we are happy the way we are. It suits us just fine, isn't that right, mum?"

"Absolutely, plus Abby owns the house anyway. So in fact she could kick me out if she wanted to."

Abby reached and kissed her mum and rubbed her arm. "Not that that would ever happen!"

Teresa smiled with confidence.

It was true though. Teresa had signed over the house to Abby a few years back and with that response Catherine discontinued that part of conversation. James was completely naïve to the fact his girlfriend was unbelievably threaten by Abby and that any offerings of friendship Abby was presenting to her, she was rejecting with force. Lost in his own world, James made a suggestion as he sat back down at the table.

"Why don't we have a ride before we head out?"

"Good idea," Abby added. "I haven't ridden for a while."

"Catherine?" James said, turning her name into a question.

"Fine with me."

Rosemary and Teresa took their mugs of Columbian coffee through to the sewing room with a look from Abby to her mum as if to say, don't leave me! However, five became three. Abby, not a big breakfast eater, aimed for the fruit bowl and helped herself to two bananas. It was then that Michael came in via the back door through the utility room. He sat down in his light tone jodhpurs, full calf leather boots and a worn denim shirt, which was just noticeable as it was covered with a thick woven jumper. Greeting Abby with a quick squeeze of her shoulder, he joined the party briefly and shared some light chat. However, his true intention for the entry was that he needed James for some business over in the office and, as Abby began to peel both her bananas ready to slice them up, James and Michael excused themselves. Catherine picked at her half a grapefruit, and it was then, when the two of them were left with just each other's company, the feisty lover of James came out with quite a peculiar statement.

"You're eating *two* bananas!" She emphasized the *two* in an exaggerated way.

A little a taken aback Abby stopped in mid chomp. "Oh, I'm sorry, did you want one?" she said in a genuinely apologetic way, although two still remained in the bowl.

"No, I don't! I've just never seen anyone eat two whole bananas like that before. I mean, two peaches, or even two nectarines, but never two bananas!"

Abby just smiled at her, wondering why she said that. It was her breakfast, after all. "I guess I must just like bananas," she said, laughing the whole thing off.

"I guess you do." Derision seeped out of all her words, and the welcome return of James prevented the need for Abby to make any further response.

For Abby the day was far from enjoyable. She felt awkward when she spoke to James and even more awkward when she tried to speak to Catherine. With

Teresa by now at home, Abby declined the offer to join them for dinner, saying she wanted an early night as she had work the next day. It was true but a little exaggerated. As James walked with Abby to the front door of the cottage, leaving Catherine in car, he asked if she was okay.

"Abby, is everything all right? You've been quiet all day."

"I'm fine." She kept it brief, not to have to keep lying when she had found the day quite a lot to take. "You get off, enjoy the meal. I'll see you soon."

"Okay. I'll call you tomorrow." James reached out to her and held her left arm as they shared a parting kiss on the cheek.

Between then and when Teresa left for Vienna, Abby didn't see them very much. The reasons she gave was that she was working or helping her mum with last minute packing. It was sort of true but her real avoidance of any further outings came because of her inability to get on with Catherine. However much she tried, Catherine just seemed to make her blood boil and, to prevent any conflict, Abby thought it was best to keep her distance for a while.

## CHAPTER 12

❀

Teresa had been in Vienna a few days now. Abby was just coming in from work on what was a bleak winter evening, the time nearing 9 p.m. She was completely exhausted. She had had a particularly rough day, with deadlines to meet and vast amounts of people to see. She slipped off her comfy loafers and just flopped her torpid body into the armchair in the living room, closed her eyes and instantly drifted off. Her messy French pleat nested in the back of the chair cushion and her trouser covered legs rested on the russet leather footstool. Some way through the night Abby must has staggered up to her bed, as come the morning she was still fully dressed but was lying in the warmth of her bed sheets. She couldn't recall the last time she had felt this tired and thought that the itinerant of the job, as well as the increased workload, along with the greater responsibility, was becoming too much for her. She had really wanted to write a novel and be working more from home, as that was just what suited her best, instead of travelling the distance to London most days; and with the recent promotion her commuting was becoming even more frequent. Abby had taken the job to bring stability and direction to her drifting career and it would have been different if she still had her heart and soul in the job. With her passion for it all fading, however, she wondered how much longer she could manage it.

Her body may have been stripped of her work suit, but her mind was still fully dressed with all her thoughts and worries. She had a quick blast in a hot shower, a hopeful act to properly wake her up. She then made her way to the stairs, her destination the kitchen for a much-needed coffee infusion. But she was about to be deterred. As she sauntered down the creaking, partly carpeted stairs to the coolness of the tiled hallway floor, a surprise was waiting for her.

On the herringbone woven doormat sat one piece of mail, the piece of mail that she had wanted since last year and the piece of mail that was about to send her into a state of utter confusion and turmoil. It was a rectangular white envelope with an airmail sticker in the left corner; and with the writing instantly recognizable from the two notes he had written to her while in Paris, which were still in a shoebox under her bed, Abby knew it was from Patrick.

The distant mail was still sitting on the breakfast table two hours since Abby had discovered it. She had a stack of emails to read and the fax machine wouldn't stop, and with the anger and frustration brewing, she picked up the long stretch of paper, which had come out of the high tech piece of technology, and threw it in the corner of the study. Running her hands through her hair, she knew what she had to do, and until she read the letter she couldn't do anything else. Her fitted jeans and pink zipped cardigan sat on the kitchen chair, which was at the head of the table, and with her heart in her mouth and her stomach hollow and empty, she slipped her finger under the seal and pulled out the white papered letter to read.

*Dear Abby,*

*I wasn't sure how you would react to me contacting you after everything, so I took the coward's option of writing; that way you couldn't put the phone down on me. There is so much I want to say but don't know where to start. I was hoping you might give me the chance to talk to you face to face. By the time you get this I will be in London on business and I had hoped you might think about coming to see me. I am staying in an apartment; the address is:*

*Penthouse Apt, Accolade Building, E21. London.*

*I have this coming Friday, the 16$^{th}$, completely free at anytime for you to come, that's if you choose to. I don't fly back until Sunday night. I extended the time a bit hoping to be able see you and talk to you. Please think about coming. It is very important to me as are you, but if I don't see you then I'll more than understand your decision. Despite what you might think of me Abby I do love you. I* *guess I just have a funny way of showing it. If I am expecting too much of you, please forgive me, it's just that I really want to see you. I really need to see you.*

*A bientot*

*Patrick.*

With the letter free from her hands, bewilderment and confusion packed into her already crammed mind. She had always wanted this letter, the letter of hope, but now, with the letter sitting in front of her, she wasn't sure what to feel. This letter suddenly sent her far away from the place she had reached, the place where she had actually started to come to terms with never seeing him again. However, now she had the chance to she was more confused than ever. She had a mixture of intense emotions, and as she pushed the chair back with the force of her body and wandered to the kitchen window, she was on the verge of an explosion. The cold February weather was even detectable through the pane of glass; the ground still look crunchy from the sharp frost and a mist still filled the air, and it was this wintry aspect that presented itself to Abby as she stared into the garden at the front of the house that provoked memories of the previous February. Her waist resting on the enamel of the deep sink, she, in her minds eye, recalled the first moment she saw Patrick again in the hotel lobby. She recalled how, when he said her name, it had sent an instant shiver down her spine, and how, when they hugged, how safe and warm his arms felt.

Her eyes fixed on the branches of the apple tree, but her mind was in a very different place—the fun they had round Paris, the first time they kissed and the first time they made love. No one had ever had this effect on her, and with all those memories flooding back her instinctive feeling was that she wanted to see him again. But in that same moment, as she sighted two blackbirds picking for grubs in the frosty white soil, something else came back—the way he blurted out that he was engaged, the way he seemed to undermine her feelings and how she saw a very selfish side of him. He'd said at the time that he hadn't meant to fall in love with her and that he didn't need this complication, and with that ringing in her ears she hurried back to the table. With those words spurring her on, she tore the letter up into small pieces, carried the bits to the cupboard and dropped them in the bin that was attached to the wooden door.

She poured another cup of coffee and with the time having passed to 10.30 a.m., she headed back to the study to make some calls and make a start on the stack of faxes that were still piled up in the corner where she had thrown them.

Relieved to be at home today, she just filled the rest of the morning with work and tried not to think about the fact that the love of her life was only a train's journey away. Just then, thinking it was work, the phone rang but in fact it was her mum. The welcome tone and sound of her mum's voice brought a much-needed smile to her distraught face.

"Abby, hi sweetheart."

"Mum! How are you? Are you having fun?"

"Fantastic!" she said with conviction, each syllable spoken with precision. "Last night we saw *La Traviata* and tonight we are seeing *Der Rosenkavalier*. My pronunciation was quite good, wasn't it?" Her tone expressed some surprise.

"That's great. I'm glad you're having a good time. How are Aunty Alice and Uncle Stanley doing?"

"They're fine. We are just about to leave to visit the barque town of Eisenstadt and the Schloss Esterhazy where Haydn lived and worked in the service of Prince Esterhazy. And then later we visit Rohrau where the composer was born, so you'll have plenty of photos to sit through—you know what I'm like!" Teresa joked.

"That's really wonderful. I'll look forward to it." However, as Abby spoke she felt overwhelmed and could feel tears welling up. It was the combination of it all, hearing her mum so far away when she needed a big hug from her and, of course, Patrick and the letter. However, she was determined not to let her upset spoil her mum's excitement, and with a deep breath she restrained the tears and was able to say goodbye without her voice breaking. She could almost feel her throat trying to close and, as soon as the receiver was down, the tears unleashed themselves. Abby's forehead rested on the hard wooden antique desk, her loose hair formimg a shelter for her face, and with her teardrops running all over her features, she flicked her head back, rubbed her reddened blurry eyes and raced to the kitchen.

Opening the cupboard under the sink, she collected together the remains of the letter, carried most of them to the table and tried to piece them together to find the address. Standing over the table she found the important part and, as she scribbled the address onto a new piece of paper, she heard a crunch on the gravel and as she glanced out the window saw it was James's Land Rover. She gathered the pieces up quickly and threw them back into the bin, covered them with some old tins of soup and then shoved the copied address into her jeans pocket. She hated keeping things from James but she didn't think he would understand why she had to go. She dabbed her eyes with a tissue and hid it under her sleeve and, as she opened the front door, she tried not to act flustered or guilty.

"Hey, this is a surprise! What are you doing up here"? Abby reached forward and kissed his cheek.

"Catherine has a stinking cold and headache, so she's in bed. I had to call in at the Lockhart's to see their Stallion and they're only a stone's throw from you. So I thought I'd see if you were in." All said as they wandered through to the kitchen.

"Cup of coffee?"

"Great. So what have you been up to?"

"Oh, just working. Mum phoned about half an hour ago. She sounds like she's having a wonderful time. I think she's taken lots of pictures, bless her." They shared a light chat while Abby waited for the kettle to boil, and with the conversation moving to Catherine, Abby confirmed what she already knew.

"It's Sunday that Catherine leaves, isn't it?" She knew it was, but she wanted to make sure that the feisty female would soon be an ocean away. She had tried hard to get on with her and it wasn't that Abby disliked her—she just found it incredibly hard to talk to her.

"That's right. She's been a bit vague, though, about her future plans. I have to talk to her." Whatever Abby felt about Catherine, it didn't stop her feeling concerned for James; so, in an honest way, she added,

"Maybe she doesn't know how you feel. Maybe she's just protecting herself."

"Perhaps. I'm not very good at reading people's emotions."

"Oh, I don't know about that; you know mine pretty well."

"That's different though," James said with a big proud smile.

"I just need the loo. Can you make the coffee?" Abby asked, passing him as she headed for the downstairs cloakroom, leaving James to make the coffee and cutting off the conversation. The morning's constant coffee drinking suddenly caught up with her.

Pouring the hot water over the ground coffee beans, he pulled open the immediate drawer to reach a teaspoon; but as he shut the drawer, with his glance downwards, a scrap of paper caught his eye. Putting the spoon in the mug, James bent down and picked up the ripped piece of paper with the words staring back at him: 'I do love…'—not catching any other words due to the tare of the paper. He had a strong feeling about whom it might be from. With the discovery of the other bits in the bin, his sapient guess proved to be accurate. With the sound of the cloakroom door closing and the faint lingering sound of the toilet flushing, Abby reappeared in the kitchen to see a readymade coffee sitting on the table. As she sat back down to an already seated James her secret was out.

"Abby, is there anything you want to tell me?" His tone clearly expressed his concern that she was going to do something she would later regret.

"Tell you? No." Her reply expressed surprise as to why he should suddenly ask that.

"Nothing at all?" His tone wasn't harsh just soft and worried.

"Like what?"

"Like maybe you had a letter from Patrick?"

"What?" She was still trying to sound baffled.

"Abby, credit me with something. I found a piece of it on the floor and I put two and two together."

Abby stood up and moved away from the table. She leant on the dresser opposite James, trying to create a distance from the questioning that was to come.

"Please tell me it's in pieces because you're not interested," he said softly.

Abby decided just to be honest and hope he would understand. "I ripped it up and then I got it out again to write down the address. I must have dropped a bit." She felt uncertain about seeing Patrick anyway, and with James dead against it, she was floundering.

"Abby…," he said with great disbelief, his whole body falling back into the chair, showing his disappointment as to how naïve and blind she was being.

"James, please don't give me a hard time about this. I *have* to see him again." There was pleading in her tone. She wanted his support.

"No, you don't have to see him again. He hurt you and used you. Why on earth to you want to go back for seconds?"

"How do you know that he'll do it again? He might *want* to be with me for all we know."

James stood up and wandered onto a small part of the kitchen floor, repeating his own steps. "Abby, you can't honestly believe that. From what you told me he's never going to change. I saw how upset he made you and that was eight months after. Why put yourself through all that heartache all over again?"

"Because if I don't go, then I'll never know—and I *have* to know, James. I *have* to! I still love him and I have to do this."

James rubbed his forehead a little and stood still using his arms to assert his argument. "He's going to hurt and use you as many times as you let him. Why can't you take him for what he is? You can be so blind sometimes."

"Blind! That's a bit rich coming from you."

The discussion was becoming slightly heated and with words they each knew they would regret later. Abby was about to blurt out her say. It was driven from her frustration as to getting the letter in the first place and because she was now arguing with James, something she hated.

"What does that mean?"

"You and Catherine! Can't you see you're dating the ice maiden whose specialist subject just happens to be being a bitch to me? What do you see in her?"

"She's not that bad."

"Not that bad! I've still got frostbite from when I touched her. I think that you're too good for her, but you don't see me saying anything. I just went along and supported what you were doing because that's what friends do."

"Well, she's not secretly engaged to another man, is she? She hasn't strung me along for a week, used me and dumped me." He felt that was a bit below the belt, when, in fact, Abby was trying to cool the mood with the latter part of her sentence.

"Fine, if that's how you feel, then you make your mistakes and I'll make mine." There was annoyance in each of their tones but also regret, for as each word came out of their mouths they each knew it was hurting the other.

"Fine, I just hope for your sake I'm wrong—but I don't think so, and I can't support you with something that I think is a bad idea. You deserve so much better than him." All said in a calmer voice. "I think I better go. Just think about it." And as he picked up his jacket from the back of the chair and headed for the door, he turned his head and added, "If you have to see him, Abby, don't do anything stupid."

Abby knew what he was implying but she said nothing.

With the sound of the front door closing, her tears got the better of her a second time. As she slid down the kitchen cupboard, her knees to her chest, she longed for the confusion to vanish and for her mum to scoop her up into her arms and make it all better. But Abby knew this was one battle she had to fight alone.

What she didn't realise was that James was very irked with himself and wished he hadn't been so harsh, given her fragile state of mind. As he got into the car he slapped both his hands onto the steering wheel, vexed by the way he had handled the situation. What added insult to injury was his knowledge that deep down Abby was right about Catherine. He wanted to shut off the fact that they didn't really have a future together and that she wasn't really suited to him. He knew it was circumstances that had brought them together, and he now knew that facing up to hard reality would part them.

He arrived back home and, not wanting to put it off any longer, the much-needed talk with Catherine took place and resulted in a sudden turn in events. Catherine packed immediately, not really upset but more put out that he got in first. She knew equally well that the sparkle had faded and there wasn't enough left to last any longer. But before she left she enlightened James with her own surmise on things, making sure he had the benefit of her perspective on his relationship with Abby.

He wanted to distance himself from all the upset that had suddenly taken place and clear his mind. He decided there and then to take an unplanned visit to his old friend Ralph. Ralph was married with one child and lived in Warwickshire. They were solid friends and knew each other well. James's trip was a little sudden but with the whole Catherine thing, and then Abby, he just wanted to escape the mess he had created. Ralph's Japanese wife Mitchiko and their three-year-old child Phoebe were visiting some family, so it left the two men the opportunity to talk freely. Ralph Grant had a delightful converted period barn in a quiet village setting. He was a physiotherapist and very good at his job, but at the same time he was a great friend to James. Ralph knew his buddy would talk to him when he was ready and it wasn't until the next evening that he really opened up.

They relaxed in the large vaulted drawing room, lounging on the comfy armchairs and sipping at a very expensive whisky. James explained about the argument with Abby, to whom Ralph had met and liked, as both James and Abby attended his wedding. He also explained how he had parted with Catherine and that she was now back in the States. However, what was upsetting him the most was that he had never argued with Abby like that before and felt regretful about how he handled it. As James conveyed the story, Ralph chipped in.

"Do you mind if I add my point?" He had an old-fashioned English gent appearance and was very well spoken and incredibly coherent.

"Fire away."

"I think, old boy, you're enamoured with a an unbridled fervour for Abby." Seeing James scrunch his forehead into a look of puzzlement, Ralph added: "You're in love with her."

"No, I'm not!" he said with conviction. "I'm mad at her for seeing Patrick and I feel bad as to how things were left. But I'm not in love with her!"

"Now you see, that instantaneous 'no'—that's a clear case of negative response denial. You see how you said, 'No,' instantly. That 'No' symbolises a depth of foreseen pain, as you feel deep down Abby will never be in love with you; so you have to reject the proposal immediately—thereby defending your true feelings. The subconscious is a wonderful thing. Plus, this Patrick you don't want her to see—a tinge of covetousness; perhaps you think you will lose her." Ralph said all this as if he were acting in a play, using his glass to drive home certain points.

"I said 'no' because I'm *not* in love with her, and I don't want her to see him because he's no good for her!" James answered in response to his friend's diagnosis.

"Ask yourself this, why haven't you had one single successful relationship? Answer—Abby! You see in her everything you want. So you go out and find the exact opposite to her. It's a way of convincing yourself it's not her you want, when, in fact, she's probably the love of your life; and for as long as you deny it, you will never find true happiness. Now I don't charge £200 an hour for nothing. I think we have our answer." He leant back and smiled indulgently. "You're an open book, James, with not many pages—and quite a dull read, really."

"I think you have a very vivid imagination, Ralph. I'm glad I didn't just pay for that." And that was the only reply James gave.

Meanwhile, miles away, Abby's head was filled with the thought of seeing Patrick. But her head was also filled with sadness because of the way things were left with James. Abby hadn't called James yet, thinking it was best they both cooled down, so she had no idea Catherine had left and no idea James was in Warwickshire. So as she headed over to the Stud in hope of seeing James, the time had just gone 8 p.m. She didn't really know what she wanted to say to him.

She was welcomed by Rosemary and sat with her in the very spacious drawing room. They relaxed comfortably on the generous sofa, Abby curling her legs underneath herself to sit in a homely way. Just as the two of them were starting to talk, Michael passed through on his way to the study.

"Hi Abby, I didn't hear you arrive." His greeting was welcoming, not just expressed out of being inquisitive.

"Oh, I came to see James, but Rosemary was just saying he's with Ralph. So I'm bending your wife's ear with my problems instead."

The couple shared a friendly smile as Abby explained her visit. Before Michael continued to the study he added with warmth but in a light-hearted way: "Well, if you need advice on matter's of the heart, don't ask me." He gave her a passing wink as he left them to it, leaving a faint smile on Abby's face.

Rosemary knew all about Patrick so it was easy to talk to her about it all. Abby felt bad that her mum knew nothing about what was going on but she didn't want her much deserved holiday to be spoilt. Rosemary was an ideal listener, impartial and never one to take sides, and knew both James and Abby would have said the things they did because they cared for one another. So she was a good alternative confidante. Rosemary had to admit to Abby that she was glad her son had seen sense about Catherine; she, too, thought he was being a tad naïve about her.

"I just wish I could have said it all a bit nicer. I was just so mixed up about getting the letter and now I don't know what to feel. One minute I'm almost excited about the thought of seeing Patrick again, and the next I feel like an idiot for seeing him again. What a mess!"

"Listen, Abby, I don't claim to have the answers, but I *will* say this. Just follow your heart this time, not what's in your head. But what's in your heart? If you want to see him, despite what happened in the past, then follow your instincts. At the end of the day, sweetheart, you'll be the one that might have to pick up the pieces, and if you're okay with that, then take a chance." Rosemary said it as if she really understood her conflict. Had she been in a similar predicament, perhaps? However, for Abby, with her mum far away and lost as to what to do, the words were just what she needed.

"So if you were me, would you go?"

"Abby, I wish I could answer that for you, but it has to be *your* decision. I can offer advice, but when it comes to the crunch *you* have to choose." Rosemary reached for Abby's hand and gave it a reassuring squeeze; the action softened the last part of Rosemary's guidance, not wanting to seem too harsh. "I've probably got the number for Ralph if you want to call James there."

"Thanks, Rosy, but I think I'll wait till he's back."

"You know where I am if you need me. When James gets back I'll tell him you were here. He probably feels just as bad as you do."

Abby was edging to the end of the deep and comfy seat, knowing she didn't want to be too late back, and when Rosemary tried to make her feel better with her kind offering, she gave a confirming nod.

"Thanks again for the chat," she said. They were heading to hallway, their final aim the front door, when they shared a friendly hug.

"Anytime," smiled Rosemary.

Abby made her way home after her helpful talk with Rosemary. She now felt even surer that she would go to London and felt confident with what she had decided. However, was her improvident decision to cost her dearly?

## CHAPTER 13

❀

With six outfits thrown out on her unmade bed, Abby finally decided and went back to her original choice. She slid the raven black tailored trousers over her clean-shaven legs and pulled her scooped neck cobalt sweater over her head. She brushed her grown hair and set about returning the unwanted garments back to the wardrobe. Lastly she flicked the bed sheets, threw over the woollen check blanket at the end of the bed and finished by returning some scattered cushions that she propped up against the white-fringed pillows. The apple and floral bedroom décor was tasteful and inviting and, as Abby grabbed her jacket and bag, draping them over her arm, she paused before closing the door. She scanned her ornate sanctuary giving a special smile to her big precious teddy Sunny. He sat in the far left corner of the room on an old wicker chair. He caught her eye as she searched the room, checking she hadn't forgotten anything.

She had been up since the early hours of the morning with uncontrollable sickness. Her nerves were really getting the better of her, having not felt this sick and anxious in a long time. Her pallid face really expressed what was going on inside and with the taxi due soon she made some quick steps down the stairs and scuttled into the kitchen. Checking everything was locked she took a final hesitant sip of orange juice and then, putting the empty glass in the near empty dishwasher, she headed for the front door.

Back in the hall and standing in front of the magnificent oval gilt mirror, she added her double-breasted coordinating jacket to her nervous body, feeling sick in the pit of her stomach, and straightened her free flowing hair. Her mum always told her that her hair was her crowing glory; so, with that in mind, she had it looking its best. She leaned in to the mirror and examined her make up, scrutinising her face to see if the foundation she had applied had covered the shadows that had formed under her normally sparkling eyes, and if it had brought some colour to her washed out complexion. She was undecided as to whether it had done the job but it was too late now, there was only so much one can do and today nothing was effectively disguising her anxious countenance. When she heard the hoot from the waiting taxi she knew it was now or never.

The train journey was a little tiresome but was over soon enough. The time was approaching 10 a.m. She had wanted to be in London early so she wouldn't have to travel home too late. The whole of the journey she fretted about how she would react to him, what to say to him, how to be, and more than once her face flushed with panic and it was only deep breaths and patience that quietened the intense feelings that were washing over her. The taxi pulled up at its destination and Abby paid and tipped the driver through the window, still clutching her scribbled piece of paper in her hand. She took in the stunning view over the Thames. Despite the low temperature the sun glistened with pride over the far from clear water. She took a deep breath and walked over to the entrance of Patrick's building.

The tall glass building exuded wealth and culture, and when Abby approached the panel doors she suddenly realised she had to use the intercom to get in. It was at this point she wondered what on earth she was doing there. Covering her hands over her now cooler face, she lent on the only piece of brickwork by the intercom. She knew now there were only a few floors separating her from Patrick, as apposed to a few thousand miles, the way it had been for the last year. However, instead of pressing the button to buzz up to him, she wandered, bemused, to a paved garden area opposite and sat down on one of the two benches. She rested her bag on the wooden slats and gazed up to the top of the apartment building. She longed for someone else to make the decision for her and, as if someone heard her, she heard a voice.

"Is this seat taken?"

Abby turned her head and there he was.

"Patrick!" She rose to her feet instantly. Surprise registered on her face but no other emotion. A smile didn't seem natural, but her heart was quickening and she could feel a burning heat filling her chest.

"Hey Abby!" When Patrick said that it almost looked like he was moving in to kiss her cheek or lips.

Such imminent close contact was something she couldn't handle and she moved subtly back to distance herself from the suspected gesture.

"I was—um—just about to—um—buzz you, then my mobile rang." She tried to be cool and confident, struggling with intense difficulty, for his presence had conjured up everything she had fallen in love with. Her heart was pounding to the beat of a fast drum, her stomach dancing to its tune.

"Shall we go inside? It's warmer in there." Patrick's burly hand gestured to the door, complemented by a smile. His casually dressed body escorted her to the door. He looked like he had filled out a bit—either that, or he had been working out; but as Abby observed him as he pressed for the lift, she tried to avoid eye contact. But she had noticed something else. It was the absence of a band of gold, which should have circled his third finger on his left hand. The concentrated silence was very apparent as they travelled up to the top floor. Patrick didn't know what to say and neither did Abby. But then, with Abby's nerves expressing themselves differently, her words came out almost without her being aware of them.

"And there was me thinking this might have been awkward." It broke the ice and made Patrick reciprocate her smile as he said, "You look really great. I didn't know if I should say so but you look as good as you always did."

There was a tinge of nostalgia in his voice as he, too, was presented with the evidence of what he had fallen for.

"Thanks," she added a smile, not really wanting to reciprocate with a compliment. She hadn't forgiven him for the way he had handled everything and the things he had said. Nor had she forgotten what she went through afterwards, and seeing him again in the flesh was making her suppressed pain resurface.

The penthouse was upon them. Patrick reached his keys from his black filament trousers and opened the door to the mighty residence, and again he gestured for Abby to enter first. The place was what one would expect from a penthouse, although Abby suppressed any impulse to look impressed. The décor was far from her taste, in any case, and it was the sparse and under-decorated vestibule that first greeted her eyes. The interior decoration apart, the place could not be faulted; it had wonderful views from the large terrace, with which she was presented as they moved through to the main room of the apartment, doors off to other rooms on every available wall space and a light and airy feel. With plenty of rooms to choose from, they just stayed in the double reception room, which was the venue for them for now. Abby had no intention of asking for a tour, pride or no pride, though she was secretly altering the scheme in her mind, thinking the place could be tens times better if she got her hands on it; but she thought to herself, each to his or her own.

The whole place felt cold and impersonal. It had a minimal and very modern look, but Abby just sat her colourful self down in the heart of the colourless scheme, which she, as an interior designer, called an Acromatic scheme, a scheme consisting of black, white and grey. She did manage to bring a smile to her face, though, while Patrick was still fiddling with his answering machine; she imagined herself as a bright and beautiful rainbow pushing its way through all the dull grey clouds—and it was true, in a way. She had instantly brought a ray of sunshine and colour into what was a bland and unfriendly room. Perched on the end of the white leather sofa, which was adorned with black scatter cushions, she removed her jacket and watched as Patrick made his way over to her. He sat on the mirroring sofa opposite her, freeing himself, too, of his outer clothing, exposing his moss-toned lambs wool jumper. The whole of the two reception rooms' furniture could have been packed into one small van. There were few pictures on the white walls and no warmth was even radiated from the silver carpet, although it was slightly more inviting than the ceramic floor in the entrance hall.

"So, is this yours?" Abby asked as she searched the place with her eyes for any pictures of Laura.

"It's on a lease." Patrick kept his response brief but started to follow Abby's glance as she surveyed the bareness.

"Very modern," she said—far from a compliment.

"That was Laura. I don't care for it much." His mottled foreign tone was still detectable and that warm voice melted the icy room somewhat. You could tell he felt awkward referring to Laura, for when he began the sentence he hesitated a little before using her name.

"So where is Laura?" Abby said with calmness.

"She's in Canada. Listen, I'm glad I was able to come alone. I can't tell you how good it is to see you." He was again mesmerised by her. "Can I get you a drink?" She didn't answer and, instead, replied with her own question.

"Why did you write to me, Patrick?" She sat forward on the compliant leather, her elbows resting on her knees.

"Same reason you're here, I guess." He was never one to answer a question directly.

"Well, right now, sat here in this penthouse, I don't know why I'm here." Abby looked straight at him. "You know, this is too weird. I thought I could do this, but I can't. We have nothing to say to each other. I just don't know how to be with you and I was a fool to come here. When you say her name it just reminds me what you did and I can't handle it. Fine, she's not to blame, but you are, and this was a big mistake. I'm looking at you and I don't know whether to slap your face or to kiss it. I'm not staying, I have to leave, I'm sorry, no, actually, I'm not sorry—why should I be sorry?" Her voice sounded out her frustration and confusion loud and clear.

Abby had the benefit of truth in her words this time and was on her feet, ready for her exit. She really was going to leave and the front door was her next destination. With just the glass and aluminium coffee table separating them and a vase of white lilies, Patrick moved quickly round it to halt her egress. With her bag on her shoulder, her jacket having been quickly pulled onto her upper body, Patrick reached out to her, his powerful grip pleading with her arm not to go. She froze at his touch and, with their bodies just that little bit closer, enough for Abby to smell his lingering scent and for them both to feel each other's breath faintly on their skin, their passion for each other quickly resurfaced. Patrick's cogent lips and persuasive eyes were becoming like an eclipse and Abby knew it would be fatal to look directly at them. But as he lifted her chin with his fingers she caught his glance and—with the words he was speaking, "Please don't go, I want you to stay"—her resistance collapsed. Her bag dropped to the medium pile carpet and, without a second's hesitation, they knew what was coming. Their body temperatures soared and their eyes fixed and then, as if nothing had ever changed, it happened, their gasping lips touched. The kiss was avid and powerful, driven by their overwhelming thirst for each other. But the kiss was incapable of quenching the fire of their passion that was inflamed by the very attempt to quench it. Their hands and arms held each other's bodies close and the contact of their lips became stronger.

It was as if the kiss was at some point inevitably going to happen and, with the build up of emotions from the previous year, it drove them to the guest bedroom, Abby being carried there by Patrick, having locked her elevated legs around his waist. The ardour of the kiss channelled their passions through their yearning bodies and, as they fell onto the bed, Abby's yielding body enveloped Patrick's unforgettable touch. He made her feel like a score of music, not just one he'd composed but one only he could play. The trouble with Patrick and Abby was that they had parted because of Patrick's strong desires and dishonesty, his need to be bigger and better than his brother, not because their feelings had changed or had died. For Abby it was a love that couldn't die because it was a love that had only just begun. With half their garments now free of their bodies, they embarked unresistingly upon a pleasurable journey, one they had travelled along many times before. But this time the time apart had acted as a strong foreplay and the potency of their magic formula had quadrupled, sending them to a heady height of pure undiluted fulfilment. As she felt his manhood slip effortlessly and deep into her, her pent-up desire for him erupted into a throbbing eternity where time ceased to exist.

Abby's contented body lay alongside Patrick's naked body, and with just the simple white cotton sheets covering their modesty their passion had only just begun. The late morning sun poured in through the skylight reflecting right over them, and with their appetite for each other far from satisfied, the kisses Abby planted on Patrick's broad chest acted as a catalyst in the temporary lull of their carnal pleasure. Her soft bare skin felt like silk as it passed over Patrick's masculine body. As she delivered encouraging and stimulating mouth contact to his quivering upper body, his head turned frequently in the pillow as the pleasure reached an all-time high. She teased his eagerness by barricading herself with an arm flung across his waist, preventing herself from any further progress below his waist. She used the palms of her hands to caress his hairy chest and her tongue to titillate his succulent nipples. He longed for her to touch him further but with her at the controls he was at the mercy of her strategy.

Abby continued with her powerful grip, which encaged both his shoulders, using the hold as an anchorage to lower herself to his pelvis. It was there she found his weak spot, just a few inches above his hips, the sensitive place where a simple lasting kiss was enough to send him into a state of utter delight. From there she invited him to turn over for her to tantalize his sultry back with the same joy she had given the front. From the base of his spine she sent her moistened mouth right up the centre of his back, finishing at the nape of his neck. Her malleable breasts pressed deep against his heated skin, her body seemingly climbing his as she shared with him her strong passion. But it was then he turned the tables on her, and his masterful turn was exhilarating in itself. Abby's relinquished body rolled to his side with her back now lying deep in to the mattress, and with a light erotic touch Patrick lifted her arms to either side of her head. He held them there while he sunk hot familiar kisses into the depth of her fragrant neck. Her rapturous head become lost in the softness of the cotton fibres as Patrick furthered the delicate kiss into the hollow of her underarm. His febrile lips carried on vertically down the side to her shapely-formed waist, leaving no doubt from Abby's pleasing moans that his action was giving her exquisite pleasure.

Patrick took the intensity horizontally to the centre of her abdomen, encircling the area with the heat and moistness of his burning tongue, all before changing direction and sinking the same pleasure deep into the bed of her belly button. He deliberately avoided temptation to touch her serenity; creating an expectancy that added even more anticipation and suspense to the titillating game they were unwittingly teasing each other with. He mirrored the same pleasure on her left side and it wasn't until their mouths touched once more that her arms were free to roam. She immediately brought each hand to his head and partially covered his ears as she intensified the much awaited touching of lips. It was then and only then that he travelled to her waiting celestial and divine tranquillity. It gave him as much pleasure as it gave Abby, and with her hands buried in the thickness of his hair, her grip tightened as the fulfilment exceeded all limits. There was no preventing their eager passion, Patrick lifting himself up her blissful body and hesitating over her firm yet liquid breasts, embellishing them with extreme tenderness; and with her alert nipples at the mercy of his touch, her head tilted back, her neck arching and her body language speaking for her.

The shared pleasure was taking on a life of it's own, and with another turn of the tables she instantly preoccupied herself with the part of Patrick that now needed her the most. This was the antecedent remuneration he had waited for, and with the heightened rhapsody and Abby's dexterity, it sent him into cloud nine. Their lusting bodies were urgent with their burning need to bring a crisis of ecstasy to their sustained pleasurable series of sensual collaboration. The unison of their effervescent bodies engaged the ultimate moment, their intentness using the entire double mattress to bring a pinnacle to their mind-blowing enjoyment. Patrick was able to give Abby manifold cherished moments all before their epicurean bodies accelerated to the eventual and unwavering finishing moment. Patrick's satiated body rested on Abby's satisfied self and with their bodies still as one, a final mouth-watering kiss brought them to the final epiphany of oneness. Their freed bodies lay wrapped in each other's arms and, as Abby relaxed her head against the side of Patrick's neck, she had never in her life felt so contented. With Patrick still feeling the warmth of Abby and with the effects of her touch still suffusing his body, the moment of release was sure to be only momentary.

Back in the Suffolk countryside James was on his way home from Ralph's. He knew what he wanted to say to Abby but he knew she would be with Patrick in London and therefore it would have to wait. Although he left before her final decision, he just knew she would have gone. However, the decision he had come to was what he felt he should have done in the first place—support her decision and just be there for her whatever the consequences. But sometimes when you know someone is making a huge mistake it's easier said than done. Meanwhile, back at home, Rosemary was trying to excuse herself from the company of her husband to be elsewhere instead of being in the Stud office for the rest of the afternoon. She shortened her private phone call at the presence of her husband and, having replaced the receiver and started to falsely play with some papers, she spoke nonchalantly.

"Michael," she said, "I'll finish these invoices off later. I want to get to the shops before it gets too late." She fiddled further with the papers on her mahogany desk that was housed in the impressive Stud office.

"Shops, what do you need at the shops? You were there only yesterday. Besides, we have the Jennings coming over soon for coffee."

"Yes, you invited them without asking me," she said in a calm voice. The ammunition she used was to the effect this wasn't the first time he had invited people over without consulting her.

"Rosemary, I really need you here."

"Why, because you *want* me here? Or because it looks good for business? All you think about is this Stud. What about my feelings for a change?"

"What do you mean? We went out last week together."

"You can't be serious. It wasn't just you and me. I had to sit through the entire dinner listening to Frank Hodges and his latest young floozy witling on about their new house. Neither of them drew breath. But because they're good for business we have to go and endure their chat all night long."

"Rosemary, how do you think we built this business in the first place? By being sociable and tolerant. We have a successful and thriving family-run Stud. You can't have the big house and the expensive cars without a little sacrifice. These people made us what we are and, like it or not, we have to continue socialising and entertaining." Michael had such a halcyon way of putting it, but that seemed to infuriate Rosemary.

"I married *you*, Michael, not the business. I wish sometimes I had four legs and a long tale—then perhaps you'd pay *me* more attention!"

"You'd never find any clothes, sweetheart." The cheekiness of his tone irritated her all the more.

"If that's meant to be funny, then it wasn't!" Her annoyance was very apparent now.

"Oh *come* on, I'm just trying to lighten the mood."

"Well, don't. I'm going out and I'll be back at about 5 p.m. and if they're here before that, well, you'll have to make an excuse for me; or perhaps you could just lighten the mood with one of your jokes." She picked up her bag and headed for the door as she finished the sentence. Outside she crossed paths with James, though very briefly, and as she left the drive her annoyance was evident in her driving. When James met his dad just coming out of the office they wandered over to the stables together. As they strolled through the sheltered enclosure they had a spur-of-the-moment chat. The coarseness of the straw block was their seat and James asked about his mother.

"Do think there is something up with mum?"

"Like what?" He was never one to face up to things.

"I don't know. Perhaps you two should make more time for each other. You hardly see one another these days."

"It's not always that easy though." Michael was in a way hiding a little behind the Stud as he was afraid if they did spend time together it would confirm what they were both feeling—that their marriage was over a long time ago.

"Make some time. You don't seem to talk anymore. I'm just worried about you both, that's all."

"I know you are, but we're fine, don't worry." It wasn't really true, so Michael changed the subject.

"So are you going to sort things out with Abby?"

"I will, yeah, but I don't know when she's back. I just hope she knows what she's doing."

"Sometimes there are just things you have to do before you can move on. You can tell her he is no good for her and that she's too special for him, but she has to discover that for herself. And if he is anything like what you say he is, then she is going to need your support."

"I know, and I *will* be there for her. I just wish she didn't have to find out the hard way, because I have a feeling she will." James may have never met Patrick, but he played on his gut feeling and his gut feeling was very accurate.

Miles away back in the avant-garde penthouse things had gone from good to better for Patrick and Abby. The afternoon had evaporated as quickly as ice on a hot day and every inch of their bodies had been adored by each other. The evening was beckoning and as Abby lay relaxing in the heat of the bathtub in the sliver-tiled bathroom she felt so happy. In the next room was the one man she wanted to spend the rest of her life with, the one man that possessed something uncountable, something that would always touch her, the part of her that only he seemed to be able to reach. In her mind, in spite of the letter, and because of the ensuing events, the absence of a wedding ring and the unbelievable love she could feel from him, his actions spoke louder than his words and she felt nothing else needed to be said. However, her surmise on the circumstances could have been taken as somewhat naïve, a trait that Abby was famous for and a trait that even with all her past hurt and disappointment, she never learned from.

Her glowing and curvaceous body lay soaking in the hot steamy bubbled water, her loose hair still damp from Abby having plunged herself into its depth. Her waterproof makeup had coped with the test and still dressed her face with beauty. Although, due to Patrick's unshaven visage, her normally smooth fair skin around her mouth had been reddened slightly by the coarseness that had grated against it all that afternoon—a small price to pay, though, for the delights it brought. The modern theme had been carried through to the guest bedroom and en-suite bathroom, although it was marginally better than the other rooms. Tall-mirrored wardrobes gave the room a capacious and light feel, which allowed for the sumptuous and deep divan that dominated the square bedroom. However, even with the continuity of the white walls and few pictures, there wasn't anything that could detract from the bright colour that was highlighting Abby's sparkling face.

She was just thinking about getting out when Patrick appeared naked in front of her. His tall muscular body was well built yet cuddly at the same time; he still had a certain amount of subtle definition around his chest and torso but by no means over the top. However, it was funny for Abby, since although she had been incredibly intimate with him, his nakedness almost seemed to embarrass her. She found herself feeling awkward looking at him, but when he slipped on his knee-length deep navy robe she instantly missed the view. He perched on the edge of the bath and lifted a hand full of bubbles and in a fun and jovial way blew them into Abby's face. She responded by moving them with her hand, only to be helped by Patrick and finally receiving his kiss on her forehead.

"We should think about dinner, you know. We haven't eaten much today."

"Well, I could do with something." Abby's eyes looked up to Patrick's half turned body. He had such a nice tone when he spoke; she could have listened to his voice all night long.

"Why don't we go out? It's still quite early and its not like you have to go home tonight." It seemed a given that she was staying the night, and with no problems from Abby she agreed.

·

"Sounds good."

"You like seafood." It was more a rhetorical question as he remembered she loved seafood. "Someone recommended a restaurant to me, so we could try there. You know, you look very sexy in there." His salubrious smile said more than the compliment did, and as he dropped his hand through the foam of the water his sensuous touch reached Abby's separated breasts. She smiled in acceptance of both the compliment and the affection. The heat of the water intensified the blooming smell of the scented bath crème, and as Patrick's pacifying touch continued, she basked in the stimulating feeling.

"I really should get out, my fingers are wrinkling." She tried to sound convincing but was clearly once again wavering under his spell.

"I was actually thinking of getting in there with you." Patrick broke the contact and pretended to smell his under arm. "Yeah, I do smell a bit." He had his mischievous grin and as he freed his gown Abby sat up and moved forward. His powerfully built and well formed legs stepped in one at a time behind her and his physically fit body slid down into the curve of the bath. Abby instinctively moved closer and was cradled against the firm presence of his aroused manhood. Her legs pressed against the side of Patrick's, her back resting on the heart of his upper body with his hands now just resting on her soft skin around her hips. The water had risen slightly due to the increased body volume, with the bubbles disappearing fast through the overflow. She used her free arms to pull his head down so she could kiss his tantalising lips. She turned her head to get as much impact from the kiss as possible, and it was then that Patrick embarked on a different form of seduction.

Their soaking close bodies remained in the same position, but Patrick started to ask her about her work and career. However, this was not a diversion from any pleasure Abby had hoped to receive; instead, it was Patrick using his lasciviousness to entice her into his web of allurement. He started slowly with his large hands still resting on her graceful and well-proportioned tummy. While she spoke of how she had started with the magazine, his hands started the journey that eventually reached her pleasure zone. She embarked further as he probed her for more details, and it was then that he began to circle his longest finger around her pleasing belly button, a place that in the last few hours had received a lot of attention. The touch was playful but very sensuous at the same time, and Abby, undeterred by the sweet distraction, continued; but as she did so all her senses went on red alert. The smell of his mannish odour lingered under her nose, the taste of him was still on her speaking lips, and his touch was agreeing with her pulsating skin. As for sound and sight, his delicate foreign accent and pleasing appearance conspired together to incite her senses. She spoke of her relatively recent promotion, but as she did the palms of Patrick's gentle giant hands caressed her hips, gently massaging them with the tips of his insinuating fingers. She faltered a little as she reached the part about too much travelling. She just couldn't seem to find the words she needed as she was becoming increasingly aroused by the entrancing hold Patrick had over her.

He asked her if she was happy with her career and what she really wanted to do. She responded by telling him she wanted to write a novel, but the words were muffled by her increased breathing as his magnanimous effect on her continued to take hold. She lifted her left arm up to pull on the back of his neck, using the grip to express the pleasure his sensitive hands were giving her, as they had now moved further down her blossoming body. He fed Abby's youthful beauty with burgeoning vigour, his indefatigable touch intensifying as the flourishing bud of her femininity bloomed into sheer elation, spreading as a hot tingling to the tips of her toes. His neck was still grasped by her along with his chest taking the force of her pressing head as he shared the rapture he had given to her; and it was then that she turned her agile body round to face him and locked her legs around the base of his spine. She advanced the pleasure by now involving Patrick in the delight that he had supplied her body with, and under the auspices of Patrick the passion continued until he felt the same intense joy she had felt.

They did finally make it to dinner but later than they first intended. The rest of the evening practically mirrored the day. Abby's head was filled with wonder and excitement that she was finally going to be with the man that made her feel like she had wings and the man she wanted to spend the rest of her life with. But as for Patrick—can a leopard really ever change his spots? His thoughts, indeed, were very different from Abby's.

# CHAPTER 14

❁

The venue for Patrick and Abby's night sleep had changed to the main suite where the view over the Thames from the sliding doors offered even more light and brightness. With Patrick still fast asleep, Abby removed her contented body and slipped on his trite cranberry cotton top and wandered softly over to the wide glass doors. Carefully unlocking and gently opening the heavy door she stepped out, her bare feet feeling the cold first. She just gazed out at the view from the balcony and pondered a while. The early morning weather was still quite dull and dreary. However, the chilly air went unnoticed by Abby as her mind went back to that morning in Paris, and then to what had happened, when she was feeling what she was feeling at this exact minute. Her perfect joy had been instantly destroyed by Patrick's errant gust; it was like a whirlwind to her, suddenly coming out of nowhere, a silent gale that had no warning and with it, it had blown her dreams to the wayside with one great swoop. And with that memory she felt the pain all over again. The recollection still seemed so real, but as she turned her head and looked over her shoulder she gave a reassuring smile that that was then, and it was in the past, whereas this was now and the future. But the gnawing thought persisted: were they really that different?

She looked over again at Patrick who was still asleep, one side of his face submerged in the bed linen with his relatively tanned skin thrown into relief by the whiteness of the sheets. His darkened and growing stumble circled his mouth and covered his jaw line and partially his cheeks too. He was oblivious to Abby's intent gaze, but as he lay softly in the bed she felt an overwhelming love for him, a love that had never gone away and a love that didn't take much to resurface. Just then, as she watched, still a short distant away, Patrick turned a little in the midst of his sleep and grabbed her vacant pillow and caressed it with his right arm, his bulging biceps and lower arm gripping it with surety. His arms were equally as splendid to look at as they were to feel around one's body; they were subtly hairy and well proportioned along with being protecting and reassuring. It was then, as Abby's stare was still fixed on him, that she knew that her feeling of security, which Patrick had given her in the past, had been short lived—and she just couldn't get this feeling out of her mind. Her cooled body was still calling to her to be warmed and so she stepped into the heated penthouse and closed the door. The flicking of Patrick's eye caught her glance. Noticing it was only 8 a.m. and that they had only gone to bed at 1 a.m., she quietly stepped back into bed, still covered in the warmness of his crew neck t-shirt, and tried to resume some sleep without disturbing him.

Having only managed to relax and just being content to lie next to Patrick, she managed to stay rested till about 9 a.m. But just as she thought of having a nice hot shower and was nearly out of the bed, she was pulled back by Patrick's masterful arm. Her body was drawn back towards his turned waist and, with him using the left side of his body as a support, Abby's stooped back was drawn against his raised hip. He used his other arm to prop himself further and rested his head on his hand and peered down at Abby.

"Where were you sneaking off too?" his sleepy voice managed to say.

"I was just going to have a nice hot shower," Abby said as she ran her hand down his exposed arm.

"Can't you stay in bed a bit longer? We could have a shower later."

"We?" Her face creased in a smile as she said that small word.

"Of course." He sometimes sounded even sexier and with that last word spoken Abby again surrendered to his charm and shuffled her body to relax in his domineering presence. After a short time of relaxing together Patrick questioned Abby's stare.

"What are thinking? Your eyes are somewhere else." Patrick noticed that Abby had her eyes turned towards the ceiling.

"Oh, its nothing," she said, dismissing his concern.

"Tell me," he said as he shuffled a bit to get comfy and to balance and readjust his weight, which was still being supported by the palm of his hand.

"It's just a friend I have. We've known each other over twenty-years and we had a bit of an argument a few days ago and I just wished I had sorted things out, that's all."

When she felt so happy Abby hated having something clouding her mind and she wished James had been more understanding, but she knew it was because he cared. But at the time her emotions were all over the place and she didn't see it like that. James, though, was a very important person to her and the sadness of their crossed words was still apparent in her eyes.

"So is this friend a he or a she?" He seemed to want to know what the gender of this friend was, more than what they had fallen out about.

"He—James. We grew up together. He was the one that I told you was in Kentucky. He breeds horses. Do you remember?"

"Vaguely. What was the argument about then?"

"Oh, just something about his girlfriend. It's just that I said some things I regret and I think so did he. Anyhow, no need to worry; we've had ups and downs before. We'll sort it out." Abby camouflaged the truth a little as she felt self-conscious about the fact that she had told James everything about Patrick. However, she didn't completely reassure herself with the part about sorting things out; deep down she was worried that their friendship may change with Patrick back in the equation. However, she was worrying over nothing, as time would surely tell.

"You *are* glad you came to see me, aren't you?"

Abby turned her body to face his and answered with great reassurance. "Do you really need to ask? I'm very glad I did."

"So am I. You know I didn't realise how much I'd missed you until now." Patrick used his free hand to run a finger from the top of Abby's forehead straight down the centre of her idyllic noise. It carried on over her closed full lips. Then, using the back of his same finger, he brushed the tenderness under her cute diminutive chin. He took the affection further and cupped her left cheek in his hand and said, "You're perfect." Abby just smiled back at him and then reached in to kiss his sweet talking lips. Patrick held the kiss longer as if he were savouring the taste, as if he knew it was the one delicacy he may not ever taste again. Abby saw a change of look mask his face and, squinting her big blue eyes a little, she questioned the look.

"What's that look for?"

"What look?"

"That look of almost terror."

"I just didn't realise how much I love being with you."

Abby kissed his coarse cheek and gave a reassuring scrunch of her noise, thinking that was sweet.

"We could have that shower now if you like?" she added hopefully.

"Sounds like a good plan. You get it going and I'll be there in a minute."

"Okay, don't be long."

Abby headed for the larger en suite room while Patrick lay still covered by the sheets. Having fallen back to be flat on the mattress, he took a moment before he got up to join Abby.

The steam from the billowing shower had, in just a just a short space of time, filled the pentagonal bathroom with force. The black ceramic tiles soon had a mist over them as well as the chrome accessories. As soon as Patrick entered the steamy room his earlier thoughts evaporated and all he could think of now was Abby in the shower and the prospect of embarking on a sensuous voyage with the woman that, despite his arrogant ways, he cared for so much. The shape of the shower space mirrored the shape of the five-sided room in a scaled-down version. The frosted doors secluded the spray and, as Abby was feeling the full strength of the powerful deluge, her expectant body felt a zephyr as Patrick pulled open the doors. He instantly moved to the spray of the water to catch up with the wetness of Abby's body, passing her with an encouraging smile along the way.

The dense tiles darkened the area, but with the inset lighting above them there was just enough luminosity. Abby reached for the new bar of soap that sat on the chrome ledge and it was as she began to lather the scented cake in her hands that the expedition of seduction began again. Instead of the sensuousness being serious, it was enthralling in a fun way. Patrick's back was taking the full impact of the pressured water, their comfortable bodies facing each other, and with the froth in Abby's teasing hands, she started to massage it into the front of his chest. His subtle hairiness became covered with the lathered substance and, as the soap descended down his body, she took him into her grasp and made it a shower he would never forget.

Far from enjoying the same pleasures, James was ringing Abby's home number for a second time. Just as he contemplated calling her mobile he resigned himself to the fact that he would have to just wait to apologize and clear the air. His suspicion that Abby had succumbed to the charms of Patrick had by now grown and, as he thought about what he wanted to say to her, concern for her had crept in. He was worried what it would do to his friend if Patrick destroyed her hopes again. However, one thing was for sure—however broken and hurt she was, he would be there to mend and piece her back together.

Lying on the unmade king-size bed of the master-suite, Patrick and Abby were dressed in the simple attire of their towels. Abby's towel was tied in a loose knot by her underarm and just about covered her modesty, while Patrick's just covered him from the waist down. They both seemed very contented and, with Abby's head full of the future and Patrick's full of the past as she began to speak, the moment had arrived that would prove to be a watershed in their relationship. With her damp hair on the white pillow, her right leg entwined with Patrick's left and her hand in the palm of Patrick's, she let her thoughts be heard.

"When I was young I always dreamed about having this feeling about someone. That feeling that even when you're with them you still can't get enough of them. That your heart aches and that everything seems to make sense, and no matter what the question, that person always seems to be the answer." Her fairytale way of looking at love was so innocent, but the reality was going to be like someone throwing a bucket of cold water over her. Her desire to be loved and her innocence and blindness with Patrick made for a lethal spell, one that was about to cast its formula all over her—again.

"The time we've spent together has been just unforgettable," Patrick said, "and never in my life have I felt this way about anyone. You're the most amazing person I've ever met." The way he said it implied there could have been a 'but'; but that didn't deter the besotted Abby.

She turned her body and prized it up a little to kiss the place where those touching words had just come from. She was in her seventh heaven and never wanted this moment to end. Their bodily contact became closer and tighter and as Patrick started to twist her long drying hair around his chief finger, he delivered the casual yet cruel statement which said, in effect, that nothing had changed.

"You know," he said, "the guy that finds you is going to be so lucky."

The way he said was everything rolled into one. In other words, it implied it wouldn't be him. What had happened in the last twenty-four hours hadn't changed anything, and in his casual way he was letting her know their relationship was finite, implying that she always knew it had no future. Abby sat up and turned round to look at him, clutching her towel to secure it so it didn't fall. She responded with disbelief.

"What's that supposed to mean?"

"I'm just saying he'll be a lucky guy," he said, again in a carefree way.

"What guy?" The disbelief was now growing with concern and she stood up, agitated. Her once smiling face was awash with fear. Was this history repeating itself?

"All I'm saying is that when you meet someone he'll be really lucky." Patrick sat up and pivoted in order to sit on the edge of the bed, his bare feet cushioned on the nondescript coloured carpet. Abby's realisation of what that actually translated to mean hit her hard and she felt her whole body become rigid.

"So, let me get this straight. That's your subtle way of saying that what has recently happened means absolutely nothing—and nothing has changed since Paris. So that was your way of making sure I knew that. Am I right?"

"It's not like that. I thought you knew that nothing had changed." His calm and arrogant way just infuriated a far from calm Abby even more. She was right back to where she was twelve months ago; only this time no tears were in sight: she was too angry to even think about crying.

"You knew that I would never have slept with you again if I thought for one minute that all it was going to be was for sex! You knew I thought it meant things could be different! Your words—' I want you to stay'—and the fact that you wrote in the first place, and the absence of a wedding ring! You *knew* what I thought it all meant and you took advantage of me. Again!"

"No, I thought you knew where we stood."

"That's rubbish and you know it!"

Abby was uncomfortable with the fact that she was close to being naked, and before he could reply again she grabbed her clothes which were lying on a wooden ottoman at the base of the bed and raced to the bathroom to dress. In the bathroom she threw her clothes on at a sure pace and in her head prepared what she wanted to say next. As she dressed in the bathroom Patrick threw on his t-shirt and some boxer shorts and waited for the bathroom door to open. He knew deep down he had been unfair but he had strong desires that hurt him as much as they hurt other people. Because, despite what Abby thought of him, he had this torturous battle going on in his head, though somehow Abby always seemed to be the loser.

"So come on then, tell me, what has been so fulfilling about the last year that you couldn't possibly bare to sacrifice?" Abby flung the question at him as she came out from the bathroom, her jacket and boots the only things missing from her disconcerted self.

"You wouldn't understand if I told you." He stood with his hands on his hips and watched as Abby put her footwear on.

"Well, you're going to tell me something! I think you owe me that much, don't you?" Her voice was far from breaking. She was hurt, yes, but at the moment that hurt was being expressed in unrestrained anger.

"For the first time in as long as I can remember," Patrick began, "I have a status, an influence and a power, and it feels better than I ever imagined. I have wealth, success and a position of superiority over my brother at long last, and to top it all the firm is in talks about taking over the company he works for. I'm the one now that people look up to. I'm the one with respect and I can't let that go. I wish I could, but something just doesn't want to let go. I do love you, but I have this mêlée going on in my head, and until it's gone there is nothing I can do." Patrick gesticulated greatly with every word, pointing to his head when regarding his battle.

Abby stood in the far right corner of the room close to the black leather chair that was near the patio doors. She was still unimpressed and, instead of just empty words, she really thought about her answer as he uttered each word. It was then, with Patrick facing her and after standing still, having paced a bit while he spoke, that she hit him with her reply. It seemed like a valediction, and as she gave her potentially futile oration she knew this was probably the last time she would ever see him.

"You know, you talk about respect—and it's a joke! You don't *buy* respect, you don't acquire it, and you certainly don't marry it. You *earn* it. What you have isn't respect, its false—and it's hollow. You're prepared to marry someone for purely superficial gain, and you' re living a life that you don't belong in. You know, you have an ego the size of China. This isn't really about outdoing your brother, this is about proving to yourself that you are equally as capable of having what he has when deep down you don't know what you want or who you want to be. You're the most lost person I have ever met."

"That's not true. I have worked all my life for this and it is what I want. If I have to marry someone to get it, then that's the way of the world."

"Oh really? You know, you think you have everything you want, but, you know, one day you're going to wake up and realise you have nothing. Money and power can buy so much, but they can never buy people. You'll be the loneliest person there is and, what's more, you will have brought it completely on your self. Thanks for involving me yet again. You say you love me! Well, pardon my French, but that's bollocks! You're in love with yourself and you always will be. I just hope that what you've done is worth the hurt and pain you have caused me."

With no more said or added from either of them, Abby grabbed her jacket and bag and walked past Patrick and made her way to the front door. However, as she approached her exit Patrick chased ahead of her and shut the door with mild force and pleaded with her.

"Abby! What happens if I said come to Canada?" He was trying to find a way to make it better when in fact he was making it worse.

"What!" Her disbelief resurfaced.

"Come to Canada! At least then we can be together." His quick thinking made him block the doorway as he waited for her to answer.

"You want me to come to Canada and have some sort of long standing affair? Is that what you're offering? You think that's what I'm worth?"

"Abby, I want to be with you, and this is the only way I know how." Despite what he was asking he sounded so lost and confused.

"Patrick, you don't know *what* you want! Now let me go before I say something I'll regret!"

"You can't go like this!"

"Watch me. One day I hope you'll know what you've just let go."

In her eyes he knew what he had just said was not the way to go, and as she made for the door Patrick moved his body to clear the way for her to leave, her last words still ringing in his head. He had this torment going on in his mind that made him lose sight of any other happiness that he could be contented with. He couldn't and wouldn't accept that maybe he just wasn't meant to follow the path he was trying to embark upon. However, this time, feeling the force of Abby's words, he wavered and in a moment of now or never, with his torture of losing her brewing, he heard the outer door open. However, as if his feet became stuck to the floor, he froze, his head having chosen never to agree with his heart as he reached to close the nearside door. Each door closed and they parted once again, but this time their once burning flame had only the embers left and there was no way they could ever be relit. Abby felt the last time when things ended a part of her would never be the same again; and now, after the last day and a repeat performance of her earlier hurt, that part had grown dramatically.

The long and tiresome journey home ended not a minute to soon for Abby. The latter part of the day was incredibly cold and foggy. She had held her at bay emotions all the way home and, however calm and collected she had seemed with Patrick, her insides were far from being composed. Her tired hair was loosely tied in a low clasp from a band she had recovered from her bag, her face bare of any makeup, and, looking decidedly white and worn out, she was cold and exhausted. She reached for her keys and was finally inside and, no sooner had the strong front door closed, when the lid on her boiling pot overflowed. Her distraught body slid down the door and tears fell from her eyes like a cascading waterfall. To make matters worse, when she smeared the tears across her face with the cuff of her slightly exposed shirt, she could still smell traces of Patrick, and that dab of salt hurt the wound even more. She picked up her crushed and devastated body and carried her sadness through to the living room.

The thick-lined curtains of the French doors were where Abby headed first, then to the windows to repeat the same action of drawing them; and, finally, she switched on a single lamp by the television. She wanted to feel enclosed and sheltered from the darkness. She was by no means a drinker, but she felt as if someone had not only given her a taste of what she could have and snatched it away, but done in such a way that the taste still lingered on her lips—and she wanted to numb the pain as quickly as possible. There were quite a selection of bottles, used for company, and with the choice staring back at her from the antique cabinet; she chose the simplicity of the vodka. The first two shots burnt her insides as the liqueur ran down her throat and inflamed her face, particularly her cheeks; however, after that the initial impact eased but sadly the pain didn't. She dropped her head down onto the arm of the sofa and her body just switched off naturally for her to sleep and be able to dream again.

She lay fast asleep, completely oblivious to the world, unaware that James had been knocking at the front door for the last five minutes. James made the trip to see her especially, wanting to see that everything was okay. It was strange—he just had this feeling, a need to see her, and acted on the feeling that was so strong he couldn't ignore it. He stood by the front door, sheltered by the overhead porch and used his mobile to call Abby. With still no answer and the light from the living room in view, he used the key he had to enter, calling out as he did so, not wanting to scare or alarm her. But nothing was going to wake her, and as James approached the living room he panicked. Seeing the bottle and Abby out to the world, he sped over to her and lifted her floppy body and called to her to wake up.

"Abby, Abby, wake up!" He had seen Abby at very low and vulnerable times and when he saw the drink and her lifeless body, panic took over. The panic was very apparent in his voice and on his face. A very groggy Abby began to stir from her few hours sleep, bringing relief to James's face.

"Where am I?" Abby rubbed her head and clutched her stomach, feeling very disorientated. There is always that first split second when one wakes up before everything comes flooding back. However that was soon to be over for her.

"You're at home, Abby. You gave me such a fright!" Her upright body was supported by the strength of his arms as he sat next to her while she regained her bearings. The last part was more for him, as he had really thought the worse. Everything started to come back and it was then that she broke down.

"Oh James, I've made such a mess of everything." Tears streamed down her washed out face.

"Hey, come on."

She fell further into his supporting arms and the tears increased as she was relieved to be held.

"Do you hate me?"

"Hate you! Of course I don't hate you!"

"But the things I said."

"We both said things we regret and it's only because each of us cares, not because we are trying to hurt one other. Sometimes things don't come out in the way they are meant to, that's all." He kissed her head and gave her an extra squeeze of reassurance.

"I'm so sorry, James. You were so right about Patrick, so right." She lifted her blurry eyes to look up at him. He moved the few loose strains of her hair off her face. He could see how distraught she was, but he didn't know what to say.

"I'm sorry too. You deserve so much better than this." With the words barely out of his mouth, Abby's tears welled up again. He held her close and tight and made her feel safe. It took only a few minutes for her to fall asleep again, but this time it was in the arms of her hero.

James's body was back on the sofa as Abby's head pressed against his chest, her half turned body cuddled up on her side. She was comfortable and contented and, not wanting to disturb her, James dropped his head back and just held Abby and didn't let go. He ran his hand down her hair and stroked it in an endearing way and looked after her shattered spirit in his repairing arms. He wondered why anyone would want to hurt her in the way Patrick had done, and how he hated the fact; that man would never know what an effect he had had on her. But right now James was just glad that he could make her feel safe and warm. It wasn't until about an hour or so later, with James also having dropped off for a while, that he felt Abby trying to move a little. He carefully removed his own body and turned Abby so she could stretch out fully and have the entire sofa to sleep on. It seemed better than moving her upstairs and potentially breaking her much needed sleep; so he draped a cotton throw over her oblivious body and, before moving himself to the opposite sofa, he tucked her growing fringe behind her left ear and paused to look at her delicate face. Even though she was fast asleep he uttered some loving words to her.

"When everything around you falls apart, I'll always be here to put it back together. I promise." The soft meaningful words floated in the air, and before standing and moving across to the other sofa he repeated an earlier affection and kissed her forehead.

He watched her sleep and rest, her eyes quivering as she dreamt, her body huddling under the fabric of the throw. He watched until his own tiredness got the better of him and then he, too, fell into the clouds of oblivion.

## CHAPTER 15

❀

The following morning brought with it the most unbelievable headache for Abby and as she stirred in the living room James came in from the kitchen carrying a strong and much needed coffee. The pattern brick throw cloaked her shoulders, with James, still dressed in his clothes from Saturday, jeans and a casual sweat top, sitting close to her while he insisted she drink the hot beverage.

"I know it's strong, but you'll feel better if you drink it."

"I couldn't have some pain killers, could I?" she said, using her free hand to completely cover her forehead.

"Sure you can." He was quick to reappear with the white tablets and a small glass of water. As he stood over Abby, passing her the much-needed pills, she gave him as big a smile as she could muster. Swapping the mug of black coffee for the glass, she added:

"I don't know what I'd do without you." Her head tilted back conveyed the words.

"Well, you're never going to have to find out."

They shared a smile and as Abby finished gulping the remedy for her aching head she stood up and left the glass on the table. Her blue blouse was all creased and hanging out of her tailored trousers and, as James placed her mug on a coaster, she opened her arms, the throw falling where she had been sitting, and surprised James with the biggest hug she could find.

"You *have* forgiven me, haven't you!" she said, still holding him tight in the hug.

"There's nothing to forgive, but if it makes you fell better, then of course I do. You forgive me, don't you?" As he said that their faces met, but their bodies were still close in the hug. James's face beamed as Abby replied:

"No need to ask." And on that final note their unshakable friendship was once again intact.

Abby headed upstairs for a much-needed shower while James drew the curtains and tidied the room, which had acted as a bedroom for them both. The bright morning sun was a welcome silver lining to the very cold air and sharp frost, and to Abby, James was like the silver lining to her aching heart. When he heard Abby finish in the bathroom he called to tell her that he would make them something to eat. She didn't want to reject his kindness and said she would have a little something. Finding what he could in the fridge, the only thing he could think that might tempt her was her favourite breakfast of all times, scrambled eggs on toast with tomato ketchup. Gentle steps down the stairs and Abby was greeted by the alluring smell of the cooking eggs, although that was now being shadowed by the smell of the toast that was burning under the grill. James was trying to do it under the grill as he knew Abby loved thick sliced bread and that the wedges he had sliced were disinclined to squeeze into the conventional toaster. She had put on her rose pyjamas that covered her whole body, just showing her bare feet and long slender neck. Her freshly washed hair was now clean and dry and hanging loose on her shoulders and, as James saw her appear at the door, he teased her as he started spreading the butter over the charred bread.

"You do like your toast well done, don't you?" The sound of the knife crunching against the overcooked breaded surface as it spread the butter embellished his passing question.

"I wouldn't want it any other way." She meant it. She was just touched by the trouble he was going to.

"I would have done some more but that was the last of the bread."

"It's fine, don't worry." She gave him a reassuring smile as she sat at the breakfast table. She had no intention of venturing any further than the house for the rest of the day, and so her pyjamas were the perfect outfit. James brought the plates over and, notwithstanding the apparent disaster with the toast, it looked quite appetising. Abby's tears had for the moment dried and, as she finished the first mouthful of her scrambled egg, saturated in tomato sauce, she looked over at James and breathed a sigh of relief—relief that other than her mum she was with the best person and that she knew she could get through this. She was stronger than she sometimes even credited herself. With James and her mum she knew she would come out of this even stronger than before, and in the midst of her pain she still was able to find a trace of laughter. As she watched as James chomped through the intense burnt flavour of the toast, he unknowingly was cheering her and in her smile and mild laughter hope was rekindled.

"What?" James knew what had made her smile but he pretended to be naïve about it all.

"Nothing."

And just then he gave her a big grin and her smile widened as she saw that all his front teeth were covered in black soot. He looked so funny without even trying and her laughter brought back a glimmer of the old Abby. James was happy that she had now eaten something and sent her to her bed to relax with her mug of tea while he cleared the kitchen. She didn't disagree and before she left the kitchen she planted a big kiss on his cheek. However, for some reason, though this wasn't the first time she had made that type of gesture, he felt awkward and just said, "Go on with you!"

With Abby heading upstairs carrying her Winnie the Pooh mug, James held his glance at the doorframe even though Abby was heading up the stairs and the image of her had long since vanished. He gave the vacant space a smile before turning back to the sink, thinking to himself how much she meant to him and how glad he was to be there supporting her.

For the rest of that day Abby just wanted the security of the inside, doing nothing other than snuggling up on the sofa and watching all her favourite films. James had insisted that he stay with her, and Abby gladly welcomed his abiding support and company. They watched Abby's favourite Murder Mystery series that she had on tape and, as they sat close to each other in the middle of the couch, the throw covering their legs that were resting on the leather footstool, James just enjoyed Abby's running commentary as to what was going to happen and when. As long as she was happy he didn't care; he had hoped, though, that at some point she would talk to him about it all, but he knew she would when the time was right. He hoped it would be before Teresa was back on Tuesday as he felt she needed to release some off of the pain before then.

The day crept on at quite a pace. The afternoon soon disappeared and in full view of them both the sun was setting, the ochre sky gleaming in through living room windows. James did have things he needed to do but nothing was more important than being there for Abby. He had already quietly phoned his dad to tell him he would not be about today, quietly, so Abby didn't think she was causing problems, for that was the last thing he wanted. Michael understood and there wasn't a problem. So with the fire blazing, the farewell sun bringing a dash of radiance to the room and the television and video now off, they just had each other and their mugs of hot chocolate for company. As James had hoped, Abby started paving the way for telling him what had happened. She told him from the beginning to the end and was very open with what she divulged; she didn't want to leave anything out and, as she reached the final part, she concluded:

"I can't believe that I thought things could be different. He even suggested I move to Canada and have some sort of long-standing affair! You know, all the way home all I kept thinking about was last Christmas. You being back, the house full of people, laughing and messing about, and how I had no idea that this was on the horizon. I guess that's why we don't know our future."

"I know that right now you can't imagine feeling better, Abby, but you will, I promise. The thing is, with time it doesn't stop you loving that person or feeling hurt and betrayed; but it helps the hurt and pain to subside. As for the love, well, you'll probably always love him in a way. But that love will gradually sink deeper and deeper down, so it's not so much on the surface and not so apparent. And there will be times you'll miss him. You may hate him now, sweetheart, but you will still miss him, but those times will become less often and, before you know it, the gap between the times you think about him again will have widened and it will get easier."

"I hope so." She didn't sound convinced so James continued.

"It may not seem like that now, because everything is fresh and sore; but once you bruise, then you can heal. Even if it leaves a scar you'll be able to touch it and, although it will always be there, you'll always remember how it happened. It won't hurt to the same degree." He was trying so hard to make sense but worried he had made it more complicated. But when Abby smiled with her mug close to her chin, he could see that the words had made sense to her, even if they sounded confusing.

James's unremitting support continued with strength and Abby knew she wouldn't have got through the day without him. The thing on Abby's mind now was work in the morning. She really couldn't face it and the only option, not to look too incapable, was to have the work emailed through and pretend she had flu. If she had to work, which with the monthly deadline looming she knew she did, it could at least be in the comfort of her of own home. James had to head home that night and couldn't stay again. Commitments with meetings were now unavoidable. However, Abby did seem brighter and she reassured him she would be fine—a little white lie, but she knew she couldn't keep him away any longer. He left about 7 p.m. just after making her another hot chocolate and her giving him a big thank you hug and kiss on his cheek that was in much need of a shave. He still smelt clean and fresh despite being unchanged from Saturday morning, but the niceness of the hug brought some tears to Abby's eyes. It was either the fact she now would only be having herself for company, or just because she felt overwhelmed by the whole experience again; either way, she stopped the tears falling and again reassured James she would be fine and also that she would probably just go to bed.

With the bright red lights shining from the back of James Land Rover fading down the drive, Abby closed the door after she heard the friendly goodbye hoot. When the door was closed she paused and just leant her body on it and dropped her head back. After a few seconds she used the weight of her body to push herself up, to stand unaided. Shutting off the lights in the living room and drawing the curtains, checking the locks on the doors, she did as she said she would and headed to her bed. Even if she didn't sleep straight away, that was the only place where she wanted to be. She lay on the side of the bed nearest the panelled door, all cuddled up in the duvet, which was protected by her checked blanket; and, for the first time since she left Patrick, she realised something was missing, not having noticed before, having been either still tired and half asleep, or intoxicated with alcohol; however, now she was quiet and calmer and knew now she had left her mum's eternity ring on the soap dish in the shower at his penthouse. Well, that was like the straw that broke the camel's back! Feeling utterly mortified that part of her mum and dad was left in that cold empty prism, it was enough to bring uncontrollable crying to her eyes. She turned her head and body to the side as the tears fell, her glance looking over at the tall chest of drawers she had behind the door. She pulled the duvet up closer to her chin as the crying intensified and used it as something to comfort her body with while her eyes wept and her heart ached.

Through some point of the crying, though, her eyes must have started to relinquish and attempted to shut, because she began to drift off. Drifting into sleep, she was able to forget the reality of her pain. It was like she grieving, grieving for a love she had enjoyed and lost in such a short space of time. But as she approached the abyss of unconsciousness, the last vision she saw in her mind's eye was the ring, and the words rang in her head: "Ever Mine, Ever Thine, Ever For Each Other."

Monday came and went with James calling nearly every hour, but the distraction of work was in fact a welcome relief for Abby. She wanted the house to look nice for when her mum returned, so the latter part of the day was filled with dusting, washing, some vacuuming and a spruce up of the bathrooms. When she came to dust in the dining room the sideboard was what needed the most attention and it was on that rich antique surface that her favourite-framed photo of her dad sat. She held the photo longer than just to wipe underneath it. She lifted it close to her face and said softly, "I miss you, dad." Her own words brought tears to her eyes and as she replaced the photo on the now polished surface she rubbed them dry and tried to find a smile for the next picture. This time it was of her and her dad: it was when she was four, taken on the day she made the rain disappear and the day she found her big teddy at the end of her rainbow. The picture was so bright, the sun almost poured out of the print and the memory was that of hope, the same hope the memory gave her when she was ill and sitting in the garden—and her face found a reluctant smile in the midst of her sadness.

With the dusting complete and with some towels in the upstairs laundry basket needing a wash, Abby climbed the stairs two at a time, heading for the bathroom for starters. Gathering the towels from the soothing cream Victorian bathroom, she headed down the landing. The floorboards, mostly covered in a thick deep bronze runner, creaked as she went. When she opened the door to her bedroom she was stunned by what she saw. In the corner to the left the wicker chair was empty, for her big teddy Sunny was sitting face down on the floor, having flopped onto the plain verdant velvet pile carpet. As she wandered over, leaving the towels on the bed, she picked him up and with both arms gave him a loving hug, a hug that she longed to share with her dad again. Replacing him to his home on the woven chair, she smiled back at him as she left the room, carrying her additional washing that she had added to the towels. She felt that although the house was empty, company was never far away.

Tuesday, and Teresa, Alice and Stanley were due to be with Abby by about 4 p.m. The house was ready and so was Abby. She wanted it to seem that everything had been okay and wanted to wait till a lot later to talk to her mum.

"Oh, it's so good to see you, mum! I've really missed you!" The big hug they shared expressed that further.

"Oh, me too! But we did have a fantastic time! You would have loved it, sweetheart."

"Shall I take these upstairs, Teresa?" Stanley's big strong hands clutched her luggage, waiting for an answer.

"That would be great, thanks."

"Stanley, one of those bags is ours," Alice called as he reached the landing, curtailing her hug with Abby a little sooner than intended.

"Come through. I've made a pot of tea and I've got your favourites, mum!"

"Oh, you didn't get Chelsea buns, did you? I've put on so much weight this last week or so. The food was out of this world!"

"Well, I'll have yours if you're not going to have it!" Alice teased her sister as she appeared at the kitchen door, hearing the conversation.

"Well, I didn't say I wouldn't have it!" she said, backtracking when she saw and smelt the buns on the dresser.

The happiness the three of them brought into the home and all the tales of their holiday, made it easier for Abby to rest from thinking about the last few days. Alice and Stanley had left their car at the cottage as they had all set off from there. It just happened to be easier at the time, so when Abby had shared in all their excitement, her Aunt and Uncle were eager to get home and unpack. With big hugs shared between Teresa and her sister and brother in law, all expressing their appreciation for the brilliant time they had had, they were on their way home. Abby and her mum shared another hug at the recently closed door with Abby reiterating her gladness that her mum had had a good time, but also that she was home again. They retired to the study where Abby finished sending a bunch of faxes and emails, while Teresa made herself comfy in one of the two striped raspberry fabric armchairs. With the last button pressed and the computer shut down, Teresa asked her daughter what she had been up to.

"So come on, what have you been up to?" Teresa came straight out with the obvious question for someone who had been away, though not knowing what the answer could possibly be. Abby turned around to view her mum and her face said it all. They sat talking for nearly the whole evening in the compact square room, making a single cup of tea last longer than one might expect. Abby had always been able to tell her mum anything and now was no exception, but she left one detail out—the fact that she had left the ring. But at the moment she just wanted to be hugged by her mum and forget the fact she had no way of retrieving it.

Over the next couple of weeks through Abby's healing period she came to a momentous decision about her work. As much as she enjoyed her career in editing, she had given her notice and decided to return to being an interior designer, resurrecting her old business. The magazine gave her a very good send off and, as a leaving present, she was presented with a weekend visit to a health farm. She still wanted to write a novel but she didn't want the weighty responsibility that the job was bringing and the endless travelling. So she intended to reunite herself with the interiors world, using the contacts she now had to make it a success again; and with her book, *Natural Interiors*, having been published two years ago, she was by no means back at the start. She was well ahead of the game and had a good status to make it a thriving business again. Abby aimed to write freelance if possible in conjunction with her revived business, with at some point embarking upon her much dreamt about novel, for which she already had a title, *A Child Hungry*—naturally based on her own experiences with anorexia. She planned to turn her true-life battle with the condition into a fictional novel.

She was confident in her change of direction and had much support from those around her. Charles had been able to give Teresa and Abby financial security and with that weight lifted, Abby was able to change her direction and find her destiny. To outsiders that security may have been envied, especially the opportunity to find what would fulfil her without the worry of money; nevertheless Abby and Teresa would both have given everything up and stood bare clothed if they could have just had Charles back with them. They found mild solace in the fact that Charles would have wanted them to make the best of what they had, as his favourite saying was just that. Of course, he had no idea that his life was going to end so suddenly, though a few weeks before the crash, when Abby was still studying, he quoted her some words by J.H Newman. He found them in a prayer book that his mother, Abby's grandmother, had given him before she died. He had articulated the meaningful words while they sat in the garden enjoying a summer lunch. It came about as Abby was questioning her future. The conviction with which Charles had spoken the inspiring words caused them to have a great impact on his daughter. He had read:

> *I have a mission, I am a link in a chain, a bond of connections between persons. God has not created me for nought. Therefore I will trust him whatever, wherever I am. I can never be thrown away. God does nothing in vain. He knows what he is about.*

He wanted Abby to have faith in her future and not have to worry about what she should be doing. It worked, because even to this day, when, at times, she felt lost and vacant, she knew she would find direction and find what she was meant to be doing. The funny thing is sometimes one comes across it while perusing something else. If one turns one's attention to other things, the answer has a way of appearing in front of one.

Well and truly back in the swing of things, it didn't take long for Abby to receive endless calls from previous clients. However this time she limited the amount of work and travel to what she felt content with, enabling her to start her novel. Two months had past since the episode in London with Patrick, but unbeknown to Abby it wasn't the end, it was just the beginning. Something else had been missing, but with the stress and work dilemmas she hadn't given it a second thought until now.

Thursday morning and Abby was late down for breakfast. When she did appear she called to find her mum and in the middle of her call she noticed a note on the table propped up against the full fruit bowl in the centre:

∾

> Abby—didn't want to wake you as you were very tired yesterday. I have headed into town. I'm meeting Rosemary for lunch. We will head back to the Stud to work on those curtains for you. See you there at about 4 p.m. James is cooking Thai tonight for everyone. Should be interesting! God Bless——Mum.

The thought of James trying to cook Thai food and the lingering smell of her mum's kippers made Abby heave. With barely a second to spare she made it to the cloakroom off the hall, just in time to be extremely sick. She stood over the small white basin that perfectly fitted into the corner, the compact circular mirror above. Cupping her clammy hands to scoop the running water, she slapped the coldness on her red flushed face, desperately trying to retrieve her normally paler colouring. The stray drips of water fell down her face and onto the collar of her pink pyjamas and, just when she thought she was over the worst, she felt the previous feeling again. She instantly dropped to her knees and relinquished the overwhelming feeling into the toilet, using her right hand to shield her hair from her face, the other gripping the rim of the bowl.

With a hot shower later and, dressed in just her blue towelling gown and coordinating hair towel that wrapped up her wet hair, only allowing a few wisps of drier hair to be detected, Abby sipped gingerly at a tepid glass of water. She sat with the glass in front of her at the table and turned and noticed the spots of rain that had emerged on the kitchen window. Turning back, Abby glanced up at the clock near the free standing fridge. She realised she was running very late but somehow it still didn't make her move. Under the clock was the calendar that Abby and her mum used for pleasure and, as Abby drank the last of her water, she had a sudden realisation. To her it wasn't obvious and she honestly hadn't even considered it, but with all the signs staring her in the face it became clear it was a very good contender to being the answer to all her symptoms. There was only one thing to do and, as she reached for the phone on the side of the dresser, opening the drawer nearby for the number, she made an emergency appointment at the doctors, knowing that she was more likely than not two months pregnant! Although not for the reason intended, she had been taking contraceptive pills, and because of that she hadn't even considered it a prospect; but as she had managed to get to see the doctor later that day, altering her plans to put herself first, the reason became clear.

"I don't see how, though. I take the contraceptive pill to regulate my periods. You suggested it." Abby sat on the edge of the hard chair in the doctor's consulting room. She had literally thrown on some jeans and an old jumper. Her hair loosely tied, she didn't even try to make her face look healthier with any makeup. Doctor Pier was a friend as well as a professional and she, too, had seen Abby through various stages of her life. She spoke to Abby as a friend and that was something Abby appreciated. Julia Pier could see the shock on her young friend's frightened face and so the buxom middle-aged doctor replied with all the warmth and kindness she could muster.

"Well, you haven't been on any antibiotics. Sometimes that can be a factor. What about a tummy bug around the time of conception? Any sickness, anything like that?" Her soft voice tried to reach out to a bewildered Abby who pondered a while and thought back, deleting the pain from the picture to remember clearly.

"Well…" she hesitated.

"Go on," Julia pressed her patiently.

"Well, I didn't have a tummy bug as such, but the night before I…well, you know, and the morning before, I was very sick. It was because of nerves. I just didn't think." Abby struggled, as although they were friends the whole thing was so alien to her.

"That seems like the answer. The sickness counteracted the dosage. The chances of you becoming pregnant as a result would have been low, but still possible."

"I just can't believe that I'm going to have a baby!"

When the news sunk in as she sat further back in the chair, Abby's reaction was that of genuine excitement—not because she thought it would bring Patrick back, but because, for the first time since Paris, all the pain and hurt she had gone through with him, back then in France and more recently in London, was worth it for this moment.

The rest of the day's jobs took a back seat and, although Abby felt excited at the prospect of having a baby, she was worried about the reaction and how her mum would take the news. With not meeting her mum till later and it being with James, Rosemary and Michael, Abby knew she would have to wait until they were alone to tell her. However, as she got in the car and looked in the interior mirror, her face had gone from that of dull and faint, to radiant and shining and for one reason only.

## CHAPTER 16

❊

"I'll be back with some toast."

"I'll come down, mum." Abby started flicking back her bed sheets and began prizing herself up with both her fists, which were pressed into the depth of her luxury mattress and were on either side of her thighs.

"No, you're staying put. No arguments." Teresa gestured to the bed with her hand and gave her pregnant daughter a warm smile as she shut the bedroom door on this early spring morning.

Abby's flowery bedroom overlooked the back garden and, as the seasoned sun shone through the sheer flowing drapes, the rays reflected onto Abby's blooming face. The start of her pregnancy had been far from easy, but that was not showing in her eyes or in the smile that started from each ear and almost covered her whole face. The need to rest and slow down came when Abby was starting a major project at Withers Gallop, one of the residences owned by Larry Golding, an acquaintance of Michael and Rosemary. As a result of their mutual friends they too had become acquaintances and, when he heard through Rosemary that Abby was breaking back into the business, he gave her first refusal on a four-room job. However, with heavy sickness and trying to burn the candle at both ends, a sudden collapse scared Abby into slowing down. The job was still hers though; she just deferred the completion date and didn't undertake any further projects, making that the last job she did before the baby was due in late October.

Telling her mum she was pregnant with Patrick's baby wasn't as hard as she feared. Abby knew her mum would always stand by her, but even knowing that, it was a relief when she was in her mum's arms listening to her reassuring words that she would be with her all the way. James was just the same and was actually excited at the prospect of Abby having a baby. She couldn't have wished for more support, though hanging over her like a grey cloud was her feelings for Patrick. Her hormones added to her conflicting emotions; she never stopped being happy about the baby but in her head she had always dreamt she would be sharing this moment with the man she loved. To tell Patrick was not an option for Abby and it was something that both James and Teresa had to respect. Abby couldn't bare a third rejection and this time it would be her baby as well; what's more, she didn't want him to think she had in some way planned it to happen and to be humiliated again was not appealing. She knew she was doing the right thing. However, she was carrying the child of the one man she loved more than anything and the happiness of being pregnant was sometimes clouded with sadness, sadness that he wasn't there sharing the joy with her. In her mind, though, she would always have a living part of Patrick to hold on to. Later that morning, as Abby lay scribbling down some rough drafts for Larry to look over, James tapped on her bedroom door. He opened it a fraction, checking first she wasn't asleep, all before he entered.

"Hey, I didn't hear the door."

"Teresa was in the garden, so I came in the back. You're supposed to be resting, not working." James walked over to the bed and kissed her cheek and revealed a big box of her favourite chocolates from behind his back.

"Ooh, my favourites! Thanks!"

"So, how are you doing?" James perched on the edge of the bed and picked up the book she had on her nightstand to see what she was reading, He held it while she answered.

"Better. I've kept everything down this morning and the doctor's coming this afternoon, so I should be able to start back at work soon." Abby became distracted as she pulled the cellophane off the milk chocolates.

"That's good. Do you think it's okay, you having those? I don't want you to be sick again."

"Yeah, one or two won't hurt." Too late, as the first one melted on her tongue and tingled on her palate.

"*The Woman in Me*—what are you reading this for?" James's jocose voice teased her.

"It's very interesting. Julia gave it me. It helps you understand your emotions. She wrote it, you know. What's that smirk for?" A second chocolate vanished in her mouth.

"It's just quite an appropriate title, coming from her" The smirk widened.

"You don't know she's that way inclined!" Abby said in defence. "She happens to make some very good points."

"Go on, then—tell me one."

"You'll only take the mickey."

"I won't—go on." His cheeky grin said differently.

"Well, sometimes we use things in our lives to symbolise what we are really feeling."

"Right, like what?"

"Like when a woman feels like a type of food or drink, or like watching a certain programme, it's a code for something else."

"Is that it? She wrote a book on that? I could have told you that."

"Well, I think it's very interesting."

"I won't argue. You're pregnant. I'll make allowances."

"Ooh, you cheeky…" She passed the box over to him.

"Choose your words carefully."

"Have a chocolate, but only one." It was all in jest and the banter distracted her from being incapacitated, which was what James was trying to do since Abby didn't find it easy staying in one place for very long.

A week later and with a "just take it easy" from the doctor, Abby was back at Withers Gallop. She had progressed with the job well and with the third stage nearly complete and just one more room to do, she felt more in control of things. However, little did she know that someone else's affairs would soon shadow her own matters of the heart. Earlier than intended, her 4x4 travelled slowly down the long drive of Larry's home. The late spring air was sweet and the bright happy sun was contagious. Abby's favourite CD bellowed from the player wedged into the dashboard and, with her voice singing completely out of tune and the light breeze blowing on the side of her face from the open driver's window, she felt calm and peaceful. His grounds were beautiful and she slowed the car to appreciate them. She was coming up to being sixteen weeks and, although she could have still just about worn her regular clothes, she now loved wearing floaty linen dresses that reflected how light and angel-like she was feeling inside. She thrived like the daisies and gleamed like the sun and felt so much better physically and emotionally.

Abby turned and parked the sturdy blue car in the circular drive and, as she gathered her bag and fabrics from the back seat, she unwittingly was about to become entangled in the web of Larry's illicit love life. Fiddling for the key he had given to her, she was startled as she opened the strong period front door to the vast vestibule. Flushed and flummoxed and coming down the stairs at quite a pace was a very uncomfortable Rosemary. She was quickly followed by a calmer and more laid back Larry. Abby looked up to them as they descended the grand curvaceous staircase. Rosemary looked like she had thrown on her clothes, whereas Larry's more brazen personality left him in just his silk dressing gown. When Rosemary met the bottom of the steps and stood on the same level as Abby, her awkward face said it all. However, Abby, even in this awkward predicament, just ignored what she knew was going on and, in her bright breezy way and just how she would have greeted Rosemary at any other time, she tried for her friend's sake not to look shocked and make her feel any more humiliated.

"Rosemary! Didn't expect to see you here."

"No, well…I…um, well." Her face flamed but Abby's smile stopped her dithering.

"Sorry, Larry. I thought you were away today." Abby lifted her sunglasses to her head, flicking back her hair in the process.

"Change of plans. Something else came up. Feel free to go through." Although the same age, Larry was like the chalk to Michael's cheese. He was known as a bit of a womaniser and, with his striking appearance, wealth and charm, it wasn't hard to see why so many women had lost all rationality around him. Nevertheless, Abby was surprised that Rosemary was one of them.

"I'm not stopping. I just wanted to match these up in the study."

"Abby, can we talk later?" Rosemary swept her fair, slightly greying hair off her pink face and held Abby's arm as she whispered the words faintly.

"Follow me home if you like. Mum's helping with the craft fair all day."

"Thanks, I'll just get myself together." Rosemary looked relieved as to how Abby seemed to be taking it in her stride. She left them as she scuttled back up the stairs.

"I have a cheque for you, Abby. It's waiting on the desk." With a yawn added at the end, it was as though he were actually enjoying it all.

"Thanks." Abby really didn't want to get too involved, but she did have some concerns. Rosemary hadn't been the first woman she had seen there and that was quite recently. She was worried that Rosemary could be on the verge of making a fool of herself. Larry changed lovers as often as his Armani suits. However, his lifestyle was not her concern before—but now, with it involving a close friend, she couldn't completely switch off to what she had seen in the past.

"Look, I'm sorry about all this." Trying to be serious with a cheesy grin at the end that he just couldn't resist giving.

"Now, why don't I believe that? You look like the cat that's got the cream." Abby broke her displeasure with a mild smile.

"Well, it's been a bonus for you seeing me in my dressing gown at least." His deep sexy voice held no weight with Abby.

"You're unbelievable, you know that; upstairs is one of my closet friends and you're flirting with me!" She whispered the words and tried to put her point across but it cut no ice.

"You know, you're actually very cute when you're displeased."

"Your incorrigible and I'm completely wasting my breath." She knew what he was like and it was all just hot air. "Tell Rosemary I'll be in the study." Abby started to walk past him, startled to hear the next word.

"Who?" The expression on Abby's turned face was enough of a response.

"It was a joke!" He gestured with his long arms out, his palms lifted.

Abby simply rolled her worried eyes and continued to the study. She finished her business there and then headed home with Rosemary on her tail. She had a feeling that Rosemary was glad that someone knew, as she had wanted to talk about it with someone for a while. Abby poured them a glass of pink lemonade each and the two of them headed for the conservatory. Sitting amongst the lavish plants, they made themselves comfy on the light green wicker cushioned furniture.

"What are thinking, getting involved with Larry! I mean, Larry, of all people!" Abby didn't want to be brutal and hadn't really intended to come out with it like that, but her true feelings overtook diplomacy.

"I know what you think of him, but he's different with me. He's sweet and tender and, for the first time in ages, Abby, I feel alive." Having had her legs crossed when she spoke, she freed them and brought her whole body forward to just sit on the edge of the two-seater wicker frame. Putting her tall glass on the table in front of her, she waited for Abby's reply.

"But I thought you and Michael were happy? I mean, it seemed that you were." The sun poured into the glasshouse and, as it caught in the eye of Rosemary, Abby got up immediately and moved over to the window and pulled the Roman blind down to remove the glair for her.

"That's just it! It *seems* like we are but I have felt so empty for years. I love Michael, I really do, but there's just something missing now. That love doesn't outweigh how lonely I feel. It's all horses, horses, and more horses. He never stops, and even when he does it's to entertain with me as the doting wife. He has no idea how I feel, even when I tell him. He thinks I just make a fuss to have something to think about. You think Larry's egotistical? Well, Michael has his moments. Michael and I may look the perfect couple, but that's about as far as it goes."

"Are you saying you're leaving him?" Abby was taken aback by her own question.

"I have to. I might not get this chance again. I'm in love with Larry. We spoke about it today and I'm going to be moving in with him as soon as I have talked to James and Michael."

"Rosemary, have you really thought about what this means? I mean, *really*?"

"Abby, I know you're concerned for me, but Larry has brought life back to my desolate soul. I feel the best I have done in years. I know he has a reputation for being a bit of philanderer—Lothario, womaniser, take your pick; but it only takes one person to make the difference."

"But aren't you risking a hell of a lot to find out if it's you?" Abby tried to plead with her rational side.

"But I *know* it's me, and I just want to have this feeling I have with him—for ever!"

Abby took in the way her greenish blue eyes lit up at the prospect of being with him for ever. Seeing her eyes sparkle with life and vitality, how could she stand in judgement with that look in her almost twinkling eyes, the same look that Patrick had given to her in the past?

"When are you going to tell James and Michael?"

"Soon. I just want the lies to be over and for Michael to understand why I have to do this. I know he's not going to like it. I just have to hope one day he'll understand. Besides, he's a very handsome man and I can't imagine he'll be on his own for long. I know women at the rotary club that will probably hardly let our bed-sheets cool."

Abby was probably the best person that could have found out, although she did feel a bit like the piggy in the middle with James's being her closest friend, as well as being fond of Michael, too. However, Rosemary needed to talk and so she was there for her. She had no intention of taking sides, though that wasn't something that would ever be expected of her.

It was a day later that Rosemary chose her moment. Abby had kept her discovery to herself, not something she enjoyed doing; however, with Rosemary promising it wouldn't be for long, she felt a little better about it, though not much. The elaborate Roman fortress kitchen was the centre stage for Rosemary's groundbreaking performance of "I'm leaving you, Michael"—but she had to get his attention first.

Michael sat at the head of the mighty table scanning some A4 pieces of white paper covered in business regarding the Stud. He was such a warm and giving person, one couldn't imagine the two of them not working things out, but sometimes it's a clash of needs and desires. Rosemary, dressed quite smartly in a long dress and coordinating red jacket, stepped into the kitchen and leant on the head chair directly opposite to a still absorbed Michael. Just as she was about to speak, James came in through the outside kitchen door, removing his leather boots before stepping onto the impeccable marble floor.

"Hey, Mum—wow, you look smart! Are you going out somewhere?"

"Not exactly, but thank you for noticing, James." Rosemary aimed that at Michael

"I was just about to say you looked nice." Michael was now looking at his wife.

"I was just going to talk to your dad, James, but I think you should stay to hear what I have to say."

James sat to the left of his dad and, with them both looking straight at her, she had a captive audience. But now she had stage fright. Somehow, as if prompted from the wings, the words eventually came out. "Michael, I'm leaving you. I have been unhappy for some time. I've tried to tell you, but you always dismiss it, and now that I'm in love with someone else I want to start a new relationship with him. James, this has nothing to do with you and my love for you will never change, and you being here this last six months has helped enormously. But soon you're going to be buying a place of your own and then it's just your dad and me again. I have to grab this chance now as I may not get another." She was strong and bold, making sure Michael knew she meant business. However, if she had drawn breath, she was afraid she would forget or stumble over the words. At the end of the day how or what she said was not going to be taken easily.

By now a puzzled look had crept across both their faces and, as Michael stood up and met her half way, the only word to come out were:

"Who?"—spoken in a calm and collected way.

"Is that all you care about? I tell you I'm leaving, and all you can say is 'Who?'"

"What do you want me to say? Beg you to stay, promise that I'll be the one to make you happy again? It seems to me you've already made up your mind."

His calm placid voice unnerved Rosemary and, as he leant on the centre dresser that accommodated a second sink and chopping area, his dark blue jeans were cooled against the fine granite. He folded his arms on his slightly opened cotton shirt as she retaliated.

"Do you know why I'm leaving you?"

"You said because you were unhappy." His nonchalant tone was his way of dealing with what was happening.

"You think it's that simple? Well, it's not! I gave you nearly thirty years of my life and you think it's that simple? We don't talk, we never go out just the two of us, and we don't even have a love life anymore. Something has been missing from us for a long time. You know it and I know it, but because you never want to face up to anything you've left it up to me to do something about it!"

"Mum, I don't really want to hear this." James stood up.

"James, please, I want you to hear what I have to say." He sat down reluctantly, but only after a second "Please."

"You didn't answer me before," Michael insisted. "Who is it?"

"It's Larry Golding!" Short and sharp, so she didn't sound ashamed, though her disguise failed.

"Said with such pride. So, he has another notch on his bedpost."

"Oh, I might have expected that from you—cheap insults cost nothing, you know! This isn't about sex, this is about him making me feel wanted, needed, and, what's more, we love each other!"

Little did they know but in the heat of their words James had headed out to the stables and left his feuding parents alone.

"Love? You think Larry loves you? He's a player. You say you want to a new live with him? Well, I give it a week. And when this menopausal crisis is over, we'll talk. But if you have to get this out of your system, then go ahead, but don't insult me with rubbish that you and him are going to live happily ever after because it's a joke!"

"I'm not laughing and this is no menopausal crisis, as you put it. I'm forty-eight, for goodness sake. I deserve more than this. With Larry I feel like a teenager again."

"Well, that's appropriate, because you're acting like one."

Their bodies faced each other and, as Rosemary turned her head in disgust, she saw James had gone.

"Now look what you've done!"

Seeing, too, that James had left the room, Michael defended himself.

"Me? You're the one who's going off with the local Casanova."

"This isn't about me being unfaithful! This is about *why* I was. How can I live with someone that doesn't give me the passion I deserve? We've lost something. Can't we both just accept that? We need different people now; we've outgrown each other. I'm leaving tonight, Michael, like it or not, and I won't be back after a week. Right now, though, I just want to find James and talk to him."

She buttoned up her jacket and left her estranged husband in the kitchen. Michael gripped the side of his neck with both hands and dropped his head back, desperately trying to take in what was happening. If he were honest, truly honest, there would be no more jokes, no more teasing or covering up; he knew something had to change and his wife was right—he had left it up to her.

Rosemary found James with his favourite horse, taking pride in brushing him down. The weather was glorious and the light cool air was a relief to Rosemary's tense heated face.

"James, please try and understand why I'm doing this."

He stopped and patted the magnificent hazelnut beast.

"What do you want me to say, mum? Congratulations, good luck? I don't know how to respond."

"I know it's not easy, but I just don't want you to hate me."

"Of course I don't hate you. I just don't want to take sides, and I don't care who's right or who's wrong. I'm not going to choose." He was adamant of that but delivered his point of view with ease.

"I would never expect you to. I just don't want our relationship to change. I love you, sweetheart, and whatever happens with your dad and I, that will never change. As long as you know that." She held his arms, wanting to hug him, but she waited to see if he would make the first move.

"I do know that." Then he did as she hoped. James wrapped his arms round his mum and said nothing else, for he knew she needed that gesture.

Later that same day Michael watched as his wife packed her immediate things and headed for Larry's house. He had conflicting emotions inside; he was saddened that this was what it had come to, but in a way relieved the pretence of a happy marriage was over. But that didn't stop it hurting saying goodbye; she had been part of his life for so long and now it was the end of a turbulent epoch.

# CHAPTER 17

Their beautiful landscaped garden was in full bloom. The sweet summer air was potent yet as delicate as Abby's alluring and misty perfume that she was wearing—a recent birthday gift from James. The charming living room was full of the spring sunshine and not one wall was exempt from the warmth of the sunbeams. The slightly opened window brought the sound of the lightly blowing trees, along with the aroma of the patio plants, the birdsong harmonising with the rustling of the leaves. Abby's gravid body just sat contented in the armchair in the far corner of the somewhat angled room. Reading through her pregnancy magazines, she stopped every now and then to look in wonder at the picture of her scan, which was never far away from her. She declined to know the sex of the baby and wanted it to be a surprise, and as for being pregnant, she was enjoying every minute, plus all the fuss she was getting from her loved ones. With all the support that James had given her over the last few months it was a nice change for her, as she was now the one helping her friend. James was finding himself caught in the middle of his parents and the realisation that his parents' marriage was not indestructible and that they had for a long time been living a lie, was harder to grasp than the separation itself.

Teresa pottered in the vegetable garden while Abby changed her venue and sat on the patio furniture, her laptop resting on a cushion on her thighs. Facing the east of the house and removing the glare but still catching the soft breeze through her hair, she started to add some adjustments to the single chapter and prologue of her flourishing novel, *A Child Hungry*. Karen Fair, a friend of Abby's, was an editor for highly sort-after publishers and, with all the contacts she could find and dig up, Abby lined them up to aid in fulfilling her dream. In fact, when Karen heard that Abby was starting a novel she was actually the one that contacted her. With Karen's arrival due in the next twenty minutes for a coffee and sneak preview, Abby finished making the final adjustments before heading to the study to print off what she had. Finishing off her trolling in the soil, Teresa moved closer to the house to sweep the front step, then removed her gardening gloves and headed around to the shed to conclude the day's agricultural tasks, taking all her equipment with her.

The fifth month of her pregnancy and Abby was showing modestly. She was now on her way to the kitchen to prepare a drink for her forthcoming company. For the first time in a long time, she was starting to feel strong enough to cope with the fact that her baby may never know its father. However, with his child growing inside her, Patrick was never far from her thoughts.

"What time will Karen be here, sweetheart?" Teresa came in through the barn style door at the side of the kitchen as she asked her daughter.

"In about ten minutes or so, but she's never on time." Abby was selecting some mugs ready for her arrival.

"Well, I think I'll have shower and then head over to Rosemary's; we're going to that antique fair this afternoon."

"Ooh, look out for any jugs! I haven't found a good one in ages." Collecting them was Abby's hobby and the dresser in the farmhouse kitchen was adorned with them.

"I'll have a look then. I think it means a lot to Rosemary, me going with her. I think she thought her leaving Michael would somehow affect our friendship and no matter how many times I tell her she still seems so insecure about it. Well, maybe today will help."

"I'm sure it will. I just hope she's done the right thing."

"I think she does as well. Let's just hope she's right about Larry and we are the one's who are wrong. Things seem to be going well so far. Let's hope for her that's how it stays." Teresa grabbed a glass of water and headed upstairs, not before sharing a parting kiss and a hug with Abby.

Proving Abby wrong, Karen arrived bang on 11 a.m. Her X-type Jaguar came sedately down the long curved drive and, as the sapphire automobile parked adjacent to the other two cars on the spacious drive, Abby appeared at the front door. Karen, who was in her early thirties, stepped out of the car, her dark designer sunglasses shielding almost half her face, with her bright scarlet lipstick almost falling off her thin narrow lips. As she slammed the door and beeped the alarm her further appearance could be seen and Abby took it all in, but in a subtle way. Karen was wearing a rather over-elaborate suit, consisting of a short jacket and even shorter skirt that needed to be at least two sizes bigger. The range of colours that completed it might have explained the thick sunglasses! She was quite a sight.

Abby's loose cotton trousers and flowing shirt seemed so white compared to the kaleidoscope of colours that were pouring off her friend's body. Nevertheless, whatever her dress sense, they got on really well and Karen was actually really pleased to see Abby. She was the one person who just took her for what she was and that meant a lot to her. Karen had this little quirk, which was quite endearing really, something she wasn't aware of: every time she said "Oh splendid" in the sweet way she did, it always brought a smile to Abby's face. Despite the visit being about the book, Abby enjoyed seeing her friend again. Her "take me as I am" was incredibly refreshing; in a way they were the two ends of the spectrum but they got on like a house on fire.

They talked for a while about each other's lives and then, when the chat ran dry, Abby produced her offering. As Karen read through what she had written, Abby got a refill of coffee for them. Carrying the full mugs back to the coolness of the living room, Abby spoke as she re-entered.

"Here we are" She carefully put the mugs down on the butterfly coasters.

"Oh splendid." Karen said, dropping the sheets of A4 and bringing a warm smile to Abby's face.

Just then Teresa popped her head round the door and said hello and goodbye before heading to the fair in the next village with Rosemary.

"Good to see you again, Karen."

"You too, Teresa"—said with a pause from the reading.

"I'll see you later, sweetheart," Teresa's voice whispered a little.

"Okay, bye mum."

"Well, I think you certainly have something," Karen beamed.

"You really think so?"

"I've been in this business a while now and you really have a flair for this type of thing. I'll take it back with me and let the rest of my team have a look. I can't promise anything but quality sells it self, so we'll see."

"That's fantastic! I really love doing it. It's such a release for me."

"Well, that comes through—and what's more, you know what you're talking about. That gives it its special essence—and this is just the start."

"Thank you so much, Karen. I can't tell you what it means to me."

"No problem, you're a good writer." The words were true and the smiles were even truer.

"I think we have some chocolate cake in the pantry. Can I tempt you?"

"Oh splendid."

The girls enjoyed the homemade baking and after polishing off two slices each, Karen had to head off, though not before making plans to stay close in touch. With the departure of one car down the gravelled drive, another made an appearance. It was Michael's Range Rover and, with the unexpected visit, Abby greeted him with surprise.

"Hey stranger, what brings you up here?" Abby started talking the minute Michael opened the car door and stepped out into the fresh air.

"I'll give you three guesses." Despite the recent change in his life he still looked just as charming as ever. His warm smile still seemed to appear on his face with ease and, with a friendly hug and kiss on the cheek, Abby knew why he had come to see her.

"James?"

"Got it in one. If it's not a good time I can comeback later." They both stood on the drive close to the canopy porch when Abby responded quickly:

"No, no, don't be daft. We'll sit in the garden if you like."

Michael's tall stature shadowed Abby as they both walked through to the back garden. His casual attire still managed to be stylish and one wouldn't think a simple short sleeve pale grey shirt and a pair of designer jeans could do so much for a man's physique. As they strolled through the open gateway, they chatted about Abby before they got to the point of why he was there.

"You're looking really well. How are you feeling?" The tips of his fingers were squeezed into his denim pockets, causing his elbows to be elevated and for one of them to brush against Abby's blowing shirt arm. They strolled through to the garden, indenting the grass with their footprints along the way, before they crossed over to the permanence of the concrete patio.

"Great, really great. After the first few months I never thought I would feel better."

"You'll make a great mum, you'll see."

"Ooh, I hope so. It's funny, really; you know you're having a baby, but sometimes you forget that means you're going to be a mum. I suppose that sounds silly."

"No, course it doesn't. It's a big thing, but you have so much love to give, Abby; it will just fall into place." They were kind words and they meant a lot. They eventually both sat on the wooden chairs opposite each other, with Michael lifting his sunglasses off his face and dropping them to the table.

"I'm sorry to burden you with all this, Abby, especially at the moment." Michael lent back in the chair and ran his hands down the front of his thighs.

"Michael, it's fine, honestly. James is just trying to get his head round it all and I know he will; he just has to deal with it in his own way."

"He just won't talk about it; well, not to me, anyway."

"He will, trust me. I'm an expert on these things." It was said tongue in cheek, but it brought a lingering smile to their faces.

"I don't want him to feel caught in the middle. That's the last thing I want him to feel." Abby didn't like to say that it had already happened. They chatted for a while on the subject before the talk turned back to Abby.

"So, have you decided on any names yet?"

"I have a few ideas but nothing certain. I like Samuel for a boy but I also like Luke, and as for a girl, I can't get past Molly at the moment; so I don't know—I'll probably change my mind a hundred times before the birth."

"My middle name's Luke."

"I never knew that!" Abby was surprised of the coincidence.

"If James had been a girl, we would have called him Jessica."

"Mmm, Jessica's nice. Sorry I didn't offer you a drink. Can I get you something?" Her own throat felt dry and with her face a little flushed, apparently from the heat, it prompted the question.

"Okay, um, a soft drink would be great."

"I'll see what we've got." A few minutes later Abby reappeared carrying two glasses of fresh orange juice. She walked over to a standing Michael who was wandering around the exquisite garden.

"Here you go."

"Thanks, Abby. That wasn't Karen Fair that I saw leaving earlier, was it?" The first sip of the orange juice came soon after the final word.

"It was. How do you know her?" Abby was taken aback that he knew her.

"I know her Father, Max. We had a couple of his Stallions a few seasons back. I met Karen a few times when they visited the Stud together."

"Oh, she's never said before. She's interested in the novel I'm writing."

"Oh, that's right, she's in the publishing game." Their chat led them back to sit down. "So have you seen much of Rosemary?"

"I wondered how long it would take you to ask that." Abby added lightness to the response.

"Sorry. I just find it unbelievable that she thinks Larry's going to make her happy." It was quite something that he had used his actual name. For the first few weeks he found some other alternatives. "It's terrible to say, but it wasn't that I was broken hearted when she left. The hurt was more dented pride. Does that sound awful?" The revelation hadn't been intended to be shared—it just came out freely.

"It sounds honest. If that's how it was, then that's how it was. You can't make yourself feel something that isn't there to feel." Abby meant her words and delivered them with reassurance

"I guess we've been on borrowed time for a while. I'm not completely innocent in all this, as much as I would like to think so." Playing with his sunglasses in his hands, he used them to scratch the back of his head.

"What do you mean?" Abby's position changed. She leant in further to the large garden table and rested her elbows on the hard surface and cupped her face in her hands, wondering what he meant.

"I knew Karen's face from somewhere else. As well as the connection with her father, I had a brief interlude from my faithful marriage, shall we say, and I became involved with Diana, her mother. I'm not sure why I just told you that. I shouldn't have told you. I mean, you're like a sister to James, and I've just told you that I had an affair with the mother of the woman who might publish your book!" Michael suddenly realised he may have been too honest, and his gabbling expressed that. He felt as though he had just removed all his clothes and sat naked in front of her and for no reason. He was not a cheat or a liar, just someone that never got it quite right.

"We all have to talk to someone, I guess. I seem to be the lucky contender at the moment." Although Abby was feeling as though she were being pulled three ways, she didn't want Michael to feel he couldn't talk to someone when he felt he could. The fact that he could be open with her could have been construed as a compliment. "How long ago was it?"

"When James first went to the States. No one ever knew, but we had a close call with Karen once—that's how her face stuck in my mind. I shouldn't have said anything—it's just that you're so easy to talk to; things just seem to flow with you. I feel really awkward now." He really wondered why he had told her but it was too late.

"Don't worry, and don't feel awkward. I'm getting used to people's revelations. I should perhaps be flattered people can talk freely to me. Besides, you don't look like it was something you were proud of. So was that the beginning of the end?"

"Kind of. I thought I was in love with Diana but she put an end to it. She said she had too much to risk. Then two years ago she divorced Max and went to live in…um…"

"France," Abby answered for him.

"France, that's it. Anyway, after it all happened the bubble of our marriage had popped. I felt bad about what had happened but at the same time confused as to what to do. Rosemary was right when she said I let her make the decision. I guess I'm just a coward in that respect."

"No one likes to face up to things, and if we can pass the buck then we will. You're not alone." Expressed with sympathy.

"You're a good listener, Abby." Michael stood up as the words followed from Abby, but as she stood she felt a sudden pain shoot across her lower stomach.

"Areh!" Abby clutched her side, folding her body down and gripped the table with her free hand, her face crippled with pain.

"Abby, what's wrong?" Michael bent down with her and held her shoulders as she grimaced with pain.

"I just felt a sharp stabbing pain. Probably wind or something. Don't worry, I'll be fine." Abby's face had turned bright red and, with long calming breaths, she resumed her full standing position after a minute or so.

"Are you sure? Should I call the doctor?" Michael's hands were still around her shoulders as they walked round to his car slowly.

"Honestly, I'll be fine. If it happens again then I'll call. It's gone now. Please don't worry."

"If you're sure."

"I'm sure."

Michael wasn't happy but he couldn't make her. As his car left the drive Abby gingerly headed inside and, as the front door closed, the same pain struck her again. This time she fell to the floor with it. She curled her knees to her chest and wept with the increased agony, her hot and sweating body contracting further with the coolness of the stone hall floor. As the pain remained with her she didn't know what to do and just then, when she knew she couldn't reach the phone, the sound of a car engine was the sound of hope. As soon as the front door opened Michael crouched at her side and wiped her brow with his reassuring hand. He had just had a feeling that something was wrong and that was what prompted his u-turn.

"I'll take you to the hospital! It will be quicker than waiting for anyone else."

Abby said nothing, and knowing she couldn't walk, Michael scooped her into his arms and carried her out to his car. It was then that her worst fear was realised—she began to bleed.

The realisation that she had lost her baby was far from sinking in. She lay in the bed of the private room, her broken and bewildered body wrapped in the sheets and warmed by the extra blanket. Her face was lifeless and drained and, as the tears streamed down her face, her vision was lost in space, vacantly staring out the window. The pain she had physically experienced was nothing compared to the pain that was making her whole body ache and almost tremble. Part of her was lost with her child, the child she now knew would have been a girl. She knew she would never be the same person again and, as she wept uncontrollably, she didn't want to be. Michael came back in at the moment her crying echoed in the compact room. He was still trying to get hold of Teresa, or James for that matter, but with no apparent luck. He had no idea what to do or say other than just go to her. He had no idea where Teresa was and with her mobile turned off and James's too, he needed to return to their cottage to wait for her. He couldn't bring himself to leave Abby, but he knew he had to. Slowly walking over to her bedside, he blocked her vacant gaze and sat on the edge of the bed close to her. He took her hand in his and with that needed gesture, with as much energy as she could find, she lifted up her shattered body and fell into his arms and sobbed her heart out. His supportive arms held her tight. All he could do was hold her.

When Michael later got hold of James, not having left Abby's side, it was he who instantly brought Teresa to Abby; and all Teresa wanted to do was hold her child and share the pain that was seeping out of her hollow body. As Teresa held her daughter tightly and close, her inconsolable inert body felt so heavy. The weight of Abby's pain fell onto her mum's chest like a violent rock. Abby's head remained cradled in her mum's bent elbow, turned and nestled in the softness of her mum's chest, her whole body still wrapped in the woollen cover. The sun faded with Abby's dreams and as dark clouds descended over the sky, the greyness of the weather filled the mourning room.

Abby remained in the hospital longer than intended, due to her severe depression and the growing concern for her state of health. She had lost her baby, the child that had given her a new lease of life. There was no explanation for the miscarriage, and Abby desperately wanted to know why. But no one could answer her that and so, instinctively, she turned the reason onto herself. As she lay with half her face on the pillow and her body turned slightly, just seeing in her right eye her mum on the bed and James on the chair next to her, she let her torment out in the open.

"Its *my* fault! Isn't that why no one will tell me why it happened?" Her voice was so calm as she uttered the words, calm in the sense that despite what anyone could say, she had made up her mind that she was the one to blame.

"What are you saying! Of course it's not your fault! Abby, you mustn't, mustn't, think like that. This was something that no one can explain. Abby, you are listening to me, aren't you?" Teresa wanted her daughter to understand quickly that this was not her fault before the notion took hold and grew. Abby's eyes filled with her salty tears as she tried to fight what her mum had said. The lump in her throat and the dropping tears made the struggle harder.

"But I had all that drink before I knew I was pregnant…and I kept on working." She broke a little more with each word.

"That has nothing to do with it. You heard what the doctor said. You can't blame yourself, sweetheart; if you do, then it will eat away at you and you will never get through this—and I know you can. You're a survivor, Abby, you always have been." Teresa had to convince Abby that she was strong enough to survive this; otherwise she was afraid of the consequences.

The day Abby was due to come home was upon them. Teresa didn't know what to do for the best; they had parenting magazines, the scan picture and some early bought things for the not yet started nursery all around the house. To move them could be potentially the wrong thing, but seeing them and leaving them could be too. Instead, she opted to contain them to one room, the earmarked nursery. On return from the hospital the midsummer month seemed more like a cold winter's day. As the car with James driving and Abby in the back with Teresa pulled up the drive, Abby's heavily dressed body made it's way in to the cottage. Her slight body entered the hall and just stopped and gazed down at the stone floor, the place where she had fallen to her knees, the place where her loss had begun.

"Lets get you upstairs." James took her arm and supported her body up the stairs.

Abby had no reaction. She was limp and empty and, as the backs of their bodies disappeared up the stairs, Teresa covered her mouth with her hand and soundless crying got the better of her. Knowing that the next few weeks were going to be tough, she moved her hand and tightly held her rosary, which she retrieved from her pocket, and in silent prayer she shared her burden and worry. Teresa knew that the recovery wouldn't happen overnight, but she knew that Abby had to let go of it all before the healing could begin, for as long as she held on to the pain and hurt and blamed herself she wouldn't be able to come to terms with it all. However, that was something Teresa knew would come in time, just as when she was anorexic, and just as when Charles died, and with her faith she was able to believe her recovery would take place—how or even when was irrelevant, just as long as it did.

Until Abby reached the point where she was able to let people in and share what she was going through, her existence didn't stretch further than her bedroom. She seemed to break in to a stage of grief where she was shutting herself away and avoiding contact with anyone, which was hard for those around her. The one person yet to visit her was the one person that was with her at the time, and the person who had never seen anyone look so frightened in all his life. His strong body and mastering presence climbed the stairs, having been warmly greeted by his son and Teresa, and with a light tap on Abby's door he entered. Seeing her lying in bed, the side closet to where he was entering, he moved slowly and gave a warm smile, which brought a weak replica to Abby's forlorn face. She sat up in her bed, dressed in her pyjamas and a bathrobe for extra warmth, and with just a faint expression on her face—which was enough, for no words needed to be said—he sat down on the edge of her bed on her right side.

"I wanted to see you before now, but I didn't know what I would say. But I realised it was better to say the wrong thing than nothing at all. Well, I hope so, anyway." He smiled nervously.

"I never got the chance to thank you for coming back and helping me," Abby said in a very characterless way.

"You don't need to thank me, Abby. I can't begin be imagine the pain you are feeling, and I know you have James and your mum; but you listened to me and if you want to talk ever then, I will always be here to listen." His jacketed elbows rested on his knees, his body slightly leaning forward and, as the words came, they were half directed to the floor, although with the last syllable of the final word he glanced up to Abby. But something inside her snapped and, as James and Teresa appeared on the landing, she lost it completely.

"I don't want to talk to anyone! I don't want to see anyone and don't want to let anything out! And I certainly don't need people treating me like an invalid. You know, I am sick and tired of people always telling me their problems. Have I got mug written across my forehead? Oh, tell Abby, she won't mind! Well, I've had enough! I've had enough of people using me. I lost my baby and there's nothing that anyone can do about it and no amount of tea and sympathy is going to change that." Abby threw the covers off her troubled body and bolted past the three of them. As she slammed the door of the bathroom her broken shell shed uncontrollable tears as it crumbled to the floor.

They all knew that the words were just another way of expressing her loss and suffering, but they all felt so useless. Abby had to battle with so much—with the fact that she had conceived Patrick's baby and he didn't know, with the reality that she had lost his baby and he didn't know; and she was going through all this pain and he didn't know. Furthermore, what she was finding hard was that it was her choice for him not to know. She was going through all of this with him completely oblivious of the truth, and it was then that she regretted having not told him. The release of her anger and sharing her excruciatingly painful feelings about Patrick with the three of them later that afternoon gave her the chance to break out of her own world and involve the ones that loved her, so much so that they were now able to share her sorrow.

Over the coming weeks Abby gradually went back to writing and took advantage of the support that was circling her. She had been pieced back together but the cracks were still visible; nevertheless, they were mending and holding together—and yet there was soon to be something else she hadn't bargained for. When things were just calming down and the summer months were on the horizon, a twist of the knife was to emerge from the shadows.

For the first time in weeks Abby was taking fairy steps to recovery, James was on a short business trip making good contacts for the Stud, and Teresa had had a week booked away since the beginning of the year to visit Prague and to see Mozart's *Le Nozze di Figaro* with Alice and Stanley—an arrangement Abby insisted she did not cancel. She was left to her own devices but she needed this time to get used to being strong when no one else was around, although with James keeping in close contact by phone and the same from her mum, she didn't feel too isolated. The house did feel quiet, though, but instead of drifting around all day she wanted to make the most of the rest of the summer and the glorious sunshine, as the seasoned days were now depleting.

With her laptop zipped in its leather case and with a casual shoulder bag and some light airy clothes, Abby headed to the grounds of a local priory, a place where she felt calm and at peace. She had visited the sacred place many times before and was always warmly welcomed. An old wooden bench catered for all of her needs and, as she typed away, the early sun just missing her bower enclosure, she felt inspired and captivated by the beauty that surrounded her.

The perfume of the air was heightened by the intensifying heat and, as Abby returned to her car to leave her materials behind, she walked back to the church. The compact place of worship was cool and serene; it had that instant smell as one walked in, a favourable smell of a church that was hard to define but one that was so wonderful at the same time. It must have been a combination of many things, the burning candles, the flowers on the windowsills, the polished pews, the remaining incense, one couldn't pinpoint it—but Abby loved it. Making the sign of the cross with cool holy water as she entered, an instant shiver ran down her spine. Goose pimples covered her body instantaneously as the blessed water embellished her skin.

She slowly walked down the isle and gazed in wonder at the hanging crucifix. As she neared the altar she diverted to the candle stand. Few were lit, but with some loose change in her pocket, she soon altered that. Picking out four candles, she lit each one with the left matches and said a pray as each flame took hold. As the fire burned in front of her eyes, she lit one more and placed it smack-bang in the centre. She used one of her lit candles to create another flame for this special symbolism. With the last candle standing alone burning, her silent prayer for her lost child brought painful tears to her eyes, and as she made her way out of the church, making the sign of the cross before she left, her head turned at the door holding her glance at that one candle. It was as if she were leaving her lost child with God and that peace she gave herself was what she so needed.

When she returned home later that afternoon the first thing she did before anything else was to climb the stairs to her bedroom and recover the picture of her early scan. She held it tight in her warm fingers and, as she walked over to her dressing table, the place where a picture of her dad sat to the left of her centred mirror, she opened the black velvet back of the photo frame. She tucked her picture of her unborn child in with the picture of her dad. She closed the frame and, before she returned it to its position, she uttered simple words but words with true belief.

"Look after her for me, dad." Abby kissed the glass, sending the gesture through to the picture. The impression of her lips lingered on the surface as she placed it back on its home position. She had given herself the gift of peace and with that release she felt able to grieve.

## CHAPTER 18

A day or so later and with a long phone call from Rosemary and another from her very excited mum, the afternoon was soon fading. Just as Abby thought about having a bath to soak away the day's heat, the door chime went.

"Michael!"

"I was just passing and thought I would see if you were about."

"Roughly translated, you've been told to keep an eye on me. Am I right?"

"Was I that obvious?" he said with a smile.

"Completely. Come in then, as you're here," Abby joked as she escorted him through the door.

"What sort of day have you had?"

"Good, actually. I worked on my novel, had a chat with…um…a friend, and then mum called; so quite eventful, I suppose." She changed her mind as he may have asked how his estranged wife was, and with what Rosemary told Abby about wanting a divorce, she didn't want to get caught in the crossfire.

"You're looking so much healthier, Abby."

"Thanks. I 'm really starting to feel better." They were in the kitchen and sitting at the table when the door chime echoed again.

"I'll just get that."

"Shall I put the kettle on?"

"Yep, go for it." Abby drifted through to the front door and turned the handle to see who the visitor was.

"Abby, sorry to disturb you." It was Blanche Lane, their neighbour to the left. Over the years they had became quite friendly. Her mature body stood in front of Abby and in her hand she was clutching a medium sized brown-bubbled envelope.

"Hi, Blanche, how are you?" Abby folded her arms with the sentence.

"Good, thanks. What about you?" Knowing what had happened recently, she kept the question very open, not wanting to be too direct.

"Better, much better," Abby replied reassuringly.

"I'm glad, really glad. Anyway…um…this came recorded delivery this morning, so Jack asked me to sign for it. I hope that was okay." Jack was their aging postman, but having done the job for over twenty years he was friends with the locals.

"Of course it was—thank you."

"Well, I won't keep you."

"Come in for a cup of tea if you like." Abby used the envelope to gesture towards the kitchen; unaware of what she was holding and who it was from.

"I have cakes in the oven, but another time. Best dash, take care."

"You too, and thanks again."

She turned and waved as she vanished from the drive.

Abby walked back into the kitchen, still unaware as to what she was carrying, as she hadn't paid attention yet to the details on the envelope. However, with Michael by the kettle and Abby now looking at the writing and standing close to him and leaning a little on the dresser, her heart quickened and her face became hot and flushed. The seal opened with ease and, peering into the opened packet, she saw a loose piece of paper and a small maroon box. Taking the paper in one hand and the box in the other, she could only hear the sound of her increased breathing.

*Abby,*

*I know I should have given you this back before but I guess I wanted to hold onto part of you for as long as I could; but I know it's too precious to you for me to keep. I'm sorry I took so long to return it to you,*

*Patrick.*

In almost slow motion she opened the square box and there, sparkling back at her, was her lost special jewel, her mum's eternity ring. As if deafened to any other sound, she was unaware of Michael and what he was saying.

"Abby, tea, or coffee?"

And as she looked up from the box, Abby seemed unable to know what to do. It was as if her body had become disorientated and panicky.

"What?"

"Abby, what is it?"

Abby passed him the note and, seeing the ring in her hand, he realised what it all meant. In spite of all the togetherness she had built over the last few weeks and recent days, it all fell by the wayside now and she just fell into the arms that were there, ready to support her body.

"Why, when I start to feel better, does this happen? I can't take anymore knocks—I just can't!" Her words were muffled by fresh tears and the fact that her mouth was lost in Michael's holding arms, his deep olive shirt taking the impact of her light tears.

"Each test you'll pass. Just think of it—you've got the ring back and that's all. Don't go back, not when you've moved forward, Abby."

She eased out a little from the support and looked up at Michael with traces of brackish tears still visible under her eyes and, using just his thumbs, Michael moved the drops with tender softness.

"I'm glad you're here. Goodness knows what I would have done without someone here to put things into perspective." Abby sniffed with almost every word, trying to clear her congested nose from the crying. Michael's hold had calmed her suddenly ridged body and, with deep breaths, she was losing some of her panic.

"See, I was meant to come over." The way he said it seemed to throw some positive light on her predicament, and he used his hand to rub her back in a sign of comfort, which invited Abby to sink her head back onto his chest. Michael was a very distinguished man and just had this very attractive appeal, not just in appearance but something else, and in that close intimacy they were sharing, their bodies instinctively drew closer.

Turning her head back to stare straight up into his piercing blue eyes, Abby had only intended to kiss him on his cheek as a sign of thanks; but with their faces touching and their lips close to each others and their bodies still compressed together, the moment was one of foolishness, yet one shared by both of them. Simultaneously their mouths were drawn closer to each other, their eyes never deterred and their tremulous lips eager to touch—and their lips met with mutual smoothness. Michael kissed Abby like a gentleman, yet at the same time with great passion, something to which Abby responded instinctively. Lost in the kiss and enjoying the intimate embrace, it took a minute or so for them to realise what they had just done. Instantly they broke free, the strong and secure hold that had gripped them releasing them both. Abby moved a few steps back and touched her lips with the back of her fingers, Michael just looking shocked. It had not only taken them by surprise that they had kissed; it was what they both felt when the kiss was in its advanced stages that stunned them most.

"Oh my goodness, Michael, I—I don't know what I was thinking." She bit her bottom lip with her front teeth, a sign of awkwardness.

"Hey, come on, it was my fault too. Best just put it down to a moment of foolishness, eh?"

"I feel so stupid." Abby rubbed her forehead and then covered her pink cheeks with her hands.

"No more than I do." The lightness on his face came from his awkwardness, but as their eyes met again the next sentence was hard to say.

"I—I guess we should just forget it happened." Abby looked at him intently. She thought only Patrick would ever be able to kiss her in that way. Never did she expect Michael to be a contender.

"Yeah, I guess we should." With their bodies a little closer and their eyes fixed, if it were to happen again it would have been then—but with resistance from them both, Michael was the first to break the moment.

"I probably…I best be heading back now," he stumbled. "I've kept you too long anyway."

"Yeah, I should…um…get myself sorted." Michael took the lead and walked through to the hall, with Abby following behind. Opening the door and stepping out into the early evening air, the sun still shining and the summer ambiance flawless, they didn't know what to do or say.

"Teresa's back Thursday." It wasn't a question—more of a statement.

"Yeah, Thursday."

"Well, I'll see you when I see you, I guess." Michael fiddled with his keys

"Okay." Abby didn't know what else to say.

"Bye then."

"Bye." Abby closed the door as Michael approached his car door.

They both knew it was a moment of silliness, but something in the kiss had struck a chord in both of them, like a question, which in that one moment together was answered. Michael had been lost and confused for years; the affair with Karen's mum was a way of expressing that. He was searching unwittingly for something or someone to capture his heart, and now it could potentially be Abby. But he knew it couldn't be; firstly, there was James, then the age difference—and the fact that he didn't believe the kiss would have had the same impact on her. It all swum around in the pool of his mind, and as he drove back to the Stud it was unbeknown to him that Abby was affected similarly by the tender caress. She had paused awhile in the hall before returning to the kitchen to gather the ring and the note. The empty mugs sat on the side where Michael hadn't finished making the drink. But that was the last thing on her mind. Until a few minutes ago she had thought no one could ever touch her in the way Patrick had, and that surmise had just been altered by the person she least expected.

She picked up the note and put it back in the envelope, feeling utterly confused. Whatever it still was, she couldn't bring herself to throw the note away, not even the envelope; so instead, she took them upstairs with her mum's ring, which she was going to return to her jewellery box, intending to put the stationery with the rest of her memories—in the shoebox she had under her bed.

But when she opened the rectangular box she suddenly realised she couldn't keep living and holding onto the past. In that moment she made a meaningful decision and took the box downstairs. The lid sat underneath it with all the contents on show, and when she got to the kitchen again she sat at the table and went through her memories of Patrick before letting them go.

The first note was the first one he had written to her at the hotel back in Paris, along with the second. The red napkin she had kept from the street café, soap from Martha's bathroom and a tissue scented with his aftershave. There were so many little things she sifted through that when added up together they equalled a happy time of her life, yet a time that would always be tainted with hurt and pain; and it was a time she had to now leave behind. Photos of the two of them were not excluded, and after all she would always have him in her memories—and that was something that could never be kept in an old shoebox. Emptying it all into the bin outside under some household rubbish, she let that part of her life go; but, at the same time, however much he had hurt her, she kept the memory dear to her heart. Patrick would always be the father of her first child and the first man she ever truly loved, and that was something that was now in the very moulding of her existence.

Abby hadn't seen anything of Michael for days, but on the horizon was something they both hadn't anticipated. When James returned from his trip he had a brainwave. Luckily his excitement shadowed Abby's awkward behaviour. She found it hard knowing she had kissed his dad and reluctantly enjoyed it, but James's idea for his dad's forthcoming birthday distracted her discomfiture. The idea was to surprise him with a holiday to the place he had always wanted to go to. The place was Egypt, and involved Abby in so far as James wanted her and Teresa to go with them.

"Come with you both?" Abby asked, surprised. "But surly it would be better for you and your dad to just enjoy it together." It was only a week since her enlightening kiss with Michael and now the thought of being with him constantly for at least a week didn't seem a good idea, somehow.

"I know what you're saying, but we can still have time together. It would just be so great if you and Teresa could share it all with us. Plus, I know you've always wanted to go there." They were sitting in the garden in the late afternoon heat when James tackled the question. The autumn season was merging with the summer, but the heat the later month brought mirrored its predecessor.

"I don't know, I've got some new clients and projects starting soon, plus my book."

"Listen, it's only eight nights, and it won't be until the end of next month. You'll have plenty of time to get sorted out. Please say yes! It would do you good, too."

"Well, I can only agree for me; we'll have to talk to mum when she's back from the dentist."

"So that's a yes?" He eagerly held her arms as he crouched in front of her while she sat back in the garden chair. It seemed to mean so much to him; she just couldn't refuse those big eyes.

"It's a yes," she said calmly but with a smile and in a tone of reluctance.

"That's fantastic! Thanks, Abby, you won't regret it, I promise."

"So how much is it all going to cost?"

"I'll tell you later, I think." He coward away as the cost might have shaken her a little.

"James, tell me now." Abby was gentle in her tone, but she wanted to know.

"Nearly fifteen hundred."

When he saw the look of horror on her face he added quickly, "But that includes everything—the excursions, the lot. It sounds worse than it is, but it *is* Egypt, after all."

"How nearly?"

"Well, just under." James wandered back to his original seat, trying not to grin.

"As in?" Abby raised her eyebrows a little, waiting for the answer to his ambiguous statement.

"As in £1499."

"So, just under as in a penny. It is with a good company, isn't it?"

"Course. Anyway, they're holding the booking till Monday, so we'll need to talk to Resa about it today really."

"She shouldn't be much longer. Come on inside. I'll make us something to eat."

They walked back inside and hooked arms along the way, and when Abby tilted her head to lean on James's thin shirt, he turned and kissed her head. With the closeness they had as they walked inside, James held his glance on Abby as she broke free and headed to the fridge to retrieve some cold meats and salad. He watched as she moved gracefully around the kitchen and listened intently as she started to talk about her latest finished chapter. Her words were echoing around the beautiful room, but James was just listening, entranced, to the sound of her voice rather than the content.

"So what do you think," Abby paused, detecting his inattention, a plump and shiny tomato clutched in her hand.

"What? Sorry." James suddenly realised that although concentrating he hadn't heard what she had been saying; instead, he had been lost in thought as he gazed at her admiringly.

"About the chapter," Abby continued, chopping the salad while James dithered.

"Um—sorry, I was miles away. I think it sounds good."

"Well, I'll let you read it later. See what you really think."

James smiled in relief that she hadn't apparently detected that he was thinking of other things. Her casually tied hair was gradually falling out as the day carried on. The wisps around her face were growing in number, yet in the middle of her casual appearance, she still looked appealing. Her face was starting to have colour again, her smile as the day progressed was widening, and James was noticing all of that, except the reason for her new radiance, which was far from what he might have ever imagined. An overwhelming feeling washed over him, a feeling that had been chasing him for years but one that he had always managed to sprint away from. But now, in this unsuspecting moment, at a time he least expected, the feeling caught up with him. With something as simple as watching Abby preparing a light dinner, his love for her had won over his dismissal of it; his sprained body had nowhere to run to. For the first time in nearly nine years he had to be honest with himself and what many people had told him, Ralph and Catherine included, he now knew for himself.

"I should have an apron really, knowing what I'm like," she said in mid flow of chopping the squashy tomato and looking down to her white t-shirt that sat on her pale washed jeans and brown leather belt. "James, you couldn't grab the one behind the door, could you?" Her messy hands gestured with the request.

"Sure—what, this pale blue one?" he said, seeing more than one apron behind the wooden door.

"That will do, thanks. You couldn't slip it on for me?"

"I don't think it would suit me," he said, teasing.

"You know what I mean!"

James moved around the dresser where Abby was standing, contentedly chopping some peppers. He softly dropped the apron over her head and passed it down her hair, and as it sat around her neck the smell of her perfumed lotion caught on his fingers. As he straightened the added fabric on her body his feelings for her were too strong for words. She was in front of him but she might as well have been a millions miles away. The tie was too long for her lean waist and so James doubled it back, turned Abby by the hips with his fingers and tied it up at the front.

"Thank you," she said.

"My pleasure." And before returning to the table he pinched a raw carrot that sat to the side of the not yet chopped cucumber. It was his way of breaking his own intenseness.

"Hey, mister! That will come off your plate."

They continued to chat freely, with James just enjoying her company and revelling in her warm presence and the fact that she was looking the best she had done in months. Later that same evening Teresa did agree and jumped at the chance to visit the ancient country.

As the date for departure drew closer, it was time for Michael to know his surprise in order to prepare—a surprise that went down very well. It was arranged by James that Abby and Teresa would meet them at the Stud on the day of the departure, and from there they would be chauffer driven to the airport. Teresa was really looking forward to the holiday but it was accompanied by memories of her time there with Charles; they were memories she always treasured and, not having been back since then, she was a little nervous to her reaction. However, all these events were leading to a fateful discovery of something that had been buried in the past. Soon, though, Teresa was unwittingly about to resurrect it.

Although over the last weeks Abby and Michael had seen each other since their kiss, it was very brief and in the company of either James or her mum. The first time was the worst, as they felt like it was written on their foreheads; but what neither had bargained for was seeing each other in a new light.

Instead of seeing Michael, James's dad and for Michael, Abby, his son's childhood friend, they were seeing one another for who they were. Furthermore, Michael was no ordinary man. He had the looks, the charm of an English gent and the warmth of the Sahara; and Abby saw a little of Patrick in him—just a way he had—but he was a more refined version. She could never see James in that kind of light, not because he didn't have those same attributes, but because he was like her guardian angel, her hero, someone that she loved in a greater way then she ever could as a lover. However, as for James—he had fought hard most of his adult life to stop himself falling in love with her. Even going to the States where he met Catherine didn't alter his feelings. If anything, it made them worse. However, there are times in life when fate steps in. Sometimes there are just two people that can't be together—and this was a true instance of that.

Michael never thought that a beautiful rose could smell as good as it looked, and once the nose has smelt something so lovable, the effects can become incurable. However, with the news of Rosemary wanting a divorce, he was preoccupied with his own thoughts. But Abby was still part of those thoughts. The concentrated time they were going to have together was to be make or break and become a true test of their friendship. With neither of them ever wanting to hurt James, their new-found feelings would just have to be ignored—that, at least, was the plan. Abby wanted them to have a few minutes alone before the day of departure, just so they could clear the air and see each other without a third party present. She had been trying to find a moment for days, so when at last the time presented itself, she took it.

With Teresa at the hairdresser and James visiting his mum, Abby was left alone to do some last minute packing. She seized the opportunity to call on Michael at the Stud. She arrived there unannounced. With no answer from the house after several tries, she made her way round the back, passing the impeccable garden along the way and finally mounting the elevated stone patio. Just as she sat on the stone wall that bordered the area, Michael appeared from around the corner, his leather-riding boots covering his calves and just finishing below his knees. His worn and tired trousers snugly fitted the rest of his lower body and, with his faint chequered shirt and thin jacket covering it, he really did have a great stature and a way about him. Abby just couldn't revert to seeing him how she used to. He had touched her and it had been through that unforgettable kiss. Her hands were struggling to stay in the pockets of her close-fitting jeans, the back of her hands lifting her fitted lilac shirt slightly; but the appearance of Michael from round the corner made her free them from the clutches of her pockets as she stood up. She tucked her loose hair behind her ears and fiddled a little with her right ear lobe. They moved in closer to each other before Michael spoke.

"I *thought* I heard a car." He was so gentle when he spoke and always had a trace of a smile on his mature face. It was difficult to believe that he and Rosemary had had the problems they did; but they also had many happy times in the beginning—they just got lost somewhere down the line, but lost in such a way that there was no way of retrieving those times again. Rosemary, in any case, had found something in Larry, and now—had Michael found something in Abby?

"I just thought I would come over, just so we can clear the air a bit better." Abby was nervous as she uttered the simple words but was quickly reassured.

"I'm glad," he said. "I wanted to too."

They walked over to the wall and sat on the cool surface, a welcome touch in the mild day air. They faced the house and looked up at its grandeur before they spoke any further. They sat modestly apart but still felt comfortable together, although when they turned and looked at each other Abby had something else on her mind—not something she had intended to voice, but Michael picked up on it.

"Are you okay? I don't just mean about what happened with us. I mean, is there anything else worrying you?"

Abby stared across at the fading flowers and, as she turned and faced his eyes again, she tried to override his concern, not wanting to fall under his mystifying spell.

"I'm fine," she said, simply.

"Look, I know things have been a bit strange between us; but I don't think that's all, is it? Please, I might be able to help."

Abby just looked down to her white pumps and added: "Its just the looming date I have to deal with."

It dawned on him what she meant. "We're going to away on the day your baby would have been born, aren't we?"

"We are. I just feel like a part of me is missing, and with time passing I keep thinking that the pain will ease—but sometimes I wonder."

"Maybe it's better you won't be here, a completely different scenery. I'm not saying it won't hurt, but it might be a minor blessing. I'm sorry I'm not very good at this."

"You're fine. I'm sorry for putting you on the spot like this. It's never easy to know what to say to someone."

Abby's hands sat freely on her lap and with pure kindness and no ulterior motive, Michael gave a gesture of his reassurance, taking her right hand gently in his left and, lifting her soft skin to his lips, he kissed the back of her hand. Not all of his lips made contact due to the twist and angle of the hold, but enough for the thought to be delivered with love and affection. Abby watched as he touched her relaxed skin, feeling how nice the contact with his lips felt and, as he held her hand as he brought it back to her thigh, she reciprocated by placing her free hand over his, creating a stack of three hands on her lap. However, with the moment growing in intensity, they mutually parted.

"I best go," Abby said half-heartedly and stood up. "I don't want to keep you from your work."

Michael remained seated and reflected a moment. "Robert should be here soon. He's holding the fort for us while we're away."

"Robert? Is that Robert Hampton?"

"That's him." Michael stood up and instantly towered over a shorter Abby.

"I'm going to be working for his wife when we get back. They're having a big extension, and I'm the lucky designer."

"That's fantastic!"

"Thanks." Abby looked relieved that the conversation had lightened the intensity between them, but she spoke too soon. When they reached her car and she opened the door, the concentrated feeling returned. They stood in the heart of the opened area, facing each other, Michael holding the tip of the driver's door.

"So, I'll see you here tomorrow," Abby said matter a factually.

"Abby, what are we going to do about this?"

It didn't need to be spelt out what he was talking about. He was taking a chance as neither of them had shared their feelings, but with the unspoken bond between them, each aware of a quickening pulse, they each knew that the attraction was mutual.

"I don't know what you mean." Abby looked to the side of his eyes and, as he moved in closer, she felt her heart miss a beat. She clenched her jaws together and blinked several times, more than usual.

"You know," he whispered.

Abby turned and put the key in the ignition, trying to avoid the confrontation of their sudden feelings for each other. He knew and she knew.

"We can't do anything. You know that."

"Abby, I'm not talking about a crush here."

"Michael, please don't say anything else."

"Abby, this isn't easy for me either. I would never in my life want to hurt or upset my son—never; but I can't look at you and not see how I can stop myself from falling in love with you, and it's tearing me up inside. James thinks I'm upset about the divorce, but the truth is I can't stop thinking about you. And for some reason I believe it's the same for you. I wake up in the morning and it's your face I see first. I close my eyes and I can still see you. You've somehow got into my heart, and how that happened with one kiss I will never know. But it has, and I don't know what to do."

"Michael, we can't do anything. Please, James has gone to so much trouble for this holiday. I'm not dismissing what you have just said, but we can't get into this."

"Just tell me one thing, does anything I've just said ring true?" Michael freed his hand, and instead of holding the blue metal door frame he held each of Abby's hands in each of his.

"You know it does," she said softly. She freed her hands and entered her car and, without looking back, she left his drive. Why this mutual attraction had happened, and one that was now growing each time they saw each other, was far from making sense to either of them. Nevertheless, it was happening, whether they liked it or not.

Abby drove back, lost in thought and fighting back some tears, wondering if she was always destined to only ever touch happiness and never hold it. Her dad dying, losing Patrick, the miscarriage, and now having love in her vision again—but a love beyond her grasp. She wished she had told her mum about the kiss, but at the time she felt that to do so would make it more real than it was. By not talking about it she thought she would forget it. But she was wrong. It wasn't that she had stopped loving Patrick. Maybe she never would, but she had seen something in Michael that just stirred something in her, and it was ignited by that one act of foolishness, which neither could forget. And neither wanted to act upon it again, afraid of where it might lead. Both found it hard to believe that something as simple as a kiss could have stirred something so strong, and the longer they fought it, the bigger and more intense it was becoming—like a rumbling volcano that would at some point have to erupt. Abby didn't see a man twenty years older than her, and Michael didn't see a woman that was the same age as his son; they just saw each other and saw something that could be wonderful.

# CHAPTER 19

❦

The temperature of the African country was kinder than it might have been on the early evening arrival as they all travelled to the five star accommodation. The holiday had been planned to precision, with arranged tours, excursions and some surprises along the way. When they arrived at the hotel they all appreciated the relief of the air conditioning, though the intensity of the hot air just added to the unforgettable experience. The journey from the airport had been a real eye opener—one really had to see Cairo to believe it: the hustle and bustle that never left the city whatever the hour, the unbelievable noise which, if it didn't come from the amount of people on the streets, it came from the excessive use of the car horn and the general amount of excessive traffic.

The distraction of where they were broke any tension between Michael and Abby. The four of them were getting on really well and that relief was pouring off Abby's face with her extreme perspiration. The people carrier, which conducted them to the hotel on the Nile, had left nothing out—the buses crammed to bursting point with Cairenes, the grand and majestic Nile that dominated the entire city, and the ancient buildings that stood so close to neighbouring modern day architecture; the extreme living conditions for many of the inhabitants, and the sight of so many people from all cultures and backgrounds; plus the ever-apparent dividing line of wealth: for example, an expensive car with suited businessman inhabiting it, still covered in dents though due to the hell raising way of driving, stopped alongside a donkey cart, which had a near blind man selling smelly old tissues whilst trying to balance on his single leg. The pollution clogged the air with force, but there was no escaping that this was the city of all cities; it had a more than twelve million people living in it, yet somehow, even with the immense population, one could feel like the only one. It just had this wonder about it. With Cairo it was as though one had a brief love affair: one took in all it had to offer, but one just enjoyed it and moved on. The tour only allowed them three nights there before they headed for Luxor and Karnak for the rest of the holiday.

Teresa and Abby naturally shared a twin room and likewise for the men. The hotel was unfaultable. No expense had been spared and, with breathtaking views over the Nile, the scene was set. After a quite adventurous dinner they all relaxed in the downstairs lounge, sipping an after-dinner drink and taking in where they all were. The hotel was potentially the best in the capital. The grand entrance took one through the open gardens before one entered the reception area; however, along the way one passed an indoor shopping complex, an informal café bar, serving locally made cakes and delicacies. There was also the outside vision of the sports complex and swimming pool. The people from numerous countries spilled out of every corner imaginable, with the air filled with many languages and cultures. The attentive waiters served the rich and affluent, the porters waited eagerly for their tips, and most of all, despite the fact that one was in an international hotel, one still knew where one was.

They all sat relaxed in light clothing, as, despite the air conditioning, the arid air still seemed to follow them. All sitting on the lounge seating, the comfort of the cushioned chairs were a welcome relief from the day's extensive travelling. In the midst of their relaxation Teresa, famous for always taking home plenty of filled camera roll, asked for some photos.

"Come on, you three, move together so I can get you all in." James and Abby's chairs were quite close together, but with Michael's further away, James made a suggestion.

"Dad, come around the back of us." Michael wandered behind them both, leant in and circled his arms around them like an eagle expanding his wings. Abby could feel the heat of his strong hand through her sheer top as it pressed against the side of her shoulder. The lingering touch of his redolent skin hovered in the air as his body lowered and created a light breeze with his motion. The time for the button to be pressed seemed to take forever. Abby could feel his breath tickling her neck as they posed and, with the flash of the camera at last, the touch of him was lifted and his presence distanced again.

"Teresa, what about one with you now?" James made a second suggestion and stood, instantly taking the camera. Teresa took James's seat while she beckoned to Michael back to mirror the same position, and in that moment an instant reply took place. Michael again could smell the freshness of Abby's loose hair, the close up vision of her angel-like neck and the electrifying contact with her body; a simple act had become a role of torment for them both. With them back to their original seating, Teresa made an enquiry.

"So what's tomorrow, other than your birthday, Michael?" Teresa asked James.

"We have to be up and ready early as tomorrow we have the Pyramids and Sphinx, and then we go on to Memphis and Saqqara. It will be a full day but a good way to spend your birthday, dad."

"It will be fantastic—help me forget I'm a year older."

"Ooh, you're not old, Michael, you're just ripening," Teresa said in jest. "That's what I tell myself, anyway."

"That's right, dad, you don't look forty eight anyway."

"I'm forty seven!" Michael quickly defended, but with a smile.

"Oh, sorry, dad. Are you sure?" he said after a little ponder.

"Of course I'm sure. I'll have you know I'm younger than quite a few sex symbols."

"What you mean, there's life in the old dog yet?" James added with fun.

"Hey you, less of the old!"

The banter continued a while. However, Abby felt as if she was distancing herself from it all; after all, she was supposed to be acting normal, and not joining in was not normal. The last thing she wanted was one of them saying to her, "Abby, you're quiet this evening"—followed by her lying and saying, "I'm just a bit tired"—a cliché in this type of circumstances she wanted to avoid. She was thinking about the forthcoming date, but she didn't want to take advantage of that in any way whatsoever. So, instead, she took the bull by the horns and added her contribution.

"Look at it this way, Michael, you're not even quite seven in animal years." Abby brought a smile to all their faces, but Michael's and Abby's lasted longer and as their eyes held a while unintentionally, James picked something up. Reading a brochure, James just moved his eyes and no other part of his body. He looked at his dad, then at Abby, and then back again to his dad—and just surveyed his observations.

The morning dawned and they were due to met in James's and Michael's room for an early room service breakfast and the exchange of some cards, plus Abby and Teresa had a gift or two of their own to give Michael. Comfortable and practical clothing was needed for the day and, as Abby walked to the side of her mum down the hallway, their different styled dresses and comfy footwear were sensible choices. However hot, they knew they needed to cover their bare arms and shoulders with a light cotton cardigan, a way of avoiding any confrontations with locals. When they arrived at the room and knocked, it was Michael who opened it and greeted them. Teresa instantaneously planted a kiss on his cheek and wished him happy birthday, and as Teresa moved in quickly, sighting a lavish breakfast and James in the spacious sized room, which was simply decorated in a hotel tradition, Abby was left briefly alone with Michael

"Happy birthday." Abby's head was a little dropped back as she directed the words up to his grand height.

"Thanks. How are you doing?" His voice was deep but light at the same time, and the words were conveyed with genuine meaning and concern.

"Good, oh these are for you, it's not much." Abby passed the two perfectly wrapped gifts and single card.

"Hey, you didn't have to this!"

"You haven't unwrapped them yet." Abby smiled, knowing that they hadn't shown that much imagination.

"It's always the thought anyway," he said, adding his touch to the chat, both finishing with a smile, and in the moment of now or never they exchanged a friendly kiss on the cheek, all before meeting James and Teresa in the eating area. The kiss was quick but not completely painless, but it seemed like the right thing to do in the moment. It was a way of feeling the contact of each other's skin, however quick and however passing.

They all enjoyed the special breakfast and then headed out to the waiting car. The sight of seeing of one of the seven wonders of the world was not all that the day would bring, as a surprise for Michael's birthday would happen further down the line—a hot air balloon trip at sunset that had been prearranged; however, that was later and this was now. The sights that filled their eyes were remarkable. The cameras were filled with the mighty views and the next stop was the imperial city of Memphis, and then on to the calm necropolis of Saqqara. The weather put on quite a show; with a sky so blue it seemed to glow, and the sun so intense it was stifling, resulting in endless drinking of bottled water, the only thing that could counteract the dryness of the air and heat. Michael was unaware of any later surprise and, with a light meal first on the agenda after the day of sights, the surprise remained in the pipeline for later. Teresa and Abby felt secure with James and Michael, but with Abby's fair colouring she stuck out like a sore thumb and could have been pestered a lot more if it hadn't been for the presence of the two men.

Sunset came and, as the sky filled with the orangey red overflow of the sun, the setting for the surprise was perfect and you couldn't have wished for a better evening. The view from the balloon was breathtaking and was completely unforgettable. The wicker basket held them all with safety and reassurance, and the silence that fell over them all came from what was filling their eyes. The distant sound of praying heard over the city was intensified from the great height and added a significant finish to the whole ambiance. The sky was so beautiful and the moment that they were all sharing would remain with them always. When they later returned to the hotel after their wonderful day, each pair retired to their rooms, but only momentarily as they thought they would have a look around some of the shops and round off the day by participating in an evening's fun at the casino.

They all wanted to freshen up on the return to the hotel but later on, with James and Michael ready and heading for the lift, Teresa was still waiting for Abby, who was still dithering with her choice of clothing. When Abby made a suggestion, she didn't allow for what might follow as a result. Teresa went ahead at the suggestion of Abby, as she would follow as soon as she was ready. Well, that was fine—Teresa met the boys at the shops and they started to eye up some bargains and thoughtful souvenirs for friends and family. However, with no sign of Abby yet, for she was still having a clothes crisis, Michael suggested he see if she was okay as he needed to get some more money from his room and, with Teresa and James both about to make a purchase, they agreed. Abby finally finished getting ready in a red sleeveless shirt dress with centre matching belt, allowing a little more flesh to be shown as they were in the protection of the hotel. She was just about to comb her hair when the knock on the door came. Thinking it would be her mum and, ready for her own departure, she called out: "It's on the catch, mum." But as she returned to the room from the bathroom it was Michael that faced her.

"Sorry, it's me. We were wondering where you had got to. Teresa and James are buying up all the shops down there." His stone trousers and predominant leather belt were finished with a soft navy shirt and, with his fair colouring, it showed he had made a good choice with his outfit. Likewise, he was thinking the same about Abby. She floundered a bit before replying.

"I was just on my way. I'll just finish my hair and we can head down." She used the fine-toothed plastic comb to point to the bathroom as she spoke and then headed there. Michael wandered around the room awhile before going to the doorway of the bathroom. Abby flicked her long hair over her shoulders and at the same time sensed Michael's presence at the doorway. Abby turned around and faced him, and the way they each looked at one other said so much and so quickly. They had a battle to fight and a battle to win, but with the moment upon them they knew they were both going to lose. She stepped into his shadow and said faintly, "I'm ready to go now."

Her words were struggling to convey meaning because of the melting look in his eyes. With their eyes fixed on one another, her sentence failed to move them to where they should be going.

Michael slowly moved closer to Abby, their waists now touching lightly and the thickness of his buckle rubbing on her thinner red replica. His large tender hands brought the contact closer as he held her slender body, feeling the definition of her rib cage under his hold. Her heart was beating for dear life, with the sound of their increased breathing outweighing the sound of the extractor fan that was still whirring at the far end of the bathroom. Their familiar lips waited for what was going to follow, but there was a short pause before the brush of their lips engaged. But once they did there was no going back. As the taste became pleasurable and heightened, their soaring senses exceeding all their anticipated expectations, the floor seemed to dissolve as they fell through space, more deeply than ever into the intoxicating presence of each other. Abby's once free hands now became lost in the back of Michael's profuse fair hair. The depth of the kiss came from the need they both had for it to happen again; but with that urgency gratified, the passion and hunger for each other grew. Their strong attraction made the whole experience lasting and memorable all over again.

They paused, momentarily resting on each other's forehead; their contact was closer than ever and not just in body but in soul too. The warmth of the kiss was running all through their bodies at speed. But they knew this couldn't go any further. They knew they shouldn't have succumbed to their desires, but in that split second it felt so right. The kiss left them hungry for more, but for the moment it was all they gave each other to survive on. Their foreheads still contacting, Michael's growing feelings for Abby were voiced out loud.

"I've never in my life had so strong a feeling for anyone. It scares me how good it feels to hold you!" The words were said with strong breathing and were finished with the same strong meaningful kiss that had recently taken them both over the edge. They knew they had to get downstairs, but with Michael's lips acting as an irresistible magnet to Abby's lips, they were finding it difficult to break free from the loving contact. After that all-consuming kiss their eyes couldn't help but watch the other's mouth—watching from where the words came out and longing to feel again the contact of the flooding, irresistible sensation. Still in the doorway of the en-suite bathroom, they had to make a move.

"I'll go down first. I'll say you're not far behind." Michael's reluctant body went to the door, but before he went to the lift he gave Abby a soft touch of his lips once again, and when she closed the door she felt so utterly confused. She covered her face completely with her quivering hands, but with the trace of Michael still on her lips, she couldn't escape her torment. After tidying her hair again and spraying her favourite designer perfume, she took the same steps along the navy patterned carpet of the hallway as Michael had done to the lift. When she arrived downstairs she headed for the casino and assembled with them all at the entrance. James noticed her flustered look. As Michael went on ahead to the bar, followed by Teresa, James voiced his concern.

"Are you okay?" Walking close by her side, he noticed a change in her eyes. The thing that Abby feared was that James had this uncanny way of knowing her so well. They just seemed to have this special connection.

"Yeah, I'm fine—bit of a headache, but that's probably all the sun today." Abby felt so awful and such a bad person, but at the same time she was just a person that had fallen in love with the wrong man, or maybe the right man in the wrong circumstances.

Any occasion for the same thing to happen again between Michael and Abby didn't seem to arise, which was probably better as they didn't find it easy curtailing the kiss. The next day went without a hitch. They enjoyed the sightseeing in the heart of Cairo, the museum, the Citadel and Mosque, finishing with some heavy haggling at the Khan-el-Khalili bazaar. However, the grand finale to the day was some very energetic horseback riding round the pyramids, another surprise. Added to the day of excitement and new discoveries, James was beginning to sense a change in the air. His astute awareness was clued up to a mystery that was closer to home. Unaware, Michael was finding it so hard to cope with the fact that he knew he was in love with James's best friend but was scared at the same time of never having this feeling about someone again. Abby was desperately trying to contain the love that was growing inside her. However, Michael, in an unsuspecting way, had given Abby new life and hope again and that, without her knowing, was making her eyes sparkle with verve. Trying not to fall in love with someone that had had such an impact on her was proving too much to bear. They may have come across their feelings by accident and at a vulnerable time for each of them, but this had gone beyond a silly act of foolishness; it had lifted on to a higher plane and was now in full flight.

They returned to the airport for their travel to Luxor and later met the river cruiser, which would be their accommodation for the immediate time. James and Abby posed for some pictures before boarding the liner. Both Michael and Abby hated being deceitful to James, and for Abby, with regard to Teresa; however, it wasn't being deceitful, as such, it was a matter of being unsure of what to do, and until they knew, they had to keep it to themselves. Although a transfer day, time was limited and so they made the best of the time available for sightseeing. They started at the Temple of Luxor and moved on to the Temple of Karnak. They were dazzled by the views that encompassed an ancient history through a span of thirteen centuries; it was an awe-inspiring vista that they were sharing together, for they were creating their very own history. After the day's excitement they moored at Luxor for the coming night.

The following day was packed full. They did a proper visit to the Valley of the Kings, taking in a whopping sixty-four tombs along the way. They continued on to the Temple of Queen Hatshephut, and when they returned to the mighty vessel later that day, Abby was unaware that James was trying to catch her on her own. With Michael in the shower preparing for dinner and Teresa writing postcards, he seized the moment and found Abby on deck leaning on the metal barrier. Lost in thought and thinking about her feelings, she had no idea James was close by. He couldn't have begun to imagine the extent of what was going on, but he had noticed little things, lasting looks, awkward moves and the look in Abby's eyes that he had seen before when she was talking about Patrick. Whatever was going on, though, he knew it was their business to sort out, and all he wanted to do was love Abby in any way he could, even if it wasn't in the way he had hoped. All this right now, however, was irrelevant as James could see that there was some more hidden mystery on her mind.

As James drew closer to her he stopped and paused and just watched awhile. Abby's cropped khaki trousers and close fitting grey t-shirt shaped her body well. The t-shirt didn't quite meet her waist, allowing a strip of her soft appealing skin to be seen. He watched as her free hair caught in the wind and her side profile defined more against the glowing setting sun. Her eyes were lost in the distance and, turning back to look straight ahead, his view of her beauty had been blocked, leading him to now move over to her. He extended his left arm and brushed her back to alert her of his presence, and instantly they exchanged a friendly kiss on the cheek. He leaned forward next to Abby on the rail, sensing what she was thinking of.

"I wish I could say something that might help you, Abby." James was looking at the calm ripples of the Nile but the blue of Abby's eyes was where his glance finally moved to.

"Honestly, I really am doing okay. I've had lots of hugs and chats with mum and I feel stronger than I thought I would." She felt so bewildered and now felt shy, talking to him about it.

"Never feel that you can't talk to me, Abby. Whatever else is happening in your life, you can always talk to me—always." For some reason he just tuned to her and could almost read her mind, which right now was unnerving for her. She did want to talk to him; she just felt guilty. However, she somehow felt a little more confident after his words and so she tried to find the words to express her feelings.

"I just can't help but think what it would have been like to have held her in my arms and to have seen her little face. But that kind of thinking doesn't help. I have to hold on to the fact that she is at peace and in safe hands. I don't think there'll ever be a day that I won't think about her, though, and how things might have been. When I fell in love with him way back in Paris, I never thought it would end like this. I thought we would get married, have children and live happily ever after. How wrong could I have been?"

"Do you still think about him"? James wondered out loud but still with care in the question.

"Sometimes. He'll always be the father of my first child and the first man I ever fell completely in love with, and for that reason he will always be part of me."

"You're a very special person, Abby, the most amazing person I know. I know that happiness will find you."

"I think it keeps getting lost somewhere or confused."

"I know it's on its way to you, you'll see. Maybe not in the way you first expected, but happiness comes in all shapes and sizes. It's tailor-made to meet our needs at different times of our lives and it changes with us. Don't search for it, let it find you—and it will." His words of wisdom and surety were delivered with great warmth and at the same time he knew the happiness that he longed for had just gone in the opposite direction.

"Thanks, James. You always know what to say." After a proud smile from him, Abby added: "Anyway, I'm glad we came. What we've seen has been out of this world." She pulled the sail and changed direction with the wind.

"I'm glad." He brought a smile to his face. "You see, my persuasion paid off." And his words brought a bigger smile to her face.

"James, you do know that you mean so much to me, don't you?" She turned and stood on her own, free from any support from the rail.

"Hey, course I do."

"And you know I would never ever want to hurt you?"

"Course I know. Where's all this come from?"

"Just getting sentimental, I guess." She couldn't go any further and halted her words.

"Come here and give me a hug." James took her in his arms and held her close. There was a time that all she ever needed was a hug from her friend to make things clearer, but in this instance it just complicated matters.

The remaining days of their trip would be taken up with Edfu and Kom Ombo and Aswan. They all took the opportunity of being able to climb to the top of the richly-carved pylon, which towered over the site of the Temples of Horus, dedicated to the falcon-headed god of the sun and planets. The view down from the mighty height was tremendous and that great experience was added to the hot air balloon and the horseback riding. Before they knew it they were back in Cairo for their last night before their flight home. The hotel was different and less elaborate, but it served the same purpose and for the first time in five days, Michael and Abby found themselves alone. Fortunately for temptation they were in the downstairs lounge, as James was having a late afternoon swim and Teresa was trying to phone her sister. They sat at opposite ends of the leather sofa, which was creaking with their fidgeting bodies. The look in their eyes and the expression on their torn faces created a silence; however, Michael suddenly leant forward, sitting on the edge of the seat, and said softly:

"Are you regretting it all?"

He looked intently at her. It was a look that betrayed how utterly smitten he was with her.

"It's not about regret, it's about knowing that we are just making it harder to forget this and close our eyes to it. We're prolonging what we both know."

"What happens if James did understand and we're walking away from this for no reason?"

"Even if we told James we had started to have feelings for each other and for some reason he was okay with that, think of what it could do to your relationship with him—and mine, for that matter. I hate the fact we have already deceived him. I feel so ashamed that he has no idea that I'm falling in love with his father." When the words came out she realised she hadn't meant to say that out loud.

"Falling in love with…" Michael looked taken aback, yet at the same relieved that he was not on his own.

"We must forget this, please."

"I understand what you are saying about feeling ashamed, but what we are keeping from James isn't driven by malice or bad intent; it's driven by love. Neither of us wants anyone to become hurt. I know that may not help us much, but don't confuse falling in love with someone as something bad, whoever it is and whatever the circumstances. To feel what I'm feeling right at this minute for you doesn't feel bad. It's feels like the most wonderful thing in the world. I don't know how to walk away from it."

Abby was leaning forward, copying his stance, and as his words drifted into the air she didn't believe she could love another man again like she was doing. There was a part of her that could and would only be touched by Patrick, but that part of her had somehow allowed someone else to come close. When this unexpected love came into her life by mistake, she was stunned by the effect it had on her. She didn't have a bad bone in her body and any misguided behaviour that was happening came from her infatuated heart and desire to be loved.

"But this wasn't meant to happen! It was by chance that we have seen each other in this way. What happens if it had been James that held me? Or Robert, or Max even? How do you know this was meant to be?" Abby was trying to find a way of escaping their love but was heading down a dead end.

"But it wasn't them. It was us, and when there is a connection, a chemistry even, between two people as strong as this, then there is a reason. Right now it seems like a complication, but one day it will be a blessing as apposed to a curse, you'll see." Michael, too, wasn't exactly feeling great about it all, but his kind tone was trying to reassure himself too.

"But what does that tell us now?" Abby looked confused.

"I only wish I knew." Michael longed to hold her hand but felt too conspicuous to move and make the gesture, and just in time Teresa reappeared.

"I hope you two don't mind, but I think I will have a nap before we have dinner. James will be a while, won't he?" She answered her own question.

"Are you sure you don't want me to come back up with you, mum?" Abby moved forward to the edge of the leather sofa, having reclined into the sumptuous curves of the seating, waiting for her mum to respond.

"No, not at all. I'll probably just catch some winks and have a freshen up. What time did we say for dinner?"

"I think we are meeting up at the restaurant at about 8 p.m.," Michael answered, coming to the same position as Abby, looking up to the still standing Teresa.

"Well, that gives us a couple of hours. I'll head up then. Will you two be okay."

"Yeah, we'll be fine," Abby said nervously.

So with Teresa on her way to the lift they had just each other for company again. They both sat feeling very awkward, but just then Abby made a suggestion.

"Look, shall we look at some of the shops or something? I saw some jewellery that I liked in one of the windows. You can offer your opinion, if you like." Abby stood up and hovered over Michael's seated body, trying to break the tension.

"Good idea." Using his hands to aid in him standing, the closeness of their two standing bodies was nearer than expected when he rose to his feet. Their lips could have so easily touched, but after a second of entertaining the notion in the middle of each other's allure, they resisted the temptation. The shops were plentiful and as they headed towards them they walked close enough together to feel the contact of each other's clothing. When they approached the shop earmarked by Abby they stopped at once and gazed into the outside window. The gold chain with a small bust of Queen Nefertiti hanging from it was simple yet very appealing, and at the same time it had found an admirer in Abby.

# CHAPTER 20

❀

The bright warm lights from the window display made the necklace look even more exquisite. The slightly tinted glass caught the reflection of their faces and, although their eyes were glancing over the jewels, their hearts and minds were somewhere else completely. They were standing in a hotel in a land of mystery and wonder, and the way they were both feeling inside was mirroring the essence of the country they were in. They were wrapped up in the wonder of what it would feel like to touch and caress each other further and in the mystery of whether the two of them could ever be happy together. This wasn't a cheap dirty fantasy between an older man and younger woman, it was literally as if cupid had cast his arrow and nothing would dislodge it. The differences between Abby's feelings for Michael and her feelings for Patrick were becoming easier to define.

The love from Patrick was different to the love she was receiving from Michael. With Patrick she always felt, even right from the beginning, that it was a one-sided love. He may have always said, "I love you," but he could give only so much, not his all—and that was of course why he couldn't and wouldn't change his life. Abby could see now, even if he had left Laura and come to England, how potentially unfulfilling his love would have been. However much she loved Patrick, her love for him couldn't make up his missing quarter, which he always seemed so reluctant to part with. It was as though he couldn't share himself completely: he had to keep back ten per cent just in case. Love is a gift of oneself, but the thing with Patrick was that he never wanted to completely unwrap himself. However, this love that was taking root with Michael was breeding new life and was shared equally by them both; their hearts and feelings were totally exposed to each other. With the paper of their fully unwrapped selves on the floor, the gift of each other's love was well and truly open and released. The fulfilment of what they were sharing, although secret, was nevertheless filling the emptiness in both their hearts.

"Let me buy it for you. You've obviously fallen in love with it."

"If only everything you fall in love with could be that simple." The poignant words fixed their eyes and, as Abby turned back to the necklace, Michael pleaded:

"Please, I want to buy it for you—a way of saying thank you."

"Thank you? Whatever for?"

"For making me feel alive again and giving me that feeling of love again."

"You don't have to say thank you for that."

"Yes I do." His soft mature skin creased when he smiled, and with the even softer three words spoken, Abby accepted the offer with Michael buying it right there and then. After the purchase they took themselves outside to the terrace and, as they slowly climbed the stone steps, James appeared from the swimming pool. His wet dripping body was just about to be completely covered in a complimentary white towelling gown.

"Hey, you two—the water's fantastic, so refreshing! Just what I needed!" James was rubbing the little hair he had and his face with the arm of his robe.

"You had a good swim then?" Abby said quickly.

"Brilliant. I'll just get showered and we'll head to the restaurant for dinner. We were going to try that Mexican one by the shopping complex, weren't we?" James glanced at Abby and then at his dad, still picking up a vibration between the two of them.

"That's right, it looks nice. Anyway, I'll leave you boys to it. I think I'll head up—see if mum's okay." Abby left them both, smiling at them on her departure and catching the eye of Michael before she vanished through the doors of the hotel, her ultimate aim the lift by reception.

James and Michael were not going to be far behind her, but Abby wanted to make her exit first and, as she entered the empty mirrored enclosure, the necklace safe in her clutch bag, a sudden feeling washed over her and saturated her body. She had become like a sponge over the last few months, one that had taken all that it could absorb and so she relinquished some needed tears to the still empty travelling lift. It was the combination of it all, the time her pregnancy should have ended, the feeling of so much guilt over her feelings for Michael, but also in a strange way she had this sadness, sadness that it wasn't Patrick that was filling her heart and mind with love anymore. She felt so confused and, when her mum opened the door, that confusion spilled out. With each teardrop that fell she was realising the turmoil that was overpowering her delicate mind, and when she fell into her mum's arms her upset and bewilderment could still only at this point be half shared. Teresa guided her daughter to the edge of the first single bed and sat her down, her arms shielding her for support. Teresa always had a handkerchief close by and in this much-needed minute she retrieved a white-laced one from her skirt pocket. Abby applied it to her eyes and spoke with the act.

"I'm sorry mum, I just became so overwhelmed. My mind is so full and jumbled, I don't know how to clear it."

"Talk to me." Teresa held her body still and tucked Abby's falling fringe behind her ear, enabling her to see her face again.

"It's just, well, it's just…" Abby was floundering but her mother's words stopped her anxiety.

"Abby, just tell me as much as you feel you can. You don't have to tell me everything, just what ever you are comfortable with." This aided Abby well and led her to follow with some of her feelings, after having given her nose a good blow.

"I'm worried that if my feelings for a certain person die down, then it means I'm forgetting about my baby." When she said the short but meaningful sentence, her tears were recalled to her eyes, although they hadn't travelled far.

"Oh, Abby, sweetheart, that's not how it is at all. You love your baby as your baby. It has nothing to do with whether your feelings for Patrick are as strong or as apparent. Abby, don't think about things too deeply, keep it simple. Your love for your baby is your love. It is completely separate to your emotions with Patrick. Listen, I haven't ever told this before and I don't even know if it will help, but it was when I'd just found out I was pregnant with you. I hadn't told your dad yet. Anyway it was our second wedding anniversary and I had planned something special and I had intended to tell him then. But when it came to the afternoon he phoned from the bank and said he was going to be later than anticipated; he was after promotion at the time and needed to be in on this new client's business. Anyway, when it got to 9 p.m., then 10 p.m., I went past the stage of understanding and it was just after my mum had died—your nana—and I really needed him. Of course, we had this huge row about it all and everything else came out with it. We weren't adjusting to married life very well; we loved each other greatly but we just weren't getting it right. Well, I stormed out and I went to stay with Alice for a few days and it took a week for us to sort out our differences. But the point I was trying to help you with, and I know it is not completely the same but at the time all I could think about was you, my baby growing inside me, a baby I wanted so much and to love so much. Even when your dad was driving me nuts and our future was uncertain, my love for you, my baby, was something that nobody could touch. Your love for Patrick might fade, but never put that love in the same box as your love for your child, because that love is separate from any love you will ever experience in your life. It's too special to compare." Abby's tears had become less frequent and she was feeling calmer and collected, but there was a question she wanted to ask her mum.

"How did things get better? I mean, how did you sort things out?"

"The funny thing was after that week apart he was so different, as if he felt guilty about it all; and after that we always talked about our problems and never ran from them, we faced them together. We were back together and settled a month before I told him I was pregnant, and it sealed the envelope to our happiness. When he worked late we would compromise and always make sure we had 'our time' and then, when you arrived, well, it was the icing on the cake. But something just changed after our brief time apart. It was as if the next eighteen years it was your dad's mission to make me happy and he did succeed. Don't forget as well on my part your dad was a very handsome man and I was always insanely jealous, and at the start of our marriage that didn't help. But we got there and trusted each other and made each other very contented. I wish we could have had more time together, but what I think about is what we had, not what we didn't; anyway, no room for anymore tears." Her true revelation was starting to provoke her own sadness.

"I love you, mum, and thank you for being so wonderful to me and sharing so much with me."

"All part of the service, sweetheart." They hugged one another well and stamped the moment with a kiss, all before realising they needed to get ready for dinner.

Abby may have not shared everything with her mum, but it was enough for her strength to have increased and for her now to be able to face her love for Michael and not to fear it. They all sat around the circular table and enjoyed the delights of the Mexican cuisine, sipping at their margaritas in between mouthfuls of the spicy fiery food. The atmosphere of the hotel's restaurant was passable as a Mexican theme and, having tried nearly all the local tastes, on their last night they delved into a taste of something more familiar. Around Abby's recently tanned neck was the gift from Michael. She fiddled with it whenever she paused from eating to talk. The head of Nefertiti dropped down into the V of Abby's lightly knitted yellow cardigan, sitting perfectly against the smoothness of her skin. Michael's eyes were drawn to Abby's whenever possible and, at the end of the courses, with James in the restroom of the restaurant and Teresa quickly fetching another film for her empty camera, Michael and Abby sat alone at the table.

"The necklace really suits you." Michael was leaning forward in his chair and broke his powerful stare at her with a sip at his diminishing cocktail.

"Thank you—and thank you for buying it for me." Abby's delivered her thanks with politeness and grace. The way they had been sitting meant there was only one empty chair between their bodies being closer and, as Abby had turned herself slightly when he complemented her, they were within arms reach of one another.

"I'm glad you let me." They both smiled warmly and, as Michael turned a little more on the wooden chair, he wanted to say something but didn't know what; and before he had the chance to say anything, James was approaching the table with the visual confirmation to his suspicion, having almost seen from a distance the aura of love that encircled both of them at the table. Teresa was a little behind him, but James had seen enough in that split second to understand why Michael and Abby had resisted being alone together during the trip.

With packing and an early night, the remainder of the time in Egypt faded with the moon and, as the stars left the sky one by one, dawn broke on the day of their departure. This unexpected holiday was to have repercussions for them all. The stone had been thrown in the Nile and the ripples it had made were going to continue and soon turn into waves.

The day didn't start well. Abby woke up at the persistence's of her mum's call, but as she stirred in the single bed she gripped her stomach tight and groaned with a very discomforting pain. Just about standing on the paisley green carpet, her body covered by her casual cotton pyjama bottoms and jersey sleeveless top, mirroring each other in lilac, Teresa wondered what on earth was wrong.

"Abby, what is it?" Teresa was dressed and nearly ready for the early breakfast as she stood close to her daughter.

"My stomach doesn't feel so good. I think I'll go to the bathroom." Some time later Abby reappeared but not really feeling any better.

"It wasn't the food last night, was it?"

"I think I know." Her face was grimacing with the gripping pain.

"What then?" Teresa said, concerned.

"Well, I woke up in the night and my mouth was so dry from all that chilli, and when we had no bottle water left I drank some from the tap in the bathroom." She felt stupid as she said it.

"Well, no wonder! Oh Abby! What am I going to do with you? You know, when I came with your dad, he did exactly the same thing!"

"What will happen?"

"It will have to work through you. Is it…up or…or down?" Teresa gestured with her hand.

"Down, but it just keeps gripping in my tummy."

"It will, I'm afraid. Well, we had the jabs. It will just take a few day's to clear from your system. How much did you have?"

"About two of those beakers." Abby pointed to the ones in the bathroom.

"Dear oh dear, I hate to be unsympathetic, sweetheart, but we have to get going soon."

"Don't worry, I'll be ready. Just give me a minute." And with a quick dash, she reacquainted herself with the bathroom.

The flight felt like an eternity and no one was happier than Abby when they were finally home. Arriving back in the much cooler early evening air, they arrived at the Stud, the place where they had originally set off from. Abby was feeling no better and just wanted to be in bed, but before they travelled the few miles home they said their thank you's to each other for a fantastic time. James and Abby were slightly distant from Michael and Teresa, who were now over at the car sorting out the luggage. However, James wanted to say something of his own and appreciated the moment before they headed off.

"I know you're feeling rough."

"That's an understatement." Despite some sun that had tanned her skin, her face looked washed out and tired.

"But I'm so glad we shared all this together."

"James, I don't deserve you." Abby gave him a great big hug, but one that was seeped in guilt and, despite how awful she felt, it didn't distract her from reeling with the poisonous emotion.

"What are you talking about? Course you do." Tight in the hug together, James knew he had to let her go and not just from that moment. His love for her, he decided there and then, would remain concealed.

"Thanks James, for everything." With Michael helping Teresa load up their car with their suitcases, James wanted to say something quickly.

"Abby, just a minute. All I've ever wanted is for you to be happy; when you're happy it makes me happy, and in life happiness comes round so infrequently that you have to grab it when you can."

"Where's this come from?" Abby wondered a little, wary of the answer.

"I don't know. I guess it's just when we were away you looked like you had a lot on your mind, more than what we talked about. I just want you to be happy, whatever, that's all." The smile between them and the expression on James's face seemed to say so much, and Abby had a feeling that her love for Michael must have been written all over her face—not only that, but it must have been read by James. She said nothing else and walked arm in arm with him to the car. As they left their extensive drive after some more thanks, James and Michael waving at their departure, James turned to his dad before they moved from the gravelled surface.

"It was a great holiday."

"It was, it really was." Michael extended his arm to his son's shoulder. "Thank you for such a great birthday. I know I don't say it often enough, but I love you, son." He squeezed his shoulder more with the final words.

"I know, I really do. I was just saying to Abby when you were helping Teresa that love and happiness is a treasured find and you have to grab it whenever you can. She's an amazing woman, Abby, and could make someone very happy." James said all the words with a gently meaningful and truthful tone, taking care to convey his understanding of the situation with refinement and subtlety. His words were caught by Michael and held with reassurance. However, at the same time in James's mind and in his heart, he wondered why it couldn't have been him and not his dad that Abby had fallen in love with. But that question, as far as James would be concerned, would always remain just that, a question. That's not to say that it didn't have an answer, of course. As with Abby, nothing else was said or added, and they made their way into the house. Life isn't always ideal and things don't always work out the way we think they should, but James felt he had no place to stand between their love; he knew they were fighting it and he didn't want them to. Abby being happy meant more to him then anything, and in that passing and indirect way, he had given the green light to their happiness, sealed with approval—something Abby and Michael so much needed.

The next day, with most of the washing hanging off clothes horses around Teresa and Abby's cottage, Abby was still feeling poorly, but was better than she had been. She thought she was over the worst until she tried eating something the previous night. However, with the morning in bed and lots of fresh water being drunk, she was getting there and was starting to feel better than she had done through the night. The sun was gracing them with its presence, although the temperature marked no comparison to what they had been used to for the last week. Teresa was eager to get the photos in and to pop over and see Alice and Stanley, so when she was about to leave, Abby just about to take the force of a hot shower, Teresa called that she would be back early evening. Elsewhere, having spoken to Abby early that morning to see how she was feeling, James was heading over to see his mum, who had some news of her own to share, having herself recently returned from the South of France. Michael had plenty to catch up with at the Stud but something, or more like someone, was praying on his mind and, until he saw her, he was no good to anyone.

Abby dressed her clean and refreshed body in her towelling gown and wrapped her hair up in a small towel. The whiteness of her new gown highlighted her tanned skin and, as she was just thinking that she was feeling brighter, the sound of the door chime filled the house. Before going to the door, aware of her attire, she looked out of the hall window and saw Michael peering back. Her face flushed instantly and before opening the front door she tightened the tie around her waist and tucked herself in more around the neck. Waiting the other side of the door, Michael was relaxed in his appearance, sporting a charmed pair of jeans and a ribbed indigo sweater that accentuated his entrancing blue eyes and suited his fairness. He passed his eyes over his clothing and ran his hands nervously through his hair. At the same time Abby took a deep breath and opened the door.

"Hey." The surprise of who it was had long since been over, but the moment had just begun.

"Hey."

"Sorry, come in."

"How are you feeling today?" Michael asked while she closed the door.

"Better. The hot shower has just helped."

"Good." Their bodies were moving closer together as they spoke and without a second too soon they broke the pretence. They were close enough for their fragrances to reach each other, to feel their passing breath on their faces and close enough for the first gesture to be made, the one that would start the sensuous trial they both longed to embark upon.

"I'm glad you stopped by. I've been thinking about you."

"You have?"

"Yeah." The words weren't really needed but it was as though they were taking a second or two to prepare for what they knew was about to happen—and then it did.

Unlike the other times when their lips touched in the profound way that they did, they knew where this one was going to take them. They broke off their searching kiss only in order for them to climb the twelve steps to Abby's bedroom, and as soon as their feet trod the thick velvet pile, their hallway kiss was about to start again. With their bodies facing each other, only a short distance away from Abby's thick mattress, her hair towel now lost on the floor, Michael placed his hands on her head and gently stroked her damp hair with softness and love. The tips of his fingers were lost in the moisture of her long locks, with the palms of his hands against Abby's rosy cheeks. Then he kissed her lips, revelling in their soft texture. His body had more garments to release than Abby and as the fundamental kiss was under way, the freeing of his clothes begun. She lifted his sweater up, aiding him in its removal, but returned to his lips instantly as the stylish top finished its journey over his head; and while absorbed in the emotion, Michael shuffled off his footwear. The moment to fall to the bed was upon them. Abby's body fell back with grace, her head taking the impact of the pillow, with Michael acting as a human blanket to her body. The passion and love was becoming even more real as their recumbent selves relished in the powerful compression of their bodies.

What was just beginning was still something that neither thought could, or would ever happen. However, it was living now, no more dreaming, for what they yearned for had become reality. The touching between them had not yet gone any further than kissing and caressing each other in the strong embrace; however, when Abby's tender hands continued to make contact with the bare skin on Michael's back, he longed to feel the same contact with her. He had stayed in good shape, with his chest and strong-arm muscles living proof of that. However, before he could take his desires further he needed to free himself from his denim trousers that entrapped his growing desire.

Left in the minimal of clothing, Michael took the next step to touching Abby's skin further. Parting from her lips to descend to where the tie of her gown was, he loosened it and separated the towelling fibres, all to view her flawless body. Both his hands enveloped her shapely waist with tender care, and as he delivered his polite, yet incredibly provoking kisses to her stomach, Abby's eyes closed with the warmth and keenness of the contact. The smell of her fresh body was reaching Michael subtly; the way her cool skin felt on his warm lips was far better than he had ever imagined. Every touch from Michael was completed with thought, every contact his hands made with her exquisitely feminine body was made with kindness and love, and as the kisses touched her skin as softly as floating bubbles, she tingled with delight.

Abby knew as soon as she felt the touch of Michael that the whole experience would be very different from her first and only. With Patrick it was heated and erotic, and although what she was now feeling was different, it was far more fulfilling and passionate than she could ever have imagined or wanted. It was so much more rewarding because of their deeper connection and their unselfish and requited love for each other. Patrick did love Abby, but in a self-seeking way, and she knew that the lovemaking with Michael would be on a completely different and higher level, one that Patrick would have been incapable of climbing to. For the two of them now, this was about bringing their love for each other to the ultimate stage of togetherness. It was bringing them as close to one another as two people in love could possibly be.

There wasn't an inch of Abby's failing essence that Michael hadn't adorned with appealing messages of his affection, and as he cupped her pliable and succulent breasts, he evoked even more fondness for her body. Her arms were never off his lightly and freshly tanned back, which was glowing with beads of perspiration. She wanted to share the contentment that he was sharing with her, but he wanted to make love to her and had no desire for her to move from her place of enjoyment. He continued to cloak her whole body in his adoration and made love to her like a gentleman, but also like a man filled with an amazing amount of passion for one person. Abby was the person who made him feel like he was the only man alive, the woman with the power to make him feel that there wasn't anything he couldn't do.

This love that they had found was going to last forever, even though, unbeknown to them, it would have to be a love that was shared in an unexpected way—in a way that neither could ever have imagined possible to happen, and in a way that was going to break Abby's heart all over again. The window on the far left wall was the source of most of the light in Abby's bedroom and that was where her glance was held. Her back was lying close up against the front of Michael's turned body. He had brought his arms around her waist to secure the squeeze further and as her head rested on his lightly fair-haired chest, she felt so happy and couldn't have wished to be anywhere else. When she tipped her head back, she smiled contentedly at his handsome face. He kissed her lightly on her forehead before she dropped her head down again. And when Michael whispered his feelings of happiness and love to her, she instantly turned to face him again.

"I love you, Abby Raycroft."

"I love you, Michael Foster," she whispered, beaming with the pride conjured up by her declaration of love.

"Well, that's fortunate."

Abby smiled at his jest and reached up to dissolve her soluble lips into his. In doing so she made the kiss last. Using her left hand and twisting her body round a little, she held the kiss even longer, caressing the side of Michael's clean-shaven cheek. She was extending the effects it was having on each of them, and it led her to turn herself in full and move her whole body to shelter Michael's instead of the cotton sheet, which until then had been doing the job. When the depth of their mouths crossed all the barriers, she took her opportunity to show her love in the way he had done. She enjoyed seeing the delight on Michael's face as she decorated his body with her own special effects, and as they brought the sensuous mission again to fulfilment, the end result mirroring the previous magic and expectation, they fell even deeper in love. When they lay deeply satisfied in the bed, Michael's back flush against the sheet and his head comforted by the raised pillow, with Abby's head resting on his supple skin around his torso, they took some time before they said another word.

# CHAPTER 21

❀

Appeased in Michael's arms, Abby's loving eyes shifted their view as she thought about how she would tell her mum about the new love in her life. One minute she was observing the inviting sight of Michael's chest, as her head still rested there, her once damp hair having now long since dried, and the next she was gazing over to the far right corner of her bedroom where she had a lavender armchair, a place where she sometimes sat and read. Her back was now to the brightness of the afternoon sun that was trying to bring some cheerfulness to the fast departing autumn air, but as long as her body was close to Michael's, she didn't care how she lay or where she was. Inside, she finally was feeling the true extent of her love for him and, with the release of their passion; they started to feel so free and weightless.

For last few months their growing attraction and then love for each other had almost been weighing them down; however, in this very contented moment, they both felt like two birds freed from a cage. Their feathery hearts fluttered at every touch they gave each other and the sound of their voices almost sang as they spoke. In Abby's flanked position, Michael lowered and pressed his chin deep into the hollowness of his neck, trying to see if she was asleep since she had been silent for a while. But when he saw her eyelids flicker and felt the tickling sensation of her eyelashes on his abdomen, he realised, like him, she was just happily hushed. Michael was the one to break the contented peace, though he had no intention of disturbing their wanted closeness.

"Why don't you and Teresa come round to the Stud tonight? We can then all spend the evening together. Will you have a chance to talk to Teresa?"

"I hope so. James knows me so well. I don't think I'd ever be able hide anything from him, not that I would want to, of course." His idea made Abby speak her thoughts about James.

"He's very tuned in to you—he always has been; must be from the length of time you've known each other, plus he is a very perceptive person."

"It's funny, really, I thought only my dad could read me like that; it's shocking when you find out that someone else can." Michael was listening but it was as if Abby was thinking out loud and saying the words to herself.

"Abby, you are sure about this, aren't you?" Michael sat up a bit more in the bed and made contact with the metal head frame. Abby followed by lifting her body up with him, leaning on her right elbow to catch her weight.

"Michael, I've never been more sure of anything in my life. I love you and I want to be with you, no question!" She sealed her reassurance with a big meaningful kiss on his waiting lips.

"You've made me the happiest man alive." An enormous smile spread across his face. He could have undertaken the tasks of the world, and all because of this amazing woman.

"Well, I aim to please," she jested and lifted her eyebrows in a suggestive way. Her playful expression triggered off their bodily contact once again.

"Come here, you little minx!" Grabbing her bare body that was warmed by the creased double sheet, Michael pulled the sheet over their heads and, with playful tickling, the magic between them began again as if a wand had been waved over them. Their jocular screams and laughing filled the room with live and vigour as they gave way to their passions again. They never thought they could feel any better than they did on this day, the day that should have been the start of things. Michael and Abby knew that he would have to head home pretty soon as the afternoon was fading with the sun and Abby wanted time to talk to her mum alone and not for her to just find them together. Michael had a business meeting he still had to attend later on as well, and so, when they finally made it down to the primrose hallway, Michael back in his attire and Abby having thrown on her tracksuit pants and rugby sweater, they were ready to part, though the parting would be for longer than either thought.

"This meeting should be finished around 7 p.m-ish; it's up at Roberts, so it isn't far. So shall we say 8 p.m.?"

"That sounds okay." They held each other close as they spoke. Michael was heading home to change before the meeting, having plenty of time to spare, but not wanting to rush.

"You're gorgeous and I love you." Michael cupped her face in his giant hands and credited Abby's lips with his richness, all before leaving her to head home, however not before giving his trademark wink at his exit.

Half an hour later and almost five thirty to the second, Teresa arrived home to find Abby at the breakfast table in their kitchen. Sitting on the rectangular table was their cockerel tea cosy, which was bulging out due to the big pot of tea it was warming underneath. Nearby were two floral mugs. One had a teaspoon popping out of the top, while a non-matching milk jug and chipped sugar bowl stood close by. Abby wanted her mum to be happy for her and, as they greeted each other, Abby poured the tea. But Teresa had a surprise of her own. Abby was wrong earlier—there were in fact three people who knew her that well. Teresa hadn't any idea of the extent of their feelings, but she too had seen the signs. However Teresa knew that when Abby felt she could and it was the right time, she would share it with her—and sure enough, now she was.

There was probably nothing the two of them couldn't talk about, although on the horizon something lurked that would test that. But now the free conversation about Michael and herself was as open and as vast as the countryside. Knowing that they were heading round to the Stud later that evening, they decided that an easy walk was a good way to clear out any old cobwebs, plus Abby's face looked decidedly pale from her recent tummy bug. As they both enjoyed the activity, neither needed much persuasion to the mutual idea, despite the cool evening air. Abby just added some trainers to her socked feet and a hooded fleece to her body. Teresa, on the other hand, just returned her woollen knee length coat to her body and, with the lock engaged on the back door, the press of the button on the answering machine and the closing of the front door, they were on their way. Arm in arm, the walk wasn't about exercise or burning calories, it was just a change of scenery and a breath of fresh air into Abby's lungs, for she had not been out of the house since their return. Their village setting made it easy to stroll freely, passing the green and local amenities along the way. However, their chatter about Abby's new love, how wonderful James had been and how Abby had such high hopes for the future, was deterring them from viewing anything around them. Just chatting and keeping a steady pace, they generated enough body heat not to be aware of the wintriness.

James was on his way back from his mother's at the time Abby and Teresa were enjoying the start of their walk. He had heard that his mother was planning to leave the country and move to Wyoming where Larry had ownership in a thriving Stud. However, that wasn't all; she wanted him to go with her. He told his mother he would have to think about it, but deep down, although he knew that his father had captured Abby's heart, he couldn't bare not having her in his life. The time when he was in the States before was a time he didn't want to relive. He had gone to flee his feelings for her, only to return and find them still there; however, he was not an all or nothing person; he wanted Abby to be in his life in any way that she could be. There had always been this invisible barrier between them, one that James never felt he could cross, long before his recent discovery about her and his dad; it was one that would always remain firmly in place. The time was speeding on and, after a quick drink at their local pub, Abby and Teresa were on their way back.

The time had just gone 7.50 p.m. as Abby and Teresa made the final strides up their drive to the front door. With the turn of the key in the door, simultaneously the phone started to ring with the rotation of the metal. Racing to the receiver to catch it before the machine kicked in.

"Hello?" Abby answered, slightly breathless. Her rubber soles fidgeted on the stone hall floor as she spoke.

"Abby, listen, it's James. There's been an accident and I'm at the hospital." James's voice was loud and yet full of confusion and distress.

"An accident! Is it you? Are you hurt?" Abby was bewildered as to what she was hearing, yet fearful at the same time. Teresa was standing close by her side and waited for further information.

"It's not me, it's…it's my dad. Listen, Abby, you have to come to the hospital. I need you here. I can't do this on my own." Abby dropped the receiver from her ear, desperately trying to comprehend what she was hearing. She could hear James calling her name down the phone.

"Abby, please."

"We're leaving now. James, how bad is it?" She was numb with the shock but had to know.

"I've not long got here, but it's not good." James's tone weakened as he fought back his own pain of what was happening. Abby dropped the phone down and failed to notice the flashing number one on the answering machine.

The endless time it took to get to the hospital just made everything feel worse, if possible. They were too shocked to understand what was happening. It wasn't until they arrived at the hospital and raced to the A&E that the extent of what was happening hit them. When James appeared in front of their panicked eyes, his own eyes reddened from his weeping, he told Abby what she had feared the whole journey. Her eyes filled with gushes of tears so quickly and as they ran down her face all she could say was, "No, please no." James and

Abby fell into each other's arms, the tightness of their hold trying to hold back the chaos in their minds and the pain that was swamping their already drowning bodies. Their torture and suffering became lost in each other's as neither broke from the tight hold. Abby gripped onto James's jumper for dear life; it was as if her own life depended on its hold, as though she were hanging over a cliff and if she let go she would fall to her death. James knew that their newfound romance was not just a flippant love and that the pain from losing his dad so quickly and suddenly was compounded by the pain he felt for Abby, knowing what she too must have been feeling.

Teresa's eyes had started to weep as the impact of what had happened hit her as well, and as she moved in closer to her godson and daughter, she used her arms to hug them as one. Their grieving selves were taken to a quiet room and it was there, as they sat close together, that James tried to relay to them what had happened. They sat as close to each other as was physically possible, when the extent of the two-car accident from Michael's short journey home from the meeting became a reality. He had left the Roberts a tad earlier and was involved in a head-on collision, the other driver dying at the scene and Michael later dying from his injuries. James couldn't hold back with the words, and neither could Abby. But in her mind, in the midst of the uncontrollable grief, she never wanted to overshadow James. Michael was his father and she felt she had no place for her grieving to take priority over his. When something like this happens unexpectedly, shock and bewilderment act as a buffer to what is accruing. The pain of losing someone who was everything and more to one at whatever time is always going to hurt. However, our bodies step in and initially protect us with shock. It cradles us and acts as a delayer to what will gradually sink in; it gives us time to gather ourselves before the reality of it all starts to hit home. To cope with the whole impact of it all would be too hard at the outset, so we are given shock and disbelief at the beginning to carry us through before the realism follows. It is only later that we are able to start grieving for our loss.

The awful formalities of what takes place in these circumstances had to follow. James couldn't do it on his own and was still unable to trace his mum. Teresa wanted to help him through it, as Abby was in no state to do it herself. In her mind she just wanted to see his face in the last way that she had seen him, smiling at her with his discerning mouth and winking at her with his right eye. She was hearing his last words echo in her mind: "You're gorgeous and I love you." She felt selfish inside but she just couldn't do it. Left with her own company, as she wanted it when James and Teresa headed off with the doctor, she broke down more freely and wept her heart out. From standing, she fell to her knees, with her left arm resting on the cushioned chair, her head supported by her arm. Again she had touched happiness, even held it a while, but unknowingly it had somehow slipped through her grasp and now it had floated away with all her other dreams. It was all too much to take in and, as her tears surged from her wounded eyes, she just couldn't accept that this was happening.

Rosemary was unaware of what was going on and was enjoying the delights of a Theatre production in London. At the hospital, though, the three mourners needed to get home, with Abby and Teresa giving no argument about James returning home with them. As they travelled back, with Teresa at the wheel and James's car in the hospital car park, it being unadvisable for him to drive, they made their way back to Abby and Teresa's cottage. Lost at the back of Abby's mind was what she had to face when she opened her bedroom door, but that, too, was about to be shadowed by the flashing light on the answering machine that they were soon to come across. When they walked through the door of the cottage they immediately went through to the kitchen; the last thing that any of them wanted was a cup of tea, but it was the only thing they could think of doing. They all felt lost and so confused. Reality had not yet sunk in and they just didn't know what to do with themselves. However, James still needed to get his mum, whose mobile had been switched off, but he later remembered she had said they were going to the theatre, which explained the unanswered calls. In the panic of everything he had completely forgotten, but as he made his way to the hall, the flashing red number from the answer machine was staring him in the face and that was soon to stir up all their far from simmering emotions.

"Abby, I think you might have a message." His sombre tone reached Abby who was in the close proximity.

"Here, I'll come and play it—it might be your mum," she said as James had left messages for her on her cell. Abby's empty shell walked weakly, her back and shoulder's stooped and her mournful body still warmed by her fleece. Close behind her was Teresa making her way to the hall to listen. As Abby pressed the button they all paused for what would follow, not one of them thinking it would be the voice that played.

As soon as the tape started and the first word softly uttered, Abby didn't know what to do with her body. She became so disorientated and at a complete loss as to what to do with herself; but James pulled her into his arms and held her tight, shielding her head with his loving hand while they listened. His own body was now being held lightly by Teresa's gesturing arm as they listened to the poignant message, which had been left before his dreadful fate. Assuming that Abby would have spoken to her mum, the message was quite personal.

"Abby, I'm sorry I missed you. I'm soon leaving, but I guess I wanted to hear your dulcet tones before tonight. I...err...also wanted to say thank you for a wonderful afternoon, and thank you for how special you have made me feel. Anyway I have to get going now, but I love you, Abby, and I will see you again soon—bye. Did I say it was Michael? Just kidding. Bye, sweetheart."

The recording was too much to bear. Tears had slowly fallen down their faces as each word was spoken, and when Abby freed herself from James she just wanted to be in the place where they had finally made their love real. However, Abby had no idea of the added pain that she was to cause herself. Teresa insisted to James that he let her go, to which he did and instead was hugged tightly by Teresa, with his own tears falling down the back of his godmother's clothing. When Abby opened the door to her orchard haven, she froze with the sight of the unmade bed. She took fairy steps to the place where she had laid so contently with Michael, her dropping tears paving her way. She had no more than five hours ago been at peace there with him, with not one foreboding feeling in her worshipped body. When she closed her eyes and just hung over the bed, swaying on her feet a little, she could still imagine the touch of him on her. Just the memory of the softness of his refined lips on her sensitive skin remained. No sparkle remained and not an inch of her doleful body was spared any of the torture she was going through.

Their love had begun with the sunset and finished with the rising of the moon, and now as the stars were settling in for the night, Abby let her body just collapse onto their place of love. The instant contact with the percale sheets took the brunt of her sorrow. Lost in all the covers, she could still feel him with her. The scent of his skin still remained on the cotton, the feathered pillow was still indented from where his head had moulded there and left an impression, the glass of water from which he had sipped was unmoved on her nightstand and still had traces of his lips on the rim. As the tears and hurt turned to anger and wretchedness as to how he could have left her, and as she gripped the fibres tightly, she was defining her knuckles with the hold and flaming her already warm face. She just couldn't understand why this had happened.

She may have not have wanted to overshadow James's love for his father, but she couldn't ignore her love for him either; and with a gentle tap on the door, James, blurry eyed, walked slowing over to the bed. When he gradually sat near the foot of the bed, Abby turned and lifted her heartbroken face from the mattress and, with a truthful gesture, James cradled her in his arms. For the first time since he had sensed the chemistry between his dad and Abby, he realised just how deeply they had fallen for each other. The fear of Michael not being in their lives was now what was most apparent—never holding him again, never seeing him smile and wink with his right eye, which he always did; and never being able to tell him just how much he was loved. The fear locked them together as one, and in one another's arms their pain and suffering merged into each other's bodies, knowing that together they would get through their anguish.

For the immediate time James stayed with Abby and Teresa, with only visits to the Stud, which was being temporary run by a manager; and when James did later that fateful day catch up with Rosemary, she too was bewildered and unable to comprehend the news. The man she had spent nearly thirty years of her life with had died. The man that she almost didn't feel entitled to grieve for, but the man that, despite their recent parting, she would always love. When two days later Rosemary called to see James, who had declined to stay with her at Larry's, Abby answered the door of the cottage; and when they instantly hugged at the sight of each other, Abby knew she would have to talk to Rosemary at some point soon, though not just then. Nobody knew what to do. Each day they would get up and sit for most of it, lost and vacant as to what they should be doing. When Charles died, Abby was so ill the whole time it was like a blur; and when she did feel better and was starting to get stronger from her second account with anorexia, she had delayed grief. It was six months after her dad's death that she was able to grieve properly. However, here and now, her loss was happening and hitting her more and more and hurting her to a greater extent by the second.

The timing never seemed right for Abby to talk to Rosemary and, as the time never presented itself, not even some day's later, Abby didn't feel she could create an opportunity. When the day of the funeral approached it was a day that would never ever be forgotten. The morning cold sky was dark and overcast, with rain forecasted for the area, so in a sense the weather was contributing to the woeful air. Dark clothing, pale faces, relations and acquaintances that hadn't been seen in years, set the scene for the day. Abby was a pillar of strength for James, with Teresa supporting Abby, who, despite her unconvincing reassurance, wasn't fine. She wasn't aiming to hide anything from Rosemary but neither was she going to make it obvious. She would try not to, anyway—but how can she hide a loss so great? However, with Rosemary caught up with all her emotions and James's, she was too absorbed to notice Abby's.

The church on the edge of the village was where they were heading. Its unassuming appearance, neat lawn and quaintness, was lost on a day like this. It was a day that was beyond their comprehension; it was happening, but none of them could believe it. It was as if they were having to act out a part in a film, a part that they hadn't ever imagined preparing for yet and any second they expected someone to yell, "Cut!"—or for them to just wake up from this living nightmare. Michael would always remain with them. A part of him was in each of their hearts, with a part of him living on and more so than Abby thought possible, as she was soon to realise. In the church memorable words of a wonderful man were being recited by the friendly vicar, and the moment was soon arriving when James had planned to add his own contribution to the proceedings. Abby's eyes never once looked at the coffin, as to her Michael was not in a box—his spirit had been lifted far beyond that. As she tightly held a dampened tissue and fiddled with the necklace he had bought for her from Egypt around her neck, she felt so empty; and although she had love and support around her, she felt so alone. However, there was company within her, company she had yet to meet—company that would give her hope again

Michael had been the one that picked her up into his arms and cradled her when she was having the miscarriage, the man that gave her faith in love again, and the man that brought life and happiness back to her heart and soul, and the man that filled her mind with dreams again. How she was ever going to feel all that again was far from imaginable, but Michael had left Abby the greatest gift of all, and that gift was a gift she would cherish and hold so greatly. Before James left the pew Abby squeezed his hand firmly and, after that comfort that they shared, he walked to the pulpit to share a poem that was a favourite of his dad's, one that he, too, found comfort in at times of his own losses. James read the words by John Oxenham with remarkable composure, but as the depth of the words took hold, his voice began to fade.

### *Adieu! And Au Revoir*

As you love me, let there be
No mourning when I go,—
No tearful eyes,
No hopeless sighs,
No woe,—nor even sadness!

Indeed I would not have you sad,
For I myself shall be full glad,
With the high triumphant gladness
Of a soul made free
Of God's sweet liberty.
—No windows darkened;

For my own
Will be flung wide as ne'er before,
To catch the radiant inpour
Of Love that in full atone
For all the ills that I have done;
And the good things left undone,
No voices hushed;
My own full flushed
With an immortal hope, will rise
In ecstasies of new-born bliss
And joyful melodies.

Rather, of your sweet courtesy,
Rejoice with me
At a soul's loosing from captivity.
Wish me 'Bon Voyage!'
As you do a friend
Whose joyous visit finds it's happy end.
And bid me both 'a Dieu!'
And 'au revoir'
Since, though I come no more,
I shall be waiting there to greet you,
At his door.

The silence in the recently warmed church was saying so much. When James returned to sit between his mum and Abby, Teresa at her daughter's side, he turned and wept in to the arms of his mother. His hand was being held by

Abby, but at the same time, although Abby was offering her support to him, his hand was also holding hers.

In life we love and we lose but we never forget. As long as we remember and treasure our memories and keep our love alive, it can't ever die; and when we meet again, our love will be reunited for eternity.

# CHAPTER 22

Christmas and the New Year came quietly and left equally as silently, and with the start of the year changes were on the horizon. Rosemary had postponed the new chapter in life, i.e. moving to America with Larry, so she could be there for James; she hated herself for thinking it, but she longed for him now to go with her. Abby had desperately been trying to continue with her book, but lost her concentration so quickly it was becoming a thankless task. She always had the feeling that she had forgotten to do something, or left something on; she just couldn't give the book her all but decided not to force it and let it come with time. James, on the other hand, just threw himself into the Stud and sought as much work as he could find and, despite what he knew his mum was hoping, he still couldn't leave England. Although his feelings about leaving weren't positive, he didn't want that to stop his mum from going, as he knew it was something she had to do. Ever since they returned from the States all those years ago she had never quite been settled and, at the end of the day, life can be so unexpected at times that one has to take opportunities when they're there to be taken.

Rosemary was still trying to come to terms with everything and sort out the move. However, at the same time she was unaware of what was to come to light in the coming days. She would have to face up to a past secret, one that she thought was only ever to be with her and no one else. If only one person knew the secret, she thought it would never dance its way into the picture, though that was just how it was to come to light—a picture. The early January afternoon was the day that someone else was to uncover Rosemary's past. James was at the stud, Abby was with him and Teresa wanted to find something to fill the rest of the day with. Just after Michael's funeral, Teresa had to collect the photos of the holiday. Not being the right time to look at them, she had put them under her bed to one side, waiting for the right time to come along. So now, with the house as clean and tidy as could be, and still recovering from the bleak Christmas, she plucked up the courage to go through them. Teresa had intended to bring the box downstairs to the dining room table, but when she knelt down on the softness of her cream carpet by her bed, she found the place there equally as suitable.

The comfort of her position extended her time there. She knew that one day Abby and James would want to see them and so, as painful as it was to see the recent holiday photos with them all looking so contented, Teresa remained on the floor to sort through them. She leant her back against her bedside table and sat all the photos and the earmarked album in the centre of her legs, which were making an effort to form a triangle but with one side missing. When Michael died so suddenly it inevitably stirred up Teresa's emotions of her loss when Charles died, and as she slowly looked through the snaps, a thought that came in her head was one that was unwittingly leading her down the path of discovery. Under her bed also was a box she knew had her photos from when she and Charles had visited Egypt. Although sometimes, as much as it hurts to see yourself with the person that made you so happy and that you loved so much, you have to look and remember the joy that that person had brought to you.

When she looked back at her past through the film of the album, having searched through a farrago of keepsakes to find it, Teresa worked out that she and her late husband would have been about the same age as Abby and James were on their recent holiday. Looking intently at her visit with Charles, she wondered if she had appreciated enough all the times they had together. Teresa thought to herself, if she had known that their time together on earth was going to be limited, would she have cherished him more than she thought she had done? Had she told enough that she loved him, hugged him enough, kissed him enough, and had she forgotten things about him that, however small, were what made him so special? The wonder crammed in to her mind to the point of bursting, until something else changed her thinking. Her rose garden bedroom suddenly became darkened by the pewter shaded sky; the alarming sound of the angry thunder made her jump and, as the mighty lightening fought for attention, it stabbed the wounded sky with determination. Teresa reached behind her and turned on her bedside lamp, trying to compete with the dimmed lighting from the gushing rainfall that was striking her windows.

It was as if the powerful downpour didn't want to be left out from the other atrocious elements.

Taking a photograph out of the leather holder, she held it in one of her hands—a print from the past—and in the other a print from the present. What hit her first was that she hadn't remembered taking the picture of James and Abby, who were in the foreground of the picture and the pyramids in the far distance. The second was uncanny; she had the exact same picture in her hand of her and Charles, a tour guide had taken it for them. Their age was the same, the location and setting was the same, and fate was twisting the knife because Teresa saw something further. The pose James and Abby had was the same as hers with Charles. James had his arm around Abby's shoulder and Abby had lifted the hand of the same shoulder to meet the tips of James's fingers, a gesture that conveyed their shared affection. And as Teresa looked at her making the same pose with Charles, her heart sank.

There was this unseen expression on James face, one she had never encountered before, because, if she had, then she would have seen what was now staring her in the face long before. It wasn't a smile with his mouth, and it wasn't a movement with his cheeks; but, however strange as it sounds, and usually the true things do, James was smiling with his eyes. In his eyes she saw a glimpse of something that she had fallen in love with in Charles. Not a pool, not even a puddle, but Teresa, for no reason whatsoever, saw a drop of Charles in James. It was a magic that to the untrained eye would have gone unnoticed; however, to the eye of the beholder it was beaming out of the photo along with the high Fahrenheit sun.

There wasn't anything about James that resembled Charles. James had always been the spitting image of his mum, and as for his build and stance, that mirrored Michael's. However, sometimes it's the less obvious things that spell out more than just features—the subtleties that carry more weight and the details that can so easily go amiss. As she held the two images tightly, the two sets of eyes were peering back at her like a startled animal caught in headlights. Teresa's body froze solid with what she was seeing; her suspicions were now haunting her troubled mind. Was she seeing something that merely wasn't there to see? Had it all just been provoked by her grief? Or was she seeing a secret that had been hidden for all this time? A chance pose and a chance holiday had equalled in a faraway discovery. But why now? Why was she seeing this now, having never seen it before? Maybe it was just her mind playing tricks with her. However, had the idea been imbedded too much to just pull it out and disregard like any other weed? Are there really times in lives when we are meant to uncover things? Or maybe we have interrupted fate, or perhaps we've just been guided by it?

Thinking that she was just being foolish, she gathered everything up and returned the recent photographs to their packets, failing to have put them into the album as intended. However, before she put her past back in its box and under the bed again and returned the new ones to the same place, she kept back the two duplicated poses to take downstairs. Sitting in the living room, having to have to light the room with an array of lamps to bring some brightness into the dulled back room, Teresa looked at them again. She wasn't able to dismiss what she now considered to be a possibility. Thinking she was being foolish wasn't stopping her from still considering it.

Teresa's back was comforted by the softness of the woven dobby brick fabric of the three-seater sofa, which she had recently reupholstered. Just as she was about to contemplate what to do next, Teresa heard Abby and James enter the hall. They had run from the car and escaped getting too wet from the torrential weather, which was not just falling from the sky but almost being thrown down with no regard for who or where it hit. When they had freed their feet from their boots and their jackets from their bodies, they found Teresa in the living room. Darkness had fallen over the daylight and, with Abby and James chatting about some of the antics up at the Stud, Teresa couldn't help but stare intently at James, but whenever he caught her eye she'd shift her look. James and Abby had plans to cook dinner but Teresa knew she had to act on her instinct; she wanted to face her fears, and there was only one way to do that.

"I won't be in for dinner, I said I'd call over to see Alice later. I'll probably eat with her." Teresa was telling a white lie. She knew where she was going but she wanted that to remain with her.

"Oh, okay; well, you know me, I always cook too much; if you're hungry when you come in you can always have something then."

"Great." Teresa was trying not to sound too vague and different but she was finding it increasingly difficult. Once one is aware of something it is virtually impossible to ignore it; and with Teresa's awareness of James, she was making herself uncomfortable.

"Mum, are you okay?" Abby asked, sitting on the opposite sofa with James.

"Course I am. I'm just a bit tired. Anyway, I'll leave you to it."

"You're going now?" Abby had noticed that her mum was acting differently.

"I think so. I don't want to be too late driving back. We can talk more later." Teresa stood up, the pictures that had been quickly hidden still in her trouser pocket; and, with Abby standing too, they shared a kiss before her mum made her unexpected departure. Abby was concerned.

"Does she seem all right to you?" she asked, involving James with her concern.

"She's a bit quiet. Perhaps she's not had a good day. Perhaps seeing Alice will help." James's words were aimed to comfort Abby who, although she resumed her seat, was still thinking about her mum.

"I'm sure you're right." Abby dismissed it for now and pulled James up to help her cook dinner. "Come on, you can help me with this new recipe of mine."

Teresa was meanwhile making the short journey to Larry's outstanding residence, hoping to find Rosemary but still none the wiser as to what she was going to say. The rain was easing up, but her worry and fears were not. Sure enough, as she approached the Grade II listed farmhouse and scuttled to the door and rang the chimes, Rosemary opened the grand door. Having to remind herself that these ideas she was having were just that—her ideas—she couldn't go barging in with accusations. For all she knew this could be just her imagination running wild and, anyway, how would she even broach such a matter? She could be risking her friendship over something that just wasn't there, and now Teresa wondered what on earth she was doing there.

"Teresa, I wasn't expecting to see you this evening." Surprise registered in her tone.

"I'm sorry, I shouldn't have come." Teresa looked like she was starting to move off the step until Rosemary came back with—

"Don't be silly, come in."

"Okay, thanks," she replied, still reluctant.

"Larry's working out in the gym downstairs so we won't be disturbed." Rosemary took them to the grand kitchen and breakfast room where she immediately put the kettle on and insisted Teresa made herself comfortable with one of the breakfast chairs. The area looked untouched from when Rosemary had moved in, although she had added some of her feminine touches to the space, but hardly. It still looked like a wealthy bachelor's kitchen—stainless steal appliances which never looked used, a very simple décor, not a lot detail, and cupboards that were poorly stocked due to the fact the occupant was always out and about; indeed, Rosemary had seemed to have adopted his lifestyle. When Rosemary joined her at the symmetrical table, Teresa was finding herself still paving the way to lead to her anxieties being dismissed or proved;

but she still couldn't imagine herself saying the words out loud as she knew as soon as she said them vocally they would just sound even more foolish than they did in her head and far to unbelievable for words.

"You must be wondering why I'm here." Teresa had draped her waterproof, which also served as a morning jacket, over the back of the chair, and as she spoke she fidgeted with the cuffs of her cable jumper.

"No, not at all, you don't have to have a reason. I'm glad of the company. I keep thinking about James. He's coming over tomorrow. Deep down I know he hasn't changed his mind about coming with me, but I have to respect that, however hard." Rosemary had upgraded her wardrobe a lot, and even in this casual appearance of trousers and feminine blouse, the outfit looked like it cost as much as Teresa had spent on clothes in a lifetime. The sad thing was she had changed, and if Michael hadn't died she was on the verge of changing even further. It somehow pulled her back a little but not far enough in the eyes of Teresa.

Although they had both always been comfortable financially, she was now in a much higher league than Teresa. *Nouveau riche* was springing to Teresa's mind, but that might have been because she could have quite possibly slept with her husband and, although, as the famous cliché says, it takes two, Rosemary was the one that was sitting opposite her. It was very unlike Teresa to have negative thoughts about her friend, but her own suspicions were driving her to distraction—and once something gets hold of one it starts to eat away—and that was what was happening to Teresa now. Something as passing as a pose and glint in a set of eyes was pestering her. It was like someone kept tapping her on the shoulder and, however much she tried to dismiss it and ignore it, it just kept on persisting.

"What do you think it is? I mean, why he's not keen to leave?" Teresa knew the answer, but she was laying the groundwork for her building plans.

"Larry, for one, but I know he would find it hard leaving Abby again. I can't blame him. She's a special young woman."

Teresa smiled with the compliment about her daughter.

"They've always been close. I wonder what it was that sparked between them?" Teresa probed.

"Maybe each being an only child, meeting at a young age. I guess time has made them close. They've been through so much together. I know he found it hard leaving her the last time and now I think it would be impossible."

Teresa longed to see a sign of discomfort on her face, but nothing appeared, and she suddenly felt so imprudent and irrational; however, she had been under a lot of pressure lately. With the recent death of Michael it had stirred all her grief again for Charles, and just as she was feeling bad about thinking that her friend was *nouveau riche*, she was about to seize an opportunity once and for all, a moment that was too easy to miss. Driven by her vulnerable thoughts she was soon to take her stand.

"When I leave, you'll keep an eye on James for me, won't you?"

"Course I will. Anyway, I think Abby will be the one he'd be more interested in looking after him." She said it in her normal tone, no other emotion added, and she waited for a reaction.

"What do you mean?" The kettle had been forgotten as the two ladies became involved in the deeper conversation.

"Well, I guess I'd always hoped those two would perhaps get together one day. I thought we all did." Teresa hadn't thought anything of the sort, but as the thought was planted in Rosemary's head and knowing she was soon to be on the other side of the Atlantic, the expression Teresa had searched for earlier was now rearing its ugly head on Rosemary's face.

"James and Abby won't ever be more than friends." The way she said it was more along the lines of they *couldn't* as apposed to *wouldn't*.

"Who knows, things change so quickly." Teresa was provoking her but for good reason.

"No, those two may be as thick as thieves, but lovers—never!" Rosemary reassured herself with the notion. Never had she even thought it an option. To her it just couldn't happen, and because of that she hadn't ever given it a seconds thought. But was that confidence now being shaken by a goading Teresa? Sometimes, when you know something can't happen, you don't even think about the possibility of it happening—and that was the case with Rosemary.

"Would it be such a bad thing if they did become lovers?" Teresa aimed that shot right at her target and it reached home. But Rosemary broke it all up with her next words.

"Teresa, what's all this about? You've never thought any of this before. We always said James and Abby were just close friends?"

Rosemary didn't think for one minute that anyone could know her secret, but she did wonder where this had all come from and all of a sudden.

"I don't know—you tell me."

"Teresa, are you okay? You're acting strangely."

"Acting—hmm—something I would say *you* were pretty good at, wouldn't you say?" Teresa stood to her feet, but she didn't move away from the chair. In fact, the back of her knees were touching the metal framed seat as she leant on the table with her hands, knowing she had the evidence in her pocket.

"What are you talking about!" Rosemary was now a little concerned, but she was still too bewildered by her friend to connect anything.

"I'm talking about you—Charles and James." She moved out from the clutches of the chair and walked round to the other side of the table. Calmly, she placed the two images in front of Rosemary and stepped back a little.

"Why are you showing me these?" Rosemary looked at the photos and then looked over to Teresa with the question.

"Because today for the first time in twenty-eight years I think I saw something that I had never seen before. I keep telling myself it's because I'm upset and distraught about things and that my mind must be playing tricks on me, but somehow I don't think so."

"I don't know what you're talking about." Rosemary couldn't believe what was happening, which was ever apparent on her face and in her tone.

"I want you to tell me there isn't the slightest chance that Charles is James's father."

"What!"

"Oh, very well done! Dismissal and shock all rolled into that one single word—clever. Now please, can you answer me? Please, Rosemary, for goodness sake, just tell me—tell me there isn't a chance." She didn't just say the words to her, she pleaded them to her and pleaded for her to answer. Teresa felt close to tears but she held them back with all her strength. Her stentorian voice was still echoing in the vastness of the downstairs room as she waited to hear an answer.

"Why are you asking me this? I mean, of course he isn't." Rosemary brushed it all off as quickly as it was implied.

"Your eyes are saying something very different. When I asked you they instantly filled with panic—panic that someone had discovered your secret. Look at those pictures, *look* at them!" Teresa picked them both up and lifted them to her bemused face.

"Teresa, please don't do this to yourself! You're upset and hurting. I can understand that, but this won't bring Charles back. You're just distressing yourself and blowing this out of all proportion."

Teresa dropped the photos back down on the table and distanced herself again from Rosemary.

"Ok, swear it, then."

"Swear it? But why? I've just told you…" Rosemary knew that she wouldn't be able to.

"Then you won't mind swearing it then, will you? You swear to me on James's life that there isn't a chance, then I'll leave."

The pause before Rosemary said anything again seemed like hours and, as she looked at the photos and then at Teresa's anxious face, she answered.

"I can't." With that short response Teresa's held back tears fell at quite a pace and all that could come out of her mouth was—

"When?"

"Teresa, it was a long time ago."

"Well, twenty-eight years, to be precise, wouldn't you say?"

Rosemary remained seated while Teresa paced the sandstone floor with the softness of her tights.

"Teresa, please sit down. If we have to talk about this, let's at least be adult about it."

Teresa reluctantly sat, this time taking the seat diagonally opposite to Rosemary.

"When did it happen? I mean, was it an affair, a fling, or what?" Her whole world was crashing down before her and she felt so let down.

"It wasn't anything like that. It was when Michael was over in the States, preparing our move. You and Charles were having a few problems at the time. I think you were staying at your sister's for a while. Anyway, Charles came round. He'd forgotten Michael had extended his trip, so we started talking and reminiscing. After lots of brandy and endless chatting about me missing Michael and feeling so alone and him upset about the problems the both of you were having, we made utter fools of ourselves. Well, I suppose you can guess the rest." Rosemary told it all to Teresa's dropped head.

Teresa's dewy-eyes were releasing tears and creating a shallow pond on the glass surface, but she whispered faintly—

"I just don't believe this."

Rosemary wanted her excuses and the rest to be heard and so she continued.

"We felt so awful the next morning. I never thought I was ever going to be able to look you in the face again. Charles felt sick with regret, we both did. But what could we do? It was a stupid thing that happened that neither of us ever forgave ourselves for."

Teresa's discomfort about what she was listening to was streaming down her face. She added nothing else and so Rosemary carried on.

"When I found out I was pregnant, Michael and I had been sleeping together, but I was never one hundred percent sure. When James inherited my features and colouring I dismissed my fears. I mean, what was the point in saying anything and ruining all our lives? You had Abby, I had James, you and Charles were closer than ever and we were off to the States. So it was forgotten and I never told Charles there could have been a chance of him being James's father. He never thought it or asked and so it was my secret—one I thought was only mine. I never thought anyone could possibly guess." Rosemary said nothing else and just waited for Teresa to respond, but when she didn't, Rosemary pressed her.

"Please say something, Teresa." She leant forward a little, trying to see her face through her growing titian hair. Teresa lifted her head up and with great calmness she spoke.

"I don't think there's anything else to say do you. There is one thing, though—how could you have been so sure that nothing would ever happen between Abby and James? You've seen the way he dotes on her. I don't understand."

"I suppose because in my mind I knew it couldn't—or shouldn't—happen. I never thought it would. I wanted to stay in America but Michael had other plans. There was nothing I could do. Then, when we all met up again, I thought everything would be okay and until now it was. To me James was Michael's son and so there wasn't a problem. I shut my mind to it and I never thought about it, never—and it doesn't have to be a problem now."

"How can you say that! James and Abby are half brother and sister and you think it's okay that they don't know? I have to live with knowing that now. If they find out it would destroy them, and not telling them is going to destroy me."

"Teresa, I am more sorry than you'll ever know."

"That may well be the case, but that doesn't really help me now, does it?" Teresa stood and put the photographs in her pocket and returned her jacket to her dazed body. As she headed to the door that led to the hallway, Rosemary called out to her, making her turn at the door.

"Teresa. Never forget what you and Charles had—that was what was real. He spent the rest of his life desperately trying to rid himself of that guilt and whether he ever succeeded, I don't know; but I do know one thing, he loved you and wanted nobody other than you. Don't let this overshadow that." She was trying to make amends but it far from helped.

The key was ready to turn in the ignition, but as Teresa sat in her car, still in Larry's drive, she broke down completely. Her head rested on the leather steering wheel, her hands clutching it at the same time and, in all her life, through everything that she had coped with, she had never felt so alone and isolated. There was no one that she could talk to, and the one person she longed to talk to is the person who could only listen to her. The hour was late and the bright lighting from within the grounds put off the darkness a little. Teresa knew she had to just get home, but she also knew she would have to lie to James and Abby and say she had a migraine so she could excuse herself to the privacy and quietness of her bedroom—and that's just what she did. But she couldn't excuse herself from what she had uncovered because that was something that was going to follow her around wherever she went until she faced it.

# CHAPTER 23

❦

Teresa's night had been far from restful and although her eyes opened with the early delivered morning paper, which she heard slide through the letterbox, she was already awake. Yesterday had far from sunk in. She just had so many feelings and emotions parading around her mind. The light patterned dusty pink pillow was propped up against her carved wooden headboard, the matching duvet close up to her waist, and as the sun had yet to reach her bedroom, she turned on her bedside lamp. She was so confused about what to make of it all and didn't know what to think anymore; her mind was overflowing, as though someone kept pouring water into a glass despite being full to the brim.

However, her memories of her life with Charles were managing to push its way to front and started to win the unplanned race. It was as though she couldn't let the new revelation alter her feelings for her beloved husband and forget all the wonderful times they had together, and how rewarding her marriage had been. She knew that they had had many tremendous and fulfilled years together, ones that would remain the best of her life. They made a beautiful and special daughter together who gave them further fulfilment and happiness. She knew the love they had shared she would never experience again with another man. Knowing Charles, and how he was, she knew, deep down, although at the time with Rosemary she didn't want to hear it, she knew he would have been mortified as to what he had done. She couldn't throw all that love away for something she knew he spent the next eighteen years making up for. He lived to make her happy, and happy she had been, and in her eyes now that was all that mattered.

The low wattage bulb was glowing on the right of her slightly more comforted, resting body. She turned to her side table to view her framed photo of

Charles and herself, the most recent one she had of them, taken on their twentieth wedding anniversary by Abby. She took it into her motherly hands and, with her left thumb, she brushed the surface over the image of his beaming smile. It was the day he had given her that illustrious ring, which for other reasons was significant to Abby; but for Teresa the words from that ring, which she entrusted her daughter with, were now very important. As she smiled over the photo, her saline tears cleansing the façade of the frame, she whispered the words softly: "Ever Mine, Ever Thine, Ever for Each Other." But Teresa had one last concern which was meddling in through her release of emotions, and it was, of course, James and Abby. Never could they know the shared secret and, knowing what it could do to them was far from consoling; and so every day Teresa knew she would say a prayer that they would never have to find out just how closely they were bound together.

By now, the time having approached 7.30 a.m., Abby was up and about. Making her way downstairs in her warm tartan pyjamas and her feet dressed in some gripping socks, she headed for the front door to relinquish the broadsheet newspaper from the clutches of the brass letterbox. Having retrieved it and tucked her messy hair behind her ears, she scanned the front cover, not for one minute expecting to see what she did. There, printed in the right slender column, was a name from the past—Patrick. Pausing before she continued, she read on silently in her head, still standing in the hallway. The piece read:

> *Samuel Copper Davis and Associates have just paid out the highest out of court settlement known to date, due to an ex-client suing them for intimidation. The eight figure sum has not only cost the firm their hard earned reputation, it has also been to the detriment of the lawyer involved in the case. Patrick Daly, 36, has since been asked to resign from his position as senior associate and, worse still, he is also to become the future ex-husband of Laura Copper Davis, Samuel's only daughter, who stands to inherit her father's fortune. The acrimonious divorce between the two has seen Daly leave the short marriage with what he came in with—nothing. The firm's reputation has in the minds of many been dented. However, speaking at a press conference yesterday, Samuel insisted: "The bad apple has been removed from the cart and it is business as usual. This has tightened our ship and we are sailing again with strength." When asked about his daughter and if the recently settled legal matter and Daly's resignation had anything to do with their marriage break up, he simply answered, "You can't build a house on rocky ground; that's all I have to add on the subject." Copper Davis are famous for some very high profile cases, but this is one they will be wanting to forget. The twist in the tale for Mr Daly, of French origin, is that his younger brother, Jacob Daly, is still thriving with the*

*company's division in Montreal. Daly was unavailable for any comments last night. However, he is believed to have left Canada and to be back in France. Cont. on page 7.*

Abby felt so strange hearing about him after all this time, but that was her only feeling. Her love for Patrick had long since been overshadowed and, without being too brutal, she thought to herself that he brought it all on himself and had no one else to blame. Inside, though, she hated the fact that she had been right—greed had got the better of him, and what had happened to him was inevitable. One attains one's dreams by working and fighting for them, not the way he did. He used deceit and dishonesty and was now no doubt feeling the brunt of his actions. Dreams have to be one's own dreams, not someone else's, and Patrick didn't know what he wanted and so he used Jacob's ambitions and turned them into his own. Little did he realise what it would result in. If one obtains things under false pretences and has something that wasn't meant to be one's own, then at some point one will lose it; or, one will have a very hard time holding onto it. Patrick could have had a life beyond all that, but he made his bed and, as the saying went, he had to lie in it. Folding the paper a little, Abby wanted to share the discovery with her mum. Climbing the stairs two at a time, she tapped on her mother's bedroom door and entered when she heard her call. Seeing her mum in bed, her first words were—

"How do you feel this morning? Any better?"

"Much better sweetheart, thanks." Although for different reasons, it was true, and having returned her framed picture to the surface closest to her, there was no trace of her recent tears.

"You're never going to believe what's in the paper!" Abby walked around the bed to her mum's right side and perched on the exposed sheeted mattress, neighbouring her mum's legs. Abby passed her the large quality newspaper and directed her mum's eyes to the side column with her own stare.

"I don't believe it—it's about Patrick" When she had filled herself with the same information that Abby had already absorbed, she passed comments. "I wonder what he will do now?" she observed, astonished. "I mean, he's ruined his career."

"I guess he will have to start again. Somehow I doubt even if he has learnt from it all. One would like to hope so, but you don't know with Patrick."

And there it was—since what happened in London and then the miscarriage, it was the first time she had actually used his name out loud. Abby had always referred to Patrick as *he* or *him* but never as Patrick, and Teresa suddenly realised this. Before she said anything about it, her face lit up with a large smile, showing how proud she was of her daughter.

"You do realise that's the first time I've heard you call him by his name since London?"

"It's not, is it?" Abby hadn't really thought about it though her mum had.

"It is, and it show's how far you've come since then. I know these last few months haven't been easy, especially with Christmas, but you're doing so well." Feelings are so difficult to put across at times, the way to phrase the words and to find the right ones and the worry for them to sound how one intended them too. However, with the expression in her mother's eyes and the reach of her hand to Abby's, the message was well received.

"Thanks mum, although sometimes I almost don't believe it's all happened. I half expect Michael to just turn up one day, having been on a trip or something, or to appear from the stables when I'm up at the Stud. I don't think I've grasped that he isn't coming back yet. I don't think James has either. I know this is a stupid thing to say, but I keep thinking that if things had worked out with Patrick, would James still have his dad? I mean, would each of our lives have taken different courses, or would the results have still been the same? But I know it's a silly thing to think. I guess you do think strange things when you're upset and hurting and not just hurting for yourself, but hurting for other people too." Abby's eyes started to water her dry cheeks but she held the majority back and dabbed her skin with the softness of her woollen nightwear. Teresa had a visit from another concern; however, this was one that she was prepared to verbalize to Abby.

"Abby, you don't think Patrick will try and get in touch, do you?" The pillow dropped a little as she leant towards her to put across the question.

"I can honestly say no, he won't. I may have been naïve about him in the past, but strangely enough I knew him better than I thought I did. He may think about it, but pride will stop him acting upon it; plus, in this respect he's like me: you go so far forward and there comes a point where it's too much to go back." Abby had a metaphor she wanted to share with her mum and so she started to pave the way. "Do you remember that time dad was taking us to where he was born in Lancashire and then up to Cumbria for a holiday?"

"I do." Teresa smiled but wondered where she was going with it.

"Well, do you remember that we hadn't long set off and you forgot your glasses?"

"Uh, how could I forget! After that your dad bought me that luminous yellow case because I was always forgetting them!" Teresa grinned as she still had the case and it still made her smile every time she saw it, remembering the teasing Charles had given her about always forgetting her spectacles.

"Well, because we hadn't gone too far we were able to turn back and get them. But there is a point on a journey that even if you do forget something, you just can't reverse; there comes a point where it is further to travel back than it is to keep going forward, and at that point you have to just leave whatever it was you forgot and hope you don't miss it too much. That's just the way it is with Patrick. He could have gone back at a point at which it was still possible to, but he chose to keep going and now it's too late—and he knows it. Our journey's over."

Abby was so wise for her years, but her insightful mind had come at a cost of years of torment and battles. First the bullying, then the anorexia, the death of her father and the serous relapse of her eating disorder and fear of food, and then came Patrick. With her first real love came her first real experience of dealing with her emotions. Falling for someone so greatly, the hurt was great. Then, losing the baby, and then finally thinking she had found happiness with Michael, and how that had that ended. She had aged beyond her years. However, she was never one to complain. She had her mum and she had James, and, with her memories in tow, she had more than many. The blackest hour is always followed by the brightest new dawn; the faintness was passing and a fresh light was beginning to shine. Hope was on the horizon and happiness was just behind it.

Abby and Teresa left the bedroom and made their way downstairs to refresh themselves for the day ahead by making a morning brew. Abby was just moving around the kitchen in the same way she did most mornings—but this morning, as she closed the fridge clutching the milk carton in her hand, she had a wave wash over her and she shared it with her mum.

"I think I will try and finish that chapter today." She had no desire as yet to reacquaint herself with her book, so this was a positive step for her.

"Good, I'm really glad." Teresa knew the day would come and, as she took the milk from her hand, they shared a much-needed hug. It was full of love and warmth and it was always the best remedy for Abby, whatever the symptom. In a hug her mum always seemed to take half the pain or worry back with her, a knack she just had, one that Abby never questioned and one that was special to them both. When they later sat at the table, Abby unwittingly put her mum on the spot, although Teresa was prepared for what was coming.

"Mum, I was wondering if I could look at the photos of the holiday? I haven't felt I could before. It doesn't have to be today—just when you get a chance."

"Course you can. I did start going through them myself but I didn't get very far. Listen, if you see any special ones you would like framed we can always hunt round some antique shops for some nice frames." Teresa was fine about it, plus she knew the sacred picture that marked her discovery was not with the collection but safely locked away in one of her safe boxes with the negatives, along with the picture of the past.

"I'd like that. I would like James to see them too, but I'll see how he feels."

"How's he managing up at the Stud?"

"Better than I thought he would, but he'd never cope without Robert. But he lives and breathes that Stud and he feels he owes it to Michael to keep it alive. Rosemary leaving won't help, but he's got us and I know he'll be fine. I just wish he would slow down a bit."

"Give him time and he will. He's frightened, frightened that if he stops for a second, he'll feel too much pain; but there will come a point that his body will make him slow the pace—you'll see." Teresa knew what she was talking about and Abby found solace in that.

The bright and sunny yet chilly morning had been a very constructive one. Abby had typed over a thousand words, plus made contact with a very worried Karen, who she reassured things were getting back on track.

And Teresa? Well, she wanted to make her peace with Rosemary before she left for the States. So, with Abby in full flow of her inspiration, Teresa made her way to Withers Gallop. The visit was to be welcomed by Rosemary, who felt terrible for what had happened yesterday. Teresa knew she owed it to herself to clear the air and, as the two ladies met at the door, Rosemary was the first to speak.

"I'm so glad you came back." Rosemary was dressed quite smartly; her ensemble of clothing was well coordinated and very stylish at the same time. Teresa felt like the poor relation in her polo neck and cardigan, but fashion was not why she was there.

"I wanted to clear the air before you left." Teresa's tone was sincere, each word delivered almost poetically.

"I wanted to, too. Please, come in." Rosemary's court shoes sounded on the wooden floorboards, creating a delicate sound as she guided them through to the living room. Teresa's more practical footwear followed in silence. "I could make a coffee or something. I just thought we would be more comfortable in here." She was a little nervous but Teresa calmed her.

"No, honestly, I'm okay, Rosemary. I'm not sure what to say, really, about yesterday, other than we best just let it all rest now. As for Abby and James, we both know what it would do to them if they found out. So we just have to hope and pray that things stay as they are." There wasn't really anything else to say. In a way the visit instigated by Teresa, along with the shared watery smiles that were spreading across their diluted faces, said more.

Their peace had been made and although their friendship may never be the same again, they had moved on to a different level of friendship—for when someone knows something so intimate about the other and the connection it brings, a closer bond is created. Teresa had appointments she needed to attend to and likewise with Rosemary. They were due to see each other again along with James, Larry and Abby, for a final farewell drink before the day of their departure; but in a way they were going to say their goodbyes now. The noon hour had lifted the temperature somewhat, though barely, and as they stepped down the few steps by the front doubled door it hit them both how much they were going to miss each other. They had known each other since they were five and, other than the four years Rosemary spent in America at the beginning of her marriage, they had seen each other practically every day. Despite what had happened in the last day or so they each knew they were going to miss their friendship terribly.

"It feels like an end of an era." Teresa could feel her tearful eyes giving up the fight.

"I know, but life passes you by if you don't grab it sometimes. I know I look selfish doing what I'm doing, but I may never get this chance again—and I do love Larry very much." Rosemary had a touch of something in her speech and it sounded like she was either justifying her actions, or still trying to convince herself she was doing the right thing. Teresa couldn't decide, but did feel bad that she had no idea what had happened between Abby and Michael. Nevertheless, she knew Abby would tell her at some point if she felt she could, but she knew it would never be her place to. Teresa more than understood why Abby hadn't said anything, but at the same time she wished she had.

"I hope you will be really happy—and I mean that." Teresa gestured with her left arm, and with that gesture came a full flown hug, one that only yesterday hardly seemed possible. And they both felt so much better for it. With promises of visits and keeping in touch through emails, although they would see each other in a few days time, this was their goodbye. Although Rosemary would only be a plane's journey away and Teresa had her sister close by, she couldn't help but feel she was the last one left of a period of her life, and that hit her hard as she left the mighty drive. Her eyes had fought hard to suppress the tears, but now they lost the battle and her crying saturated her once parched face.

When the day came for the last goodbyes it finalised the string of events that had been happening to all of them. James was going to miss his mum terribly but he just couldn't bring himself to leave, and as much as he didn't have a great deal of time for Larry, he could see his mother was contented. For his mum's sake he offered his hand in true gentlemanly form to Larry, who accepted graciously. Larry, in his unassuming way, had to date proved them all wrong. In his own way he had found a woman who had tamed him. Whether his wild and unruly days were behind him for good only time would tell. Their farewells were at Withers Gallop, which was now going to be managed and run by Larry's niece and nephew, as airport goodbyes were not favoured by any of them. When Larry's driver exited the drive with the couple bound for the States, after some tender warm moments in the brisk morning air between all, James still knew he had made the right decision and found immediate comfort in the arms of Abby.

It wasn't until three days later that Abby found herself looking at the pictures—and she wasn't alone. James was sitting close by her side as they flicked through the prints that were taken nearly three and half months ago. The lunchtime sun was adequately lighting the drawing room at Abby and Teresa's cottage for the two of them to view the snaps. Teresa was not with them, for she was taking some time out with her sister. They were hitting the shops in London and catching a show to round off the day, a boost Teresa needed. Looking back over the holiday was harder than they both thought it would be. It provoked too much pain. Although it would always hurt, the day would come when they would be able to smile with the tears—but right now that wasn't possible.

"I'm sorry, James. I thought I would be able to cope seeing them. I thought I had given myself enough time." Abby stood up from her seat and left the packets of photos on the table as she wandered over to the double doors, which led to the garden. She wasn't going anywhere—she just wanted to remove her hurting and take it somewhere else. James followed her to the place and answered her with thought.

"Abby, don't apologise, we'll get there. Anyway, it's not important. You don't have to look at the pictures to be able to see his smiling face. All you have to do is close your eyes. One day you'll be able to look at them. We both will, but right now he's in here and in here." James touched his heart and head with the last six words and then continued. "He will always be part of us, both of us." However, with those last words came a release from Abby. She just fell towards him all of a sudden and, although James wasn't expecting it, he still caught her with both his able arms. With Abby landing onto his chest she uttered faintly, "Oh James, you have no idea." Little did he know that more of Michael was living on in Abby than James could have ever imagined, and with her fears from her first experience, she shared her worry with her soul mate.

"Abby, what is it?" He was shielding her head with his arm and, as she lifted her head up, her hair became statically attached to his sweatshirt, and with tears flowing gently from her big blue eyes, she told him.

"James, I think, no, I know…I'm three months pregnant and I am just so scared. Scared of going through what I did the first time, scared of telling you and what you will think of me, and…" And before she could carry on he stopped her by kissing her forehead. It was as if with that kiss he found her mute button.

"Listen, I can understand your fears because of what happened last year, but as for me, that is the best news I have heard in a very long time." His enormous smile backed up his claim.

"You mean it?" Abby's arms were still holding on to his waist as she heard him say what he did and with more words from James soon to follow he brought his hands to her shoulders and with great reassurance, he added—

"Of *course* I mean it."

Abby was visibly relieved, the tension seeping out of her. It was as if she became pounds lighter, and all because of James's true happiness at the news. For her James was like her knight in shining armour, the one person that was just always there for her. She looked to him as her brother. Little did she know, he was.

# *Epilogue*

❀

**Six months later**

The conservatory, which came off the sitting room, had never before been filled with so much love. Luke Charles Raycroft, born a healthy 7lbs 6oz, was being held proudly in the arms of his adoring grandmother, with a proud James sitting right next to him and an even prouder Abby on the other side. None of them seemed to be able to feel close enough to the small bundle of joy—the bundle of joy that had given their lives new birth and new hope, being a special part of Michael. Despite the midsummer day the rain, which started early in the morning, was cascading down on to the roof of the glasshouse. James very reluctantly had to make a move because of a commitment at the Stud, but promised he would be back later that same day. With James having left and Luke back in the arms of his mother, Teresa needed a shower and to get dressed, and so Abby and Luke continued their comfort in the conservatory. But instead of staying seated, she took him slowly in her arms to the closed outside doors of the outhouse. Clothed only in her loose blue nightwear, she spoke softly to her son.

"You know, you're a very lucky boy, yes you are. You see, you have me, your mummy who loves you very, very much, then you have my mummy, your nan who simply adores you, and thennnnn…"—she drew out the word—"you have James, and he loves you very much too. And although they're not with us here, up there in heaven you have my daddy, your grandpa, you have a little sister, Jessica and, last but definitely not least, you have your daddy, Michael. And your mummy wishes he was here to share this moment with us, but we know he's with us in a different way; and without him this moment wouldn't have been possible, and in you I will always have a part of him. And I promise to tell you as much about him as I can, because he was a wonderful man and I want you to be able to know that one day. So there you go—all that love for someone so tiny!"

Abby said each word so lovingly that she brought tears to her own eyes, tears that fell in harmony with the light rain. With Luke's eyes closed and him fast asleep, Abby moved her own eyes to the grey sky and all she added was, "I love you, Michael"—and for Michael's reply he sent the one thing he knew would make Abby smile, and that was a rainbow. When the sun pushed it's way through the mean clouds, the most beautiful rainbow arched the happier sky, bringing a hopeful smile to Abby's face and respite to her aching heart. The blue sky took over from the clouds, the rainbow peaked in all its glory and each colour exceeded all limits by shining with clarity and Abby received her message loud and clear. However, not just from Michael, but from her dad too, who she knew was looking after everything. With Abby holding her son in her arms and feeling ungovernable love for him, happiness was not elusive and intangible, but something that could be held. It was not just something that can be touched for a few seconds. But how happiness reaches us and what route it takes—that will always remain a mystery.

## The End

# About the Author

Having recently bought a house with her mother Pat, the author exercises her talents in interior design and creating a home for both of them and their two black Labradors Charley and Molly. Apart from writing she has a huge passion for travelling and, with family in Egypt, USA, South Africa and friends in the Lake District, she has a wide range of holiday venues. She loves the simple things in life, too—taking her dogs for a walk, bird watching and photographing scenic views.

0-595-28803-0

Printed in the United Kingdom
by Lightning Source UK Ltd.
9796600001BA/331